Dark Revenge

by

Glenys O'Connell

Dark Revenge

Cover Art by *Diana Carlile*

The Wild Rose Press, Inc.
PO Box 708
Adams Basin, NY 14410-0708
Visit us at www.thewildrosepress.com

Publishing History
First Edition, 2023
Trade Paperback ISBN 978-1-5092-4626-7
Digital ISBN 978-1-5092-4627-4

Published in the United States of America

"Then let me spell it out for you," Fern hissed back at him, refusing to allow him to see how disconcerting his proximity was. She could almost feel the heat of his gaze on her skin, feel the force of his sharp intelligence pushing at her mind, trying to convince—or intimidate? Which was it? No, no, I can't let him confuse me like that!

"I don't believe in your innocence, Joel. But while ever there may be a tiny, tiny iota of doubt, or while there may be anyone—" She aimed a glance at Glory. "—who may be taken in and believe you may be innocent, while there's the slightest chance that some clever lawyer could come up with a means of getting you off the hook, I want to make sure all possibilities are covered. When I've erased all possible doubt, I'm going to make sure you're punished."

Glory squirmed in the heavy silence. Seeing these two staring at each other, locked in mental combat, she found herself holding her breath wondering what would happen next. Would the emotions roiling in the room explode? She'd never before realized how close hate and love could be, but the intensity of emotions that hammered between Fern and Joel made her wonder what was driving them. Could it be that the feelings growing between the two before Rose's death still lingered? And just how did Fern Adams intend to carry out her threat to see that Joel was punished?

Dedication

To TWRP who welcomed me back into the fold after a long writing absence, and for the freedom they offer in writing in different genres. And to the excellent Frances Sevilla, a very special editor.

Chapter One

Dr. Fern Adams tossed and turned in her sleep, struggling to escape from a nightmare.

Helpless to look away, she watched as her dream-self mounted first one stair, and then another. Then she faltered on the third step, listening to the sound of heavy steps rushing toward her. In the dream she looked up in time to see his face—the wild eyes, the cruel, twisted mouth. The blood on his sweatshirt.

Now Fern's heart fluttered like a wild thing in her chest in concert with her dream self's reaction. She knew that face.

Panicked, Fern watched as in the dream she grabbed for the handrail to save herself from falling backward as he shoved past her.

Fern moaned a warning to her dream-self, *No! No!* But the dream Fern continued to slowly make her way up the stairs to her sister's apartment.

Then she paused, good sense clicking in as she stopped to stare at the open door.

And then waking Fern pulled herself from the clutches of the nightmare with a scream fading on her lips.

She lay in the tangle of sheets, sweating, heart racing so hard she feared a heart attack, trapped between nightmare and the reality of her twilight bedroom. Rubbing her gritty eyes, she remembered.

Tomorrow. Tomorrow was the day that justice would be served. But would she have peace then, no more nightmares, knowing that the man who murdered her sister was suffering in prison?

****

The small-town courtroom was silent, almost sleepy, with dust motes dancing in the beams of sunlight entering through the tall, narrow windows. Oak-paneled walls, darkened with age, and hard-wearing blue carpet muted sounds from the street outside and gave an added air of elegant sobriety to the business of the day. To the right of the judge's box the Canadian flag, red maple leaf prominent on white background, hung dispirited as if longing for the kiss of a breeze to set it free.

Fern sat alone in the room, trying to relate this mundane scene to the drama that had been played out—was still being played out—in the dignified courtroom. She knew that this day, this scene, the sounds, the smell of the courtroom, would be burned into her memory forever. She sat alone as an island, wondering if the scene would become the doorway to nightmares that would again torment her sleep. A doorway that led to the horrific picture of her sister lying naked and dead.

And the looming face of the man who killed her.

Joel Alvarez. Tall, dark, and classically handsome. Broad shoulders, big hands. Strong hands designed to hold, caress, protect. A destiny he had perverted to choke a woman as he raped her, choked her, raped her, again and again, until she lost consciousness. Powerful enough, cruel enough, to slit that woman's sleek white throat and leave her bleeding and beyond the help that was only moments away.

A door opened, and a momentary hush fell on the crowd as the prisoner shuffled in, flanked by two hefty guards. Fern startled out of her reverie to see the defendant staring at her, trapping her gaze. In that moment she fancied she saw an appeal in his eyes.

She shivered and quickly turned away as ululating noise levels rose around her. The crowds settled down on the hard seats, a signal that the jury had finished its deliberations and was returning. She watched as the twelve good men and women of the jury filed back and took their places.

Judge Michaels, a sun-bronzed, silver-haired man with half-moon glasses and a stern cast to his mouth, seated himself on his high perch, flicking back black robes, getting comfortable. He poured a glass of water, took a sip, pushed his eyeglasses back on his straight patrician nose, and all the while Fern wanted to shout, *Get on with it! Tell Me! End this!*

Once this was over, once the verdict was delivered and a killer punished, she would have her life back again. Only it would never be the same, not now that her sister Rose was dead. Murdered. Until this moment it had never crossed Fern's mind that the jury would say anything but "Guilty" in response to the judge's ritual question.

Yet when the pudgy, middle-aged man who'd been elected their foreman rose to his feet, a quiver of anxiety shook her. *Shouldn't they look more righteous, surer of themselves?* The seven women and five men looked merely uncomfortable, as though they were no longer a cohesive group but strangers who couldn't wait to get back to their own lives and never see this place again. *What if they found him not guilty?* Fern's throat swelled with fear as the room seemed robbed of oxygen.

"Are you all right, Miss?" the man sitting next to her asked, obviously concerned. Fern recognized him as the older man who'd testified to Alvarez's good character, the fire chief who'd spoken of the man's heroic behavior. Briefly she wondered how he must feel at this moment, having heard the testimony of a brutal murder by the man he'd claimed was like a son to him? Fern muttered her thanks for his concern and forced herself to breathe steadily. *Was he one more person Alvarez had wounded?*

She noted that the only person who looked directly at the man in the defendant's box was the strait-laced matronly woman, the one who'd taken her vow with such righteous devotion, her hand on the Bible and her strong voice proclaiming her God-given duty. She cast a steady, unforgiving gaze at Joel Alvarez before settling into her seat.

Fern's heart settled into a steady thud, thud as her tension grew. Tension that was also evident in the stiff set shoulders of Glory Jordan, Alvarez' defense attorney, and the frown between the eyes that belied the apparently relaxed posture of Dan Bradshaw, the prosecutor.

Alvarez sat with his hands tightly folded together as if he was holding himself from flying apart. Fern looked at those hands and shuddered as she remembered what those hands had done. Witnesses had testified he had been a firefighter, decorated for his bravery, a responsible citizen—the kind of man any girl's mom would be happy to trust with her daughter.

Not like the kind of man who would seduce his

way into the feelings of a young woman, then rape her and leave her dying in a pool of her own blood. Risking another glance at the defendant, Fern once more felt the horrified disbelief that had dogged her all these months. This man...this monster...looked so...well, *ordinary*. Like a nice, attractive young guy. Her gorge rose as she remembered she had dated him, had enjoyed his company, had dinner, taken a long walk on a Sunday afternoon. Laughed together at the same jokes. She'd found herself then, hoping for more, and now she knew that all this time she'd been courting a monster. And Rose had paid a terrible price for her blindness.

But then, what did a monster really look like? Did anyone know? If we could identify the monsters, we could control them and save their innocent victims. Perhaps. Fern had believed herself to be a good judge of character, but boy, had Joel Alvarez fooled her! She clenched her fists so tight the marks of her nails bled on her palms like stigmata. *Would the jury be as misled by the man's clean good looks and heroic record as she had been the first time she saw Alvarez?*

"Members of the jury, have you reached a conclusion?" Judge Michaels' deep voice shook Fern from her thoughts. She laid a hand on her abdomen as anticipation tightened her stomach.

The jury foreman rose and spoke. "Yes, Your Honor, we have."

"And how do you find?" A redundant question, really, since the judge had already read the slip of paper the bailiff had handed him and knew what the jury had decided. But ritual is a vital part of the open delivery of justice, and Fern forced herself to curb her impatience.

"We find the defendant, Joel Alvarez, guilty of the

5

murder in the first degree of Rose Adams."

Time stopped. The moment froze. Then the courtroom crowd let out a collective sigh, and the minutes began to tick by again. Swallowing hard as tears threatened to overtake her, Fern glanced over at Alvarez, the man who had been the focus of her hatred for so long—and was shocked at his bewildered expression. *Was he so evil, so arrogant, that he was unable to believe he'd be found and punished for his crime?*

The courtroom erupted into life, people in the public gallery chattering, a couple of journalists rushing outside, fingers already dialing on cell phones as they went.

****

Joel sat staring at the judge, waiting for someone to jump out from behind the Canadian flag and shout, *Joke!* Waiting for the nightmare to be over, his hands tightly clenched into fists. Every fiber of his being rejected the idea that this was for real, that the nightmare of the last few months had really happened. It simply didn't seem possible.

He struggled against the bile that rose in his throat as a couple of hefty prison officers came over to his table. His lawyer paused from packing files into her battered leather case, her face closed as she turned to him. He heard her speaking, but the words didn't resolve themselves into anything meaningful in his numbed brain.

"We'll appeal, of course we will," she was saying, as much to herself as to Joel. "Don't you worry, we'll…" and without finishing the sentence, she tucked a last yellow legal pad into the bulging briefcase, patted

Joel on the shoulder, and walked away. It seemed that no one liked a lost cause.

From the corner of his eye, he saw Fern Adams, surrounded by friends and well-wishers, comforted by gentle pats on her back, by fingers on her arm, by soft words. Her face was pale, but a grateful smile hovered around her lips.

Joel hated her even more in that moment.

He rose, his face gray with shock, too numb to fully realize that his life was over as the two officers pulled him to his feet and snapped manacles on his wrists.

"Come on, son, get with the program—you'll need your wits about you now. Prison's hard on killers like you," the tall gray-haired guard whispered cheerfully as he led Joel away. Still shell-shocked from the verdict, from the sheer injustice of it all, he stared numbly at the pretty woman who had moved forward and now stood behind the rail that separated the actors from the audience in the farce that had just taken place.

"Does she haunt your sleep? Does she keep you awake at night?" Fern spat in a harsh whisper as he passed by. He focused on her, and their eyes locked for a moment. Even numb from the shock himself, the misery and pain in her eyes held him. Her words were quietly spoken, but they burned into his soul as if she had branded them there.

He wanted to scream that he was innocent. It seemed so important to have her believe him. More than anything, he wanted to ask her why she was doing this to him. Why had she lied to the police and the court? But his tongue was too big in his mouth, the words could not pass, and the guards hustled him away as an older woman laid a comforting arm around Fern Adams' shoulders.

There was no comfort for Joel Alvarez.

****

Joel paced the cell that would be his home until the sentencing and worked on stoking the rage that boiled within him. The rage that centered on Dr. Fern Adams, the woman whose testimony had been the clincher in convincing twelve men and women—the jury of his peers—that he was guilty of so terrible a deed.

Her face swam into view before him; he had no difficulty conjuring her up each time he thought of her. *Why, why, had this woman wanted to see him jailed, his life ruined?* What was in it for her? Why had she told the police, told the court, that she had seen him running away from her sister's apartment that terrible night?

Was she protecting the real killer? What kind of woman would lie to defend the murderer of her sister and put an innocent man behind bars for the same reason? Had Glory Jordan, his lawyer, been right in her questioning of Fern when she suggested the woman had identified him as the killer out of revenge because she believed he'd dropped her to date her sister? Surely, she'd have to be insane to take jealousy to such a level.

He closed his eyes as he went through the testimony Fern had given. The terrible words were carved on his mind but made as much sense to him as hieroglyphics.

Glory had questioned Fern closely about her relationship to the accused.

The Witness: Yes, I dated Joel Alvarez a couple of times. Yes, I introduced him to my sister.

Ms. Jordan: How did you come to meet Mr.

8

Alvarez?

The Witness: I was duty doctor that afternoon at the ER, and he brought Jed Simpson, the mechanic who had been working on his car, into the ER with a bad cut on his hand.

Ms. Jordan: And was that injury severe?

The Witness: Yes, Mr. Alvarez did the right thing— it was bleeding profusely and needed six stitches.

Ms. Jordan: And is that when Mr. Alvarez invited you out for a drink?

The Witness: Yes.

Ms. Jordan: And you had no anxieties about meeting the man?

The Witness (pause): We were meeting in a very public place.

Ms. Jordan: Even so, nothing about his behavior had given you any anxiety about seeing him again.

The Witness: No.

Ms. Jordan: Had you been angry that he started dating your sister behind your back?

The Witness: No, I wasn't aware that he was seeing Rose.

Ms. Jordan: Had he ever given any indication to you of being anything other than a normal, amicable man, a newcomer to town wanting to make friends? Did you notice any propensity for violence, anything that made you feel uncomfortable?

The Witness: No, nothing like that.

Ms. Jordan: Did you want to punish him for abandoning you by identifying him as your sister's murderer?

Dan Bradshaw, for the prosecution, had jumped to his feet then, objecting to the line of questioning. "The witness is being harassed, Your Honor," he declared.

Ms. Jordan: You are sure that your identification of Joel Alvarez as the murderer was not colored by the fact that you held some ill will toward him for, to all intents and purposes, dumping you for your sister?

The Judge: Ms. Jordan, you are on dangerous ground, and belaboring this issue is not helping your case any. Save this for your closing statements.

Joel went over the words again and again, but still they made no sense. Just what was Fern Adams up to? She had to have a motive, a reason for doing this to him. He'd been attracted to her the moment he saw her in the hospital ER and thought she had shared that attraction. He sure as hell hadn't dumped her for her flighty sister. He'd been introduced to Fern's sister once, and he'd never been in her apartment.

But obviously he had made a very serious error of judgment. Someday, if he got out of here alive, Joel swore he would track Fern Adams down and find out just what game she was playing.

And make her pay.

****

A victory party was the last thing Fern wanted to go to, but her friends and supporters had gone to so much trouble to arrange it that she felt obliged to at least show her face there.

"Even if it's just for an hour or so; these people have been very good, working hard to get press publicity for the case, stirring public opinion, and showing up in court every day for the trial. You need to draw a line under everything now and get on with your life, Fern. Maybe this party will be just the thing," Dan Bradshaw urged. The public prosecutor had worked so hard to get a guilty verdict, and now he offered to accompany her to the celebration. Fern had a sneaking suspicion that maybe Dan would like their relationship to go up a notch or two, especially now the major obstacle to that—the trial of her sister's killer—was over.

She accepted his offer gratefully, even though she had no intention of dating the man. She might never want to date again! But she couldn't face the party alone, felt little reason to celebrate. Dan had been her rock during the trial, after all, and what could a few more hours in his company hurt? The trial was over, the monster jailed, but her sister was still dead.

Maybe with Dan to shield her she could spend some time with the people who had been so kind to her in the past few months. She had grown to lean on Dan and her friends and neighbors a lot during the evidence gathering and the trial. Once more wouldn't hurt.

It was a relief the court case was all over. It had been gruelling—not only listening to the details of her sister's character and murder fought over by the lawyers like hungry dogs with fresh meat, but the time she herself had spent on the witness stand.

Especially when the defense lawyer, Glory Jordan, had questioned her about her relationship to the accused, going so far as to suggest that Fern was lying because she wanted to punish Joel for "dumping" her. Fern squirmed at the humiliating memory of the questions.

The party was to be held in the event room at the Richmond Hotel, which was decked with flowers and streamers. It reminded Fern more of a football victory party or a bridal shower—it seemed inappropriate somehow. Because her sister, Rose, the one who really loved parties, was cold in her grave. And the man who had killed her was going to rot in prison until he, too, was dead. Or as good as.

Fern shivered, and without warning Joel's face flooded her mind, his shocked expression when the jury foreman gave their verdict. Not for the first time, a little worm of suspicion wriggled in her consciousness. She paused and turned to the prosecutor. "Dan, you don't think there's a chance that…well, that Alvarez is innocent, do you?"

Dan gave a snort of amazement. "Where the hell did that come from, Fern? Your testimony was the glue that pulled all the evidence together, that and the fact that Alvarez's DNA was found at the crime scene. "

"Just that—well, he seemed such a nice guy…what if he'd found Rose and panicked?"

"Psychopaths are often very charming. And the man is supposed to be a hero firefighter—would he panic like that? Wouldn't he be more likely to try to help her, call for help?' The prosecutor put a reassuring arm around Fern's shoulders.

"There's no doubt that that was his DNA? I mean, only his DNA, you know…" Fern choked on the words. "I mean, the semen…"

"None at all. DNA doesn't lie. But without your identifying him in the first place, giving us the suspect, we might never have been able to build the case. You gave the eyewitness testimony of seeing him run from your sister's apartment; and you remembered Rose saying she was dating an out-of-towner. He'd told you the truth about being a firefighter in Toronto. Thank goodness there are DNA records for emergency services people."

"I, well, he just looked so…shocked.'

"Probably too damned arrogant to think that he'd ever be convicted. Guys like him think they're invincible. Is that it? Just his expression? You're not thinking you made a mistake in identifying him?" Dan's eyes were narrowed in shock as he studied her face.

Fern shook her head. If she closed her eyes, she could see again Joel Alvarez barreling toward her down the stairs to her sister's walk-up apartment, feel the sharp nudge of his elbow as he pushed her out of his way, feel the cold movement of air as he rushed past.

And see the bloody red stains on his blue sweater and on his face and hands.

How many times had that scene replayed itself in her dreams? How many times had she woken up sweating, the raw stench of blood and rage in her nostrils as clear as if Alvarez were really there?

Fern sighed. No, there was no possibility that Joel Alvarez was not the man she'd seen running away from her sister's murder scene. Whatever else might be fallible, this was one thing she could never get wrong, not in a thousand years.

****

Richard Phelan rushed to his computer as soon as he got home from work. Cursing that fool of a supervisor who'd kept him late and had him go over work again, had held him up as he burned with impatience for the news he hoped would be waiting for him on the small LCD screen. *One day soon he was going to tell that man exactly what he thought of him and his fucking pathetic job rules, but right now wasn't the time.*

Anticipation danced in his chest as his fingers worked the keyboard to bring up his email program. A burst of pure pleasure washed through him as he saw that at the top of his list was an email from his contact. Haste made his fingers clumsy as he pressed the computer keys to open the message.

'Joel Alvarez was found guilty of murdering Rose Adams in the Primrose Hill, Ontario court today. Sentencing will be in two weeks' time on the 25th. Do you want me to be there?'

Phelan enjoyed the rush of victory that flooded through him. *Joel Alvarez was going to pay for his sins at last. He was going to suffer the pain and loss and humiliation that Richard had suffered for so long.* Phelan punched the air in a victory salute before pouring himself a generous glass of good rye from the bottle he kept in his home office desk drawer. He wanted to savor his victory before he replied to the email.

A titillating thought popped into his mind as he toasted himself in the mirror over the shoddy kitchen sink. *Could he, was it possible, that he could travel to Primrose Hill and be in the courtroom himself to see Alvarez's face when the sentence was pronounced?*

Chapter Two

It was a kind of déjà vu. Fern sat in the same courtroom, in the same seat, and watched as the dust motes carried on their endless dance in the wintry sunlight. Her heart was tight in her chest as she waited for all the players to take their seats: Dan Bradshaw, looking dapper and pleased with himself, and his young assistant, pretty, blonde Laura McKie, at the prosecutors' table.

Glory Jordan, the lawyer who had represented Joel, came in late, her feet dragging, a woman looking defeated as she dropped her files on the desk and flopped down into her seat. Then the star player, the man they'd all come to see, Joel Alvarez, was led into the room, manacles on his hands and feet.

Fern was shocked to see the effects that the time spent awaiting sentencing in prison had had on the man. He was thinner, almost gaunt. The effect was to fine tune the granite planes of his face, making his chin square and determined, his mouth a thin line, his eyes cold and hard over the blue shadows of sleeplessness under them.

A jagged bruise raged on his left cheek. It was obvious that the man had been fighting, was still violent, even in jail. Fern looked away as he turned, and his hard gaze came to rest on her. She couldn't meet his eyes for fear she'd break down in the face of the broken fury that resided there.

Judge Michaels' voice quieted the court room. The defendant and his lawyer stood, as did prosecutor Dan Bradshaw and his assistant.

Looking at the defendant over the rim of his half-moon reading glasses, the judge shuffled papers, cleared his throat, and began: "Joel Alvarez, you have been found guilty by a jury of your peers of the crime of murder. We have heard testimony from a number of people about the death of Rose Elaine Adams, and we have had heartrending victim impact statements from those who were close to Ms. Adams. There is no doubt in my mind that this was a heinous crime deserving of the highest punishment under the law.

"This has been an extremely puzzling case because I find it difficult to understand how a man of your apparent high caliber, a man who has worked in a dangerous profession such as firefighting and who has risked his own life to save the lives of strangers, should find it within himself to rob a young woman of her life and destroy the peace of mind of her family in so brutal a way. This is perhaps something for you to think about in the years to come. It is therefore my judgment that you be held in Her Majesty's prison for life, which is twenty-five years. However, in view of your previous good standing, I am not recommending against parole at some point in the future. If you are fit to be released before the sentence is up, that will be something for others to decide."

****

The room around him spun, his vision fading until he could only focus on the face of the judge who had just handed down a sentence that was beyond his ability to understand. *Surely, he wasn't to be sent to that hell hole of a prison for a quarter of a century?*

The only good thing was that he was sure he wouldn't live that long. Joel Alvarez felt the room close in around him, constricting his beathing and blurring his vision. And on the edge of his sight was Fern Adams. The woman who had brought him to this. The thrust of fury that followed the sight of her was the lifeline that kept him from falling apart. *Someday he'd make her pay...*

Fern Adams sat back on the hard courtroom bench, feeling as if all the strength had been drained from her. At last, it was here—the day the evil man who robbed her of a sister in a terrible, nightmarish way, was going to start paying for his crime. For her, the nightmare was over. For Joel Alvarez, it was just beginning.

So why didn't she feel even a little bit elated, even when her friends gathered around, congratulating her, and offering words of relief and pleasure that the murderer would pay for his terrible crime.

"Justice has been done," murmured Mrs. Kanjorski, the elderly neighbor who'd faithfully attended court each day with Fern.

"Nah, justice would have that bastard hung," said a gruff voice behind her, and Fern recognized Bob Mather, Rose's boss at the garden center where she'd worked on odd occasions. A shy, quiet man she'd always thought had a bit of a crush on her sister.

"No, Bob—justice would have Rose restored to us, alive and well, and erase the nightmare we've been living through. Nothing can achieve that," Fern said, realizing that this was the truth that had robbed her of a sense of victory when Alvarez was sentenced.

"He ought to be made to suffer every bit as much as he made Rose," Bob insisted.

"I think you'll find that Mr. Alvarez will find prison a very unpleasant place—for some, they say, life there is a living hell." A tall man with a long-billed baseball cap pulled down low on his head murmured into her ear. Fern reared back, annoyed that the stranger had been so…so intimate, whispering to her.

And there was something disturbingly familiar about the man. She turned to get a better look, but he was already walking away, his back toward her, a broad back that somehow reinforced her sense that she knew him. Perhaps they'd met in the corridors of the courthouse, or passing through the courtroom doors, or maybe in the cafeteria. Fern shrugged. She'd been in such a fog throughout the trial, she could have been sitting next to the man all these days and probably wouldn't recognize him.

****

What a rush this was! Sitting in the crowded courtroom, watching all these small-town hicks gather together like vultures screaming for the blood of the stranger who'd killed one of their own! Richard Phelan briefly wondered what their reactions would have been like if the killer had been one of their neighbors, their friends, the kid who delivered pizza, the guy who cut their hair, the auto mechanic down at the small main street garage, the high school teacher who coached their kids in soccer in his spare time…

Would they have howled for blood in the same way? Would the qualities of mercy have fallen like the gentle rain for one of their own, or would the fear-fueled fury at this abomination have been even more aggressive? As one of those people who had always been on the edge of society, Richard Phelan really wanted to know.

Phelan watched the crowd that had filled the courthouse on a cold late November day to witness the sentencing of Joel Alvarez. He wondered if the woman who had been murdered, Rose Adams, had been an out-of-towner, or a woman of ill repute—the very phrase made him smile—instead of a born-and-bred Primrose Hill woman with a snow-white reputation, would the feeding frenzy of revenge have been anything like this savage response?

His thoughts were interrupted as the defendant was brought into court and he got his first live look at the man he had hated since he was three years old and first learned of his existence. His nerves had been jumping like firecrackers every time the door opened, expecting to see Alvarez, as he called himself, hustled in. It had taken much of his considerable acting talent to keep up his cool, calm exterior and not draw unwanted attention to himself. His heart thrilled at the risk he was taking just coming into this courtroom.

It was okay now to stare at the man, even to allow some of his hatred to seep through his gaze, because if anyone saw him, they would simply think he was reflecting the same disgust and horror that they felt at the monster among them.

What they probably wouldn't understand was the immense disappointment he felt. This person he'd been raised to hate was just a clean shaven, dazed looking man who was struggling to hold his head high while dressed in prison clothes and wearing manacles. *Why, Joel Alvarez looked just the same as any man in his late twenties—in fact, he looks just like me!* Phelan grinned.

Then the judge entered the room and began the sentencing procedure, describing the crime and its effects on the local community, expressing his disgust which he knew was echoed by everyone there. Then he pronounced sentence, and Richard experienced the return of a deep sense of satisfaction flooding through his bones, making him feel his own strength as he watched the blood drain out of Joel's face.

Twenty-five years in prison seemed like a fair way to punish a man who'd robbed him of the life he should have had. Phelan leaned back in his seat in satisfaction, thoroughly savoring the look of utter shock and despair that flashed onto Joel's face.

When you've only ever had good things happen for you, having the gods give you a good slap in the face must be quite a shock, Phelan thought, battling the big grin that fought to transform his face.

Suddenly Joel's anguished expression fixed on a member of the audience, and a look of utter bewilderment and pain flashed across the handsome, haggard features. Curiously, Richard followed the direction of Joel's glance and gave a little shudder of excitement when he realized Joel was aiming the look at the murdered woman's sister, the woman who'd found Rose Adams' body. The obvious shock and grief that she was still experiencing had worked to cement in the minds of the jury that here was a distraught woman who nevertheless was seeking the truth, revealing to them the face of the murdering bastard who'd pushed past her in his flight down the stairs and out of the apartment building after his terrible deed.

Phelan put a hand over his face to stifle the bark of

laughter that threatened to erupt and pulled the billed cap he wore farther over his forehead. What a stroke of luck it had been, that Rose's sister should choose to visit her at the moment her murderer was making his escape! Her testimony had been the clincher in sealing Joel's fate, even more than the DNA evidence. This small-town hick jury was suspicious of the science yet more than willing to believe the eyewitness testimony of one of its own. Next to Fern sat the barmaid who'd sworn that Joel was the man who sat drinking with Rose for several hours that afternoon—she even told the court that the man had given her his name as Joel and said he was a fireman from Toronto...Phelan grinned again. *He just couldn't help himself.*

On the other side of the star witness was an older woman who'd been in court with Fern Adams every day, supportive in a grandmotherly type of a way. It seemed that this little town was all about family. Phelan's mouth turned down in a sour pout. *Family.* The very word made him want to puke.

He couldn't resist moving closer to the crowd and eavesdropping on their conversations. He wanted to feel a part of the excited, chattering group. A burly, heavyset man who'd given testimony as a character witness for the deceased, Rose's boss, had joined Fern and the other supporters, and Richard heard him say, "He ought to be made to suffer every bit as much as he made Rose."

"I think you'll find that Mr. Alvarez will find prison is a very unpleasant place—for some, they say, life there is a living hell," Phelan stated knowingly, watching as Fern whirled around to look at him. He'd startled her, getting so close without her realizing it, and Richard could have kicked himself for the *faux pas*—until he looked into her wide green eyes and was momentarily transfixed. She was so very like her sister…he wondered if she was as soft and warm and giving…or if she had that sweet, sexy, throaty laugh.

Then he pulled himself together. He had to get out of there, for there was a remote chance that she'd recognize him, and he didn't want that at all. Besides, it was hot in the courtroom, and the thick woolen hoodie and peaked hat with earmuffs that he'd kept on throughout the proceedings were beginning to weigh him down. Right now, he was starting to long for the wide-open places and the dim, silent spaces of the woods that had sheltered him in the many times he had run away from home. He'd left that place, his own personal hell. It had taken him too long to escape, but not long to find and punish Joel Alvarez!

A brief image of the blazing shack he'd left behind flashed through his mind, his mother's funeral pyre. The picture added to his sense of satisfaction as he watched Joel struggle to keep his shoulders straight and his head high.

****

"We will appeal, Joel. There must be evidence out there that will show that you are innocent. We'll appeal the sentence," Glory Jordan, Joel's attorney, said in the interview room just before Joel was led away to the bus that would take him to prison. This time he would be an ordinary member of the prison population, not a man awaiting trial or sentencing. Joel shuddered. The orange prison garb confirmed he was a convicted felon. His complexion looked even more sallow, like a very sick man who was scarcely holding things together.

"There would have to be new evidence to bring to an appeal," he told her roughly, "If you and your investigator and the police haven't been able to come up with anything so far, what makes you think you can get something that will convince a judge of my innocence in an appeal hearing now?"

Glory's look was fierce. "There must be something!"

For a brief moment Joel felt sorry for her but found himself then wishing she had shown this much fire, this much passion, at his trial. If his lawyer had had this much determination to win then, maybe he wouldn't be facing this nightmare now.

That's not fair, he berated himself. He was only too well aware that he hadn't been much use in the trial preparation. For weeks he had been unable to believe this was really happening; after that, it seemed all he could say was, "I'm innocent. I didn't do this." Words that sounded hollow even to his ears.

But when they asked him for some lead, some proof, some independent shred of evidence that would explain why all the evidence the police had collected pointed in his direction, he could only shake his head and lapse back into his numb stupor.

Now he shook himself back to the horrible reality of his situation. Placing a hand on Glory's arm, he said quietly, "We'll be in touch. If I think of something, I'll use my one weekly phone call to contact you. Otherwise, I'd appreciate you dropping by and letting me know of any progress—or lack of it."

She looked at him, her brown eyes brimming with tears, knowing he was asking her to visit or call not just for the updates but to help relieve the loneliness that surrounded him like an aura. "This has been such a fucking awful case, Joel. I've not known where to turn. There's been nothing to get a grip on. Everything that has been brought into evidence says that you're a brutal killer and guilty as hell. But my gut says you're an innocent man. And I stand by that. It's just so damn frustrating."

"It means a lot to me to hear you say that," Joel said truthfully. It was the first time in an such a long time anyone had shown faith in his innocence. His eyes filled, and he hid the emotion by standing up and turning away as the two guards came to the door. "I'd better be off...Wish me luck."

She reached up and planted a kiss on his cheek, her arms going around him for a moment before the guards separated them. It tore her up to think that somehow there had been a monstrous miscarriage of justice and she, with all her training, all her intelligence, had been unable to stop it.

"Good luck, Joel," she whispered, knowing all the while that this man would need more than luck to survive in prison.

Moments later the guards escorted him away. He shuffled in the heavy manacles on his feet and hands, and it took all his strength not to turn back and beg Glory to do something—anything—to achieve the impossible and get him out of there.

****

Back in the tiny Toronto basement apartment he called home, Richard Phelan smiled in satisfaction as he relived the court experience over and over by reading the screaming headlines in the newspapers he'd gathered on his way home:

Hero Firefighter Turned Vicious Killer Jailed!
Toronto Firefighter Convicted of Brutal Murder!
Savage Killing of Pretty Singer – Hero Fireman Jailed for Life!

Ah, now you can experience what life is like in a prison, with no hope of redemption, Phelan muttered. He'd have found the headlines more satisfying if there's been fewer "hero" comments, but even so, he spent a happy few hours searching the Internet for all the available information, articles, letters, and other documents about Primrose Hill Penitentiary that he could find. He wanted to immerse himself in the grim reality that was now Joel Alvarez' life.

And would be for the next twenty-five years unless a parole board took a shine to him… Richard laughed. If that happened, then maybe he and Joel could have some fun together.

For the briefest of moments, Richard wished he could be present at the jail to see how Joel got on—and perhaps to make the man's life even more miserable. Then a truly inspired idea struck him, and he hurried back to the keyboard to write a brief email to his contact, outlining yet another assignment he knew the man would take on without question, so long as the money was right.

Chapter Three

Fern thought she'd find closure once the trial was over and her sister's killer was shut away in prison for so many years. But doubts assailed her, thoughts of how different things might have been. Could she have saved her sister by not chattering about Joel to her? She knew Rose was a flirt, and it wouldn't have been the first time she'd made a deliberate play for one of Fern's boyfriends. But losing Joel to Rose would have been so much less painful than losing her sister to the murderer.

Halloween, Thanksgiving, and then Christmas were fast approaching—Rose's favorite times of the year. A time for endless parties, dressing up, drinking, and gifting. Fern dreaded it this year, without Rose to shepherd her more introverted self through the partying and socializing. Tears filled Fern's eyes. Her heart ached with longing for her sister, and she had no idea how she'd manage to get through the Christmas season without her.

One bright beacon stood out for her. She was going to fly to New York for a medical conference the week after Thanksgiving. When she'd first heard about it, she'd thought of cancelling. Fern had always considered this to be the start of the Christmas season, family time! She and Rose would get together with friends and…suddenly, her heart was breaking all over again. The idea of the season without Rose was just awful. Maybe she'd take the holiday time she was owed and stay over in the Big Apple for a week or so, lose herself in crowds of strangers, maybe visit the museums and art galleries, do some shopping.

But at her core, no matter where she was, no matter what exciting events she could take part in, she knew she'd always be on the periphery without Rose. Rose, the extravert, who would throw herself into the celebrations and take her shy sister with her.

****

The days in prison flowed into each other as slowly as if the world time was set on a new timetable of slow. Joel settled into the grinding routine of daily life behind bars. Being a self-disciplined kind of guy, he found it hard to adjust to the fixed and unwavering, daily events in which he had no choice of his own. On top of that, the occasional sudden alarms of lockdowns, cell searches, and random drug tests sent his blood pressure soaring because of their effect on the men around him. Any small wave of excitement or change in routine played on their nerves sending awareness into high gear in a manner that meant that any little extra thing, change, or stressor, could set them off.

And that little extra thing, some small or imagined slight or betrayal, could mean a beating in the showers—or worse—a shiv between the ribs. These were rare indeed, but he'd been in jail less than a month when he witnessed the horror of such a beating, and it never left his mind. The knowledge of the sudden, mindless rage and violence left him constantly wary and on edge.

One thing he did have was plenty of was time to himself—time after lights out when bile rose in his throat as he listened to the sounds of other prisoners snoring, crying, screaming, having sex with themselves or with another inmate. Sometimes that inmate was unwilling and there were brutal sounds of violence followed by animal guttural sounds of sex. He tried to close his eyes and ears, but he couldn't shut down his imagination. Hypervigilance ruled his days and nights.

He'd been lucky in that being a lifer gave him a special sort of status, and he'd been placed in the cell of another lifer who spent most of his time lost in a book. Jack Godsell had been in jail for fifteen years of a life sentence for beating his wife to death with a meat hammer. The guards had joked that the two of them would have lots to talk about when Joel had been assigned the lower bunk bed. But they hadn't had much to say to each other. Jack definitely preferred his own company, and Joel didn't want to be best buddies with a murderer. But they got along together in uneasy silence.

All that changed the day Joel came upon his cellmate being jumped by two other guys—younger, heavier, and meaner—and looking like he wouldn't survive the fight. Jack was a slender, middle-aged guy with a small pot belly and muscles atrophied from lack of exercise and use. Somehow, he'd managed to offend one of these guys. In prison lingo, he'd dissed the man. Joel could tell from Jack's wide and terrified eyes that he hadn't a clue what he'd done, but that wasn't going to save him from the beating that would restore his attackers' dignity.

"Hey guys, what's up?" Joel asked quietly. All three pairs of eyes swung toward him in the cramped space under the stairwell.

"What's it to you, buddy?" one of the men

demanded.

"Nothing, just looks like you and old Jack aren't feeling too friendly towards one another. Jack, sometimes his mouth runs off faster than his brain."

"It sure can. Bastard looked at the book I was reading and asked me if I wouldn't rather see the movie, like as how I couldn't read!"

"That's not what I meant!" Jack protested, his sentence ending in a whump as a fist struck his belly and he doubled over retching.

"Well, you know, Jack's seen a lot of movies. He's always down there on a Friday night. Even watches the kissy-kissy-chick flicks." Joel illustrated by making kissy sounds with his lips.

"Yeah, I bet he likes that kind of thing," sneered the other guy who'd been quiet up till now.

"Nah, he likes to watch the ladies in their little skirts. And sometimes less than that."

"Them movies have ladies in little skirts? Or show their knickers?"

"Ah, yes, and sometimes they even take all their clothes off…"

"They do?"

"That's probably why he asked if you wouldn't rather see the movie. Er, you know, he's maybe already seen it and, well, there's nothing like seeing the babes naked on the big screen…nothing, except seeing them in the flesh." Joel grinned.

"So he wasn't saying as how I couldn't read proper?"

"Nah. Not at all. Everybody knows who you are, Tupper. You think a little weasel of a guy like Jack would diss you? Not a chance. Don't rightly know that anyone would. He was trying to make nice, you know, get on your good side by sharing something he thought you'd maybe like."

The two men stared at Joel, then at Jack, and back again at Joel, digesting what was said. Then Tupper pulled Jack upright with a beefy hand, making Jack wince with pain. The other guy handed Jack the glasses that had fallen on the floor, and they both grinned and slapped the little man on his back. "Well, well, and maybe next time there's one of them movies due on, you'll be a good little man and tell us," Tupper said. "One of them with the girlies."

"Er, yeah, sure…They're not on often, but I'll be sure and let you know."

"And you, you're that guy who raped and murdered the bitch out in Primrose Hill, right? Maybe there'll be a movie that's good for you, you know, one where she gets it rough…" And the two men slouched off laughing and punching each other's arms.

"Thanks, kid. I owe you one."

"Not at all. Us lifers must stick together," Joel said, knowing the bitterness sounded in his voice. It was strange that, in order to get respect in this place, he had to let people think he'd done a brutal, horrendous murder.

"You're wrong about one thing, though," Jack said as he walked back toward the cell clutching his new library book.

"What's that?" Joel said, following him.

"I did mean to diss him. That big oaf could hardly read words of more than one syllable. He was sounding the words out loud as he went along. It was painful to listen to, and I'd had enough."

"That kind of behavior could get you badly hurt in here! Or killed."

"Yeah, well, after a while that doesn't seem like such a bad thing. You'll see." And Jack climbed up onto the top bunk, opened his book, and lost himself in the faraway world of the story.

****

The need to keep a low profile in prison meant long hours sitting on the bunk, reading, writing letters, or playing solitaire. For Joel, there was a lot of time to reflect on the past, on the miseries of the present, and project into the future. He found himself going over and over his life, wondering what little deed, what chance meeting, what joke of the universe had led him to this point.

What had started out as a mission to reunite with his unknown past had become a living nightmare, and he hadn't a clue how to wake himself out of it. Hitting his fist against the hard iron side of his bunk, Joel clenched his teeth against the physical pain that momentarily distracted him from the awful reality he was living through.

He wished to God he'd never bothered going through his mother's things. He'd started looking for comfort, hoping to find something in the stacks of well-organized papers that would ease the pain of losing her so quickly after his father's death. It had been a bittersweet consolation that she'd not been able to live without the man she'd married and loved for forty years. Joel had fought against the pain that she hadn't loved him enough to live without her husband and fight to stay with him a little longer. After all, he was a grown man now, and he'd been grateful that he'd had the parents he had been given.

He'd always thought there was just the three of them, so it was a shock to find the first evidence that he might have a relative he'd never met, letters sent to his mother many years before. Strangely, as lonely as he was feeling, that offered the crumb of comfort that somewhere he might have another family, that he wasn't all alone in the world. The last of his tribe.

For a while, the tantalizing idea that when they knew his parents were dead, they'd welcome him into their family circle. He'd even written to the address on the letters he'd found, letters from a doctor treating a woman named SueAnne who seemed to be a relative of his mother's and was about to have a baby. Nothing ever came of it, though, and his heart had ached with disappointment from what seemed like a new abandonment that left him feeling even lonelier than ever.

Then the anonymous note had come. The short message galvanized him into the mission that had led him into this mess.

You should visit Copper Junction, the note said, *where you might learn something about your family.*

There was no name or address on the letter, nothing to give him a clue about why he'd received it. Or the intent of the person who sent it. But the reference to "family" piqued his interest.

Why not? he'd thought to himself, setting aside anxieties about the note not being signed. He'd had some holiday time due to him from the city fire department, so he'd set off from Toronto on a voyage of discovery. He planned to search for his mother's relative, this SueAnne, or the doctor who'd sent the letters his mother had saved. Perhaps he'd find that he wasn't alone in the world. He did pause to consider, if he had family in Copper Junction, how they might feel about an unknown relative showing up out of the blue, but he set that thought aside.

He'd made it just as far as Primrose Hill before his world caved in on him.

Right now, he had never felt more alone in his life. His heart ached to think of the effect his conviction would have had on his parents had they lived to see it.

One thing he knew for certain was that he had to find some way to get out of here before he lost his mind.

****

Fern Adams was lonely. She and her sister Rose had been best friends since they were children and remained close even when Rose, two years older, had moved ahead first to primary school, then high school, then university.

"You must miss Rose terribly," Angie Rainier, manager at Glorious Gardens Garden Centre, where Rose had worked part-time, said. Rose had an eye for design and her talent and light-hearted banter brought in customers to the florist's shop that was part of Bob Mather's landscaping business. Fern had dropped in to see Angie a few days after the trial, wanting the comfort of connecting with someone who had known her sister well.

"Yeah, it's an ache that never goes away," Fern admitted. "Sometimes I see something and think, *can't wait to tell Rose about this*! Or I see a shirt or scarf or some little thing in Rose's favorite color—she adored orange—and I get all the way to the checkout to buy it for her. Then reality hits me, and I feel like I can't breathe. Like somehow the guy who killed her punched a hole in the universe which keeps opening up in front of me when I least expect it."

"Well, at least the vicious bastard is in jail now. He won't get a chance to hurt anyone else."

"I hope it's hell on earth for him," Fern replied fervently, then paused. Even as she said the words, she saw Joel Alvarez' pale, shocked face on the day he'd been found guilty.

"What's wrong, Fern? You've gone quite white." Angie put her arm around the younger woman. "Don't you feel well?"

Fern bit her lip to hold back the emotions that threatened to swamp her. "It's weird. I know it was Joel Alvarez I saw running away—he almost knocked me flying back down the steps, he was in such a rush. And he wouldn't have cared if I'd fallen backwards and broken my neck. Yet he had seemed like such a nice guy. I dated him a few times, you know?"

Angie nodded, chewing her bottom lip as she fought the tears that sprang to her eyes. Fern looked out at the luxurious rainbow of flowers and shrubs for sale at the garden center greenhouse. "It's just, you know, he did seem like a straight up guy. I wasn't surprised to hear he'd been a hero fireman. And his face when the jury foreman said they'd found him guilty…he looked so shocked. Like he never expected it could come to that. Angie, you don't think…?"

"That they got the wrong killer?" Angie gave a sharp bark of laughter. "Do me a favor! You said it yourself, dear. You saw him with your own eyes running away. And then there's the DNA evidence.

They say that can't lie, and it pointed right to Joel Alvarez. And the barista who identified him, too, said he'd been drinking with Rose at the tavern all afternoon. Psychopaths can lie without blinking and think they're too smart to ever be caught. That's probably why he was shocked. Don't lose any sleep over that monster, not after what he did to poor Rose."

Fern bit her lip. "You're right. I don't know why I'm even thinking of him." She fiddled with a pot of bright chrysanthemums, comparing them to several other similar pots like a customer with nothing else on her mind but choosing something pretty for a late autumn display in her home. She handed the pot and its vibrant scarlet cargo to Angie and smiled. "It's just that he didn't seem at all like the kind of man who'd kill someone. And all the guys who testified about his bravery, including the young woman who came forward to tell how he'd risked his life to get her out of that burning apartment."

"They say that psychos are like that, honey." Angie wrapped the pot in a big sheaf of paper and refused Fern's tendered banknotes. "He's probably worked hard to fit in as a hero, and all the time there's been this dark side to him struggling to get out. You just got taken in, the same way Rose must have been."

"But why Rose? Why travel all the way here from Toronto? Why not find a victim in the city or even go to New York, Chicago, somewhere big where he could have been anonymous, done what he wanted, and left?" Seeing Angie's narrowed gaze, Fern forced a smile she didn't feel. "I'm sorry, I'm a bit maudlin. It's almost the first anniversary of Rose's death, and it still feels like there are more questions than answers. Like why did he date me and then kill Rose? Why not me?"

"You're just a tender-hearted soul, Fern, but you'll have to understand that sometimes there are no answers. It's time you got on with your own life and put all this behind you. You'll never forget Rose, but you'll never know why he chose Rose and not you as his victim. I know there's probably a lot of guilt involved, but it's not your fault. You go on to your conference in New York and enjoy some down time away from Primrose Hill. Maybe get some perspective, but you shouldn't spare another moment's thought to Joel Alvarez."

Chapter Four

Richard Phelan paced around his small, rented apartment in a less desirable area of Toronto. The insatiable hunger that had returned so soon was ravenously gnawing at his mind, denying him rest. He ached with the hunger to see Joel Alvarez punished even more. It had grown back into his brain like a cancerous tumor, spreading its murderous seeds throughout his existence so that it seemed his entire body, his whole existence, throbbed with the need for revenge.

Or, should I say, even more revenge? Richard grinned as he booted up his computer and opened his email server to click on the instant message application. One thing you could say for sure about having money, lots of money, was that you could buy anything you wanted. And anybody. *What a shame my dear old Mom didn't live long enough to enjoy it.* The smile that accompanied the thought carried a searing flash of hatred.

Richard's smile grew wider as he saw Slater's IM message pop up, under that silly name. *Facilitator, indeed! What a dumb nom-de-plume his agent had chosen.*

Facilitator: *What can I do for you, Mr. Brown?*

Oh, how he loved this anonymous persona he'd adopted. *What would Slater think if he knew my real name? Doubt he'd be smart enough to put two and two together.* And for the first time, Richard experienced a little shiver of insecurity. *Maybe there would come a time, perhaps very soon, when he would have to do something about Slater.*

But in the meantime:

Mr. Brown: *About our mutual friend who's, shall we say, housebound?*

Facilitator: *Ah, yes. Poor man. :-)*

Mr. Brown: *I was wondering if there was anything we could do for him, say, to let him have a breath of fresh air?*

Facilitator: *Get him out and about, you mean? Are you kidding?*

Mr. Brown: *I beg your pardon?*

Facilitator: *It's just that you were so keen to see him...er, housebound, that I'm surprised...*

Mr. Brown: *I'm not paying you to think, Slater. I just want to know if you're up for this.*

Facilitator: *I thought we weren't going to use names, you know, in case...?*

Mr. Brown: *Getting nervous, are you? Stress is bad for a person's health.*

Facilitator: *Sorry, sir. But you should know it would cost you to, er, help our poor friend. There'd be a lot of people who who'd need...a lot of people I'd have to hire.*

Mr. Brown: *But you're up for it? You can do it?*

Facilitator: *It won't be easy.*

Mr. Brown: *Just say whether or no—I am sure I can find someone else.*

Facilitator: *No, no—er, no, I mean yes. I am sure we can do it. It will just take some finesse, that's all.*

Mr. Brown*: Expensive finesse, I assume.*
Facilitator: *LOL! Yes.*

Mr. Brown*: Well, listen closely, I have an idea how I want this done. I will leave detailed instructions at our usual drop spot. Pick up on Friday, okay?*

Facilitator*: Okay. Will do. Mr. Brown? I will need some upfront cash for this one. Hiring the staff you need won't come cheap.*

Mr. Brown: *That will all be in the package.*

Facilitator: *Thank you, sir.*

Richard logged off, grimacing at that last sentence from Slater. The man would do better if he wasn't so obsequious! But he had to admit, he kind of liked it. For the first thirty or so years of his life, he'd been kicked around like garbage, having to eat shit for people like Slater and the likes of Joel Alvarez. His mother used to say that turn around was fair play. *Well, in that, at least, dear old Mom was right.*

****

Fern Adams entered the room that had once been her sister's childhood bedroom when this old house had been their family home, shutting the door behind her as if she was trying to shut herself in with all those boxes. *As if a door would prevent her from turning and running from the task she'd been dreading!*

A shiver of freezing rain, early forerunner of the cold winter weather that was closing in, rattled against the windowpane. *Lord, but she wished she didn't have to do this.* She'd put off going through her sister's stuff for months now and, if she had her way, she'd never do it. But Angie was right—it was time she got on with her own life. There was nothing more she could do for Rose except keep her memory in her heart. That would have to be enough. When she returned from New York, the room would be empty, and all trace of her sister's life would be eradicated except for a few small mementoes. She wasn't sure how she felt about that, but her heart told her she would always have a connection to her wild, warm-hearted sister.

Rose had rented a furnished apartment, so all they'd had to do after...afterwards, was to just pack her clothes and odds and ends into boxes and move them over to the old family farmhouse where Fern could deal with them when she was ready. She hated the sorting she must do, but she couldn't just leave everything here. Rose was never coming back to claim her belongings, and that was thanks to Joel Alvarez. "I hope that jail time is hell every minute for him," she muttered as she used a craft knife to slit open the tape of the first box. Giving everything away would seem like letting her memories of Rose go, and tears streamed down Fern's cheeks and landed with a patter on the cardboard. She could just give everything away without looking at the stuff, yet what if there was some personal stuff of Rose's? Something that might embarrass her or her sister... or tossing away mementoes that she might later wish she'd kept would be heartbreaking and foolish.

So, she'd set this afternoon aside to do the least distressing of the two choices.

And she might have put it off even further if Mrs. Kanjorski hadn't reminded her gently that the children's hospital charity—one that was close to her sister's heart—had a fundraising sale coming up soon. It would be fitting, Mrs. Kanjorski had suggested, for Fern to donate anything that she didn't want to keep from her sister's possessions.

"I just know this would make her happy," Mrs. Kanjorski had said. "And it will help you, too, dear, to let go of her things and move on."

First Angie, and then Mrs. Kanjorski. *Am I really that transparent? I had high hopes that that seeing that animal, Alvarez, sent to jail would lift this burden of grief from my heart and let me go on. But he's been in jail months now, and I still can't let go.*

The first box she opened was a stark reminder of the differences between herself and her sister. The slinky evening clothes, the sexy tops, and the short, tight skirts for daywear. *All very fitting for her fun-loving sister.* Rose had been so full of life, so full of vitality and… Fern's eyes filled with tears that escaped and fell onto the deep red low-necked halter topped t-shirt dress she'd pulled from the box. The musky perfume her sister had worn, so different from the light floral fragrances Fern herself favored, filled the room as if Rose were there with her or had just stepped out for a moment and would be back with a joke or a teasing invitation to her to join her and the gang for an evening of clubbing.

Fern knew that the contents of every one of these boxes would stab painful memories into her heart. Because despite being so different, the two sisters had been close as children, had remained close even as they grew older and followed different paths. Fern had taken her medical training seriously while Rose had drifted from job to job, picking up hostess work on cruise ships and bar tending work in high-class clubs, day work at the garden center. Always on the brink of being broke, Fern's sister had flittered through life like a beautiful butterfly, and the world was darker for her leaving it.

If Fern had one regret it was that she hadn't spent more time flitting around with her sister. And if she had one hope, it was that Joel Alvarez, with his sharp, innocent expression and killer's heart, was suffering every minute he spent behind bars.

She shuddered as she recalled how she'd enjoyed her time with Alvarez, their dates, their kisses...*how could she have been so wrong?*

****

The greasy spoon diner was busy with the evening traffic and redolent with the smell of fried food when Slater walked in and ordered coffee to go. As he paid at the cash register, he kept his voice casual as he asked; "A friend of mine was leaving a package for me here— guy by the name of Brown?"

"Ah, yeah, let me see. Here it is." The plump cashier with the long graying blonde hair and deep red lips smiled at him as she straightened her short skirt after rummaging under the counter. She held out a large, fat, brown envelope. "This must be what you're looking for."

Slater grasped the envelope, but the woman held on, smile never faltering. With a muttered curse, Slater handed her an extra ten-dollar bill along with the price of his coffee. With a smile and a cute *"Thank you ever so much, sir,"* she let her fingers slip from the package. Slater wanted to slap the bitch but knew that he might need her again to pick up more instructions from his very generous client. So instead he said a casual "Goodnight, sweetheart, and thank you" and walked out of the restaurant, hoping that no one had noticed the little scene.

Then the thought occurred to him that the same woman had been on the cash register each time he'd picked up information from Mr. Brown. How much did she know? Would she be able to identify Mr. Brown if he ever needed to know who his client was?

A sharp pain tightened his stomach as he realized that the woman could also identify him, not only to the cops, but to his client "Mr. Brown." He crunched two antacid tablets, something he was doing more and more as he worked with 'Mr. Brown'. For there was no doubt in Slater's mind, especially after his last chat with Brown, that he was getting way too deep into something more criminal than he'd ever tackled before. It wouldn't be the first time he'd skirted the law, but this was well into criminal waters, and he wasn't comfortable with it. After all, there were witnesses.

He might, one day soon, have to do something about that restaurant cashier. And maybe, just maybe, he'd need to do something about Mr. Brown, the cash cow.

Or Mr. Brown might just decide to do something about him, and a man needed to keep his options open and his powder dry.

His anxiety heightened when he read the assignment Mr. Brown had given him, and the large wad of cash that accompanied it only slightly mitigated the fear that was uncurling within him.

It took Slater a while, a lot of phone calls and discreet questions, before the wad of money was much depleted and everything was in place to ensure his client's demands were facilitated.

But somehow to Slater, the company name he'd adopted, The Facilitator, was beginning to seem less like a sick joke and more like a very dangerous venture indeed. He emailed his client to tell him all the arrangements were under way and he was sure he would be pleased with the result.

And then he swallowed another handful of antacid tablets that did little to ease that queasy feeling that persisted in his stomach.

Chapter Five

Clanging sirens filled his head and Joel choked on the bile that rose in his throat as pain swamped him again. He struggled to open his eyes, trying to shake his head to free himself from the dream.

The noise disoriented him, and he struggled to grasp a reality that seemed to dodge his attempts to pin it down. *Where was he? What was the noise? Was he racing toward a fire call? Where were his teammates? Why couldn't he move...?* Sour bile filled his throat again and he managed to swivel his head sideways as he vomited.

"Oh, God...I should have seen that coming!" A thin-faced man in a dark uniform moved into Joel's line of sight and began to wipe Joel's chin and the sheet with a warm, damp towel. Joel tried to push out a thank you, but the words were mangled.

"Don't worry, son— you're not the first to vomit all over my nice clean ambulance," the cheery voice assured him.

Concentrating hard, Joel slowly forced his foggy brain to clear enough for him to see that he hadn't been dreaming. He wasn't racing to a fire call. He was strapped to a gurney in an ambulance, the siren singing an urgent song for him, blatting out the need to get to hospital as fast as possible.

"He's awake," a voice somewhere off towards the

foot of his stretcher said, and a face came into view. *The prison guard who'd made it his mission in life to make Joel's life more miserable than ever?* A name eluded him, but the shiver of fear connected to the man rushed through him. "Well, Alvarez, looks like someone else dislikes scum like you, too. One of your jail buddies put a shiv in you. Pity they didn't do a better—"

"Knock it off, officer. This man is in my care, and I'll be damned if I'll let you harass him." The thin-faced man moved back into Joel's line of vision and the guard was pushed aside. "Can you hear me? Take it easy, son. Can you tell me your name?"

Joel's head swung from side to side in an attempt to clear his thoughts, struggling to find the answer to the question. And then it was there. "Joel," he mumbled, although it sounded more like a gurgle to his ears.

"Do you know where you are?"

"Amboolas," he tried.

"That's fine. You're doing good. Now, Joel, you've lost a lot of blood, and we need to get you to ER as fast as we can. I want you just to lie still and try not to worry. You're in good hands." The paramedic gently wiped Joel's face with a cool, damp cloth.

Somewhere toward the end of the stretcher, Joel heard a grunt. He understood without seeing him that the other person wasn't as sympathetic as the paramedic who'd been questioning him. Without warning, the fog cleared, and memory flooded back, forcing his heartbeat to race. The voice belonged to Officer Dan Meade, a mean bastard if ever there was one. And Meade was riding in the ambulance with Joel because

46

Joel had been…had been…

Yes, he remembered now. He'd been in the line-up for meals, and it hadn't seemed too big a deal when Fuggy Armstrong and another guy he didn't know pushed in ahead of Jack and behind him. Certainly not a big enough deal to risk challenging the two thugs even though they'd jostled him. He'd catch up with Jack once they'd picked up their food. He'd learned a prudent prisoner picked his fights carefully.

Then out of nowhere…pain. Searing pain ripped into his back, and he cried out—falling, crumpling really—while the grinning faces of Fuggy and the other guy floated above him before they disappeared. Then Jack was kneeling by him screaming for a guard, screaming for someone, *any fucking someone, get an ambulance, a doctor, do something!*

After that, he remembered nothing until he woke up to the screaming of the sirens, the calm voice of the paramedic, and the heartless grunting of Meade. He closed his eyes then, not caring if he ever opened them again…

But inevitably he did. He awoke handcuffed to the steel frame of the hospital bed, his chest bandaged so tightly he could hardly breathe, and an IV streaming fluid through a clear tube into the back of his hand. Every bone in his body ached, every muscle and sinew had melted into rubber that wouldn't obey his commands.

"What the hell happened?" he asked, but no sound came from his mouth. There was no one in the room to hear, anyway, and he drifted back into that welcome darkness.

To wake again later—minutes? hours? weeks?

Learning that he was still alive was a painful experience; raising his head from the pillow high enough to have a full view of the white-walled hospital room sent shock waves of dizziness through him and the taste of vomit cramped from his stomach into his throat to burn like the ghost of a bad meal just above his breastbone.

He collapsed back into the bed and drifted off again into a deep, blessed sleep, only to come wide awake a short time—or maybe again it was hours, days later?—when deft fingers palpated his stomach and chest, and the pain shot through him like high voltage lightning. The doctor who was examining him stepped backwards at Joel's sudden movement, looking apprehensive. It was that look, as much as anything, that spun Joel into full memory. He was a prisoner, had been stabbed several times with a homemade shiv, and had been transported by emergency ambulance to hospital.

Where he remained a prisoner, handcuffed to the bed.

And the reason the pretty young doctor flinched when she saw he was awake, the reason for that look of horror mixed with fear and disgust on her face, was that he was a convicted rapist and murderer.

"Why didn't you just let me die?" he croaked, realizing painfully how dry and bruised his throat was.

"We don't let people die. We save them," the young doctor said crisply.

Self-righteous bitch, Joel thought and winced as his mind flashed back to a time when he'd made a similar comment when asked why he'd rushed back into a burning building to save a woman trapped there.

48

"The reason your throat may be painful, Mr. Alvarez, is that we had to intubate you for surgery. You had been stabbed in your back just below your ribs, and we had to access through your chest to repair some tissue and stop the bleeding. To do so, we had to put tubes down your throat. Here…take a small sip of water. It will help."

She offered him a glass of water with a bendy straw in it, holding the glass while he took a drink, but taking it away before he had had enough. "Not too much, or there's a risk you'll vomit.

"Now, the surgeon who operated will be along later to discuss with you the consequences of the surgery and if there are any long-lasting effects."

"Ah, so Sleeping Beauty is awake, is he?" a harsh voice asked. Joel didn't need to lift his head to know that the dreaded Officer Meade had entered to room. "Well, Alvarez, don't think this is going to be your ticket out—you'll be handcuffed to that bed, except for potty calls, which you'll do with some lucky sod of a corrections officer or cop in attendance. And there'll be an officer guarding your room at all times. Then we'll be taking you back to your cell for the next 25 years." The gloating laughter in his voice was unmistakable.

The young doctor—Dr. Louisa Havisham, her name tag said—gave him a quick, pitying look before her professional mask was back in place.

"So, son, if you feel like trying anything like an escape, remember two things. One, you're wearing a little short hospital gown with a bare ass—that's a pretty noticeable outfit outside in the wide world. Two, me or one of my fellow guards will be sitting outside. And no-one will hesitate to use necessary force to prevent a killer like you from escaping. Even in your current delicate condition."

"Officer Meade, I think Mr. Alvarez gets the picture."

"*Mr. Alvarez* brutally raped a pretty young woman who looked a lot like you, blondie, and when he was done having his fun, he slit her throat like she was a pig for the barbecue. You want to be careful where you put your sympathy, girlie." Joel heard the door slam back against its hinges as Meade stamped out, and he flashed the doctor a look of gratitude which was met with a cold, stony glare.

"Are you in pain?"

Was he in pain? Hell, yes. "Not a lot," he replied, not knowing why he denied the truth, perhaps one last shred of dignity or pride.

"Good, well, there is some pain killer in your IV. If it gets worse, ring the bell. I'll leave instructions with the nurses that you can have something more for the pain if you ask."

Joel didn't bother to answer. He had the feeling that, once Meade had finished broadcasting the grisly details of the crime Joel was supposed to be guilty of, the nurses would let him wait until Hell froze over before they would bring him pain medication. He'd just have to live with it.

Exhausted, he fell back against the pillows again and drifted into a fragmented sleep haunted by images of a dead woman lying in her own blood. His dreams left him confused about whether these images were from the photographs of the scene that he'd been shown, and which had been displayed for the jury in court, or whether he had these pictures in his memory because he had actually been there and killed the woman.

Hell, no—I didn't kill anyone! I'm innocent, he murmured over and over again in his sleep. Before he fell into deeper, dreamless sleep, he heard another woman's voice say, *"Does she haunt your sleep? Does she keep you awake at night?"*

And saw another face painted on the backs of his eyelids. In that moment, when he hung in the balance between drugged wakefulness and the blessed oblivion of deeper sleep, he cursed the woman who'd spoken those words to him in court. The woman who'd laid her hand on the Bible and lied about him. Convincing the jury that he was the one she'd seen running from her sister's apartment, branded with a young woman's blood.

The next day his thoughts were clearer, even though his body seemed to ache worse than when he'd come out of surgery. At least he could recognize the difference between reality and nightmare without the few pain killers that he'd been offered and steadfastly refused. But when he tried to get out of bed, he staggered as his legs threatened to give way under him.

The officer detailed to guard him that morning grinned as he saw Joel struggle but made no move to help or support him. Fearing the man would let him collapse to the floor—and perhaps kick him in the ribs, claiming he'd tried to escape—Joel managed with supreme effort to hold himself upright, holding onto the bed rail as the guard unlocked the handcuffs. Joel gave a brief thought to the weapon strapped to the man's side, wondered if he could make a grab for it, but knew he was as weak as a kitten and would be about as effective.

"Don't even think about it," the guard, a seasoned oldster by the name of Ted Maguire, told him as if he could read Joel's mind. "No, I'm not psychic. You were just having the same thoughts every other con in your position has had. Wondering what the chances were you could make a grab for the gun. Well, forget it— you'd be dead before you knew you'd screwed up."

Even in his weakened condition, Joel knew the man was right. Worse, he suspected that, even if he had been able to grab the weapon, he would not have been able to use it and would have wound up surrendering and facing even worse consequences. The thought of taking another human life sickened him. God knew, he'd saved lives in his career, not taken them.

Besides which, Joel held on to his burgeoning determination to live. To live and make Fern Adams— *Dr. Fern Adams*—recount her accusations and confess why she had done this to him. Yes, he had to live for that…

He clenched his fists as far as the handcuffs would let him. Why was he serving a life sentence in jail for murdering and raping a beautiful young woman? He was an innocent man. And why had Fern Adams, that woman's sister—a woman he'd admired and dated— lied to the court about seeing him running from Rose Adams' apartment?

As he made his slow and painful way toward the small bathroom, he realized with a frisson of shock that his earlier death wish had evaporated like the haunted dreams of his sleep.

In its place was a deep and bitter commitment to stay alive until he was able to find Fern Adams, his supposed victim's sister, and force her to tell the truth about what she saw the night Rose died. He'd never use violence against a woman, but he would find a way to make her exonerate him—and make her regret every word of the false testimony she had given.

****

Fern gathered up her notes from the last session the Psychology of Crime—Information for Medics conference she was attending in New York. The large lecture room was already emptying as other convention goers rushed to get out before the weather worsened.

"It's great to see you again, Fern." The lecturer for this session, Dr. Kyle Witburg, was an old friend from college days, and she had been delighted to see his name on the roster of presenters.

"And nice to see you, too. How is life in the Big City?"

"Oh, you know how it is – lots of pressure. You gotta run to keep up."

"Oh, if I remember right, you thrive on pressure," Fern said, giving him a hug. It felt good to connect with old friends again.

"And are you still out in the sticks in the Great White North?"

"It's not exactly the middle of nowhere, Kyle. And the slower pace suits me," Fern told him. "I'm doing up the old farmhouse that I inherited from Mom and Dad, and I have plenty of friends and a good job. Keeps me busy and out of trouble."

"Ah, I can remember the days when we thrived on getting into trouble." He winked at her.

"I doubt you go getting into much trouble these days. I'm sure Alice keeps you occupied," she teased, smiling. Kyle's wife, Alice, was also an old friend from college days.

"Alice, and the two rug rats. You'll have to come and stay for a few days and meet them. I know Alice would be thrilled to see you."

"Maybe later, in the spring when things calm down. I'd love to see her again, and I can't believe you have two little ones." A little murmur of envy surprised Fern.. What must it be like to have family?

"Sometimes it surprises me, too. Especially at two a.m. feedings…" Kyle gave a dramatic grimace.

"Admit it, Kyle, you love it."

"True enough." Kyle cupped her elbow with his hand and moved them towards the doors. "I hope you got something out of my talk today. Did you find anything of relevance to your practice?"

She paused, thinking about the session material. "You know, I really wanted to hear about this issue. Even out in the sticks…" she grinned and poked him in the ribs. "We're finding an increased number of psychiatric cases being brought into the ER as more suitable facilities are either underfunded or over stretched. So yes, I found your information very useful and will be passing some of your recommendations on to the hospital medical board when I get back."

Kyle, tall and slender and still youthful, with only the slight graying of the dark hair at his temples to give away his approaching middle age, nodded. "It's a story we're hearing more and more, especially in these days of cutbacks. And nurses and doctors are often under equipped and untrained to cope with the various forms of psychosis and other mental health ailments that they are faced with."

Fern paused for a moment at the door, a hesitant frown marring her forehead. "You know Kyle, I came across something…it's, well, a bit personal…"

Kyle frowned. "Alice and I did send condolences, but I wanted to tell you in person how sorry I was to hear about your sister. Rose was a lovely person and didn't deserve to fall foul of some crazy person…"

Fern blinked back tears. "I'm sorry, it's still fresh even after all these months." She paused a moment. "Listen, let me buy you a drink and pick your brains over something."

"Might be slim pickings, but sure. Let's go to the bar downstairs, and you'll be able to get a cab to the airport. When's your flight?"

"Not until early this evening, so long as we don't get snowed in." She glanced through the glass doors at the street outside, where winter was making itself felt in a deepening cover of white flakes.

They sipped their drinks in silence for a few minutes, watching as other conventioneers slowly drifted away, most of them carrying overnight bags and briefcases.

"So, what is your ulterior motive?" Kyle asked.

Fern played with the serviette under her drink. "Oh, you might think this is silly, but you know you talked about the use of hypnotism to help people dealing with all sorts of issues…"

"That's usually the victims of crime we're talking about, although it can work at times with people experiencing some sort of mental dislocation. However, in that case, it's used to try to induce calm."

"What if…what if someone who was convicted of a horrible crime insisted they were innocent. And yet there was all the evidence in the world to prove that they were guilty?"

"You mean, someone who appears to sincerely believe they're innocent, such as someone who's in a fugue state?" Kyle sipped his drink. "Are you talking about the man convicted of Rose's murder? I understand he was a hero fireman, and had no other convictions?"

"That's true. Joel Alvarez doesn't have so much as an outstanding parking ticket, and yet he has been convicted of a most...brutal..." Fern stopped to swallow back the tears that promised to swamp her. "It seems to be so, well, out of character, although I saw him myself, running away from Rose's apartment." Fern shivered. "He had Rose's blood on him, but he claims he was never there, had met Rose, and didn't even know where she lived."

Kye patted her hand. "Sometimes, after a very traumatic experience, the mind can split off to hide the terrible thing. But that's usually some kind of post traumatic experience, and in general it affects the person who is convinced they are in mortal danger. I'm afraid it doesn't sound like your man would be in that state of mind."

"What about Borderline Personality Dissociative?"

"Again, you'd expect there to be other incidents, times when he acted and thought as if he were someone else. I'm afraid your guy may simply be a killer. Perhaps with psychopathic tendencies, which makes him a dangerous creature. Or perhaps he was on a drug high, lost his temper and didn't mean to do what he did."

"Could hypnosis reveal another personality?"

"Is this the guy you were also involved with?"

"Oh, you're quick, aren't you?" Fern wished he hadn't guessed, hoped her questions hadn't been too obvious. "Yes, I did date Joel Alvarez for a few times and that's why it's so confusing. He seemed such a nice, normal, sane character, not a murdering madman. And when he says he's innocent, it all seems so…true. It's hard to reconcile the Alvarez I thought I knew with the animal who murdered my sister."

Kyle touched her hand, a sympathy pat. "It's hard. I can see that. It sounds like you're feeling torn about who this guy really is." Kyle thought for a moment. "Obviously, without meeting with him, I can't diagnose. But I did read about the trial, and the man's background, the hero fireman, makes him sound like anything but a crazy rapist and killer.

"But on top of that, he was examined by a psychologist, and the court had ordered a psychiatric exam. If there was some issue like this, some mental health problems that led to him being in a fugue state or another personality, when he murdered Rose, they would at least have suspected something. The clincher is that you witnessed him running away from Rose's apartment. There's evidence that he was seen with Rose that afternoon in a bar. Does he have anything to say to contradict that?"

Fern chewed her lip to try to stop the tears that welled up in her eyes. Everything still hurt like a fresh, open wound. She shook her head. No, Joel had not a single shred of evidence to prove he was innocent. "He claims he was hiking around the lake, alone, and didn't see another soul. And no-one came forward to support that alibi."

Kyle sighed. "So no, dear Fern. I think the man is just plain well a murderer, and you should be happy he's in prison."

"He's just so convincing in his claim to be innocent. Is there no other explanation?"

Kyle sighed. "Not unless he has an identical twin. A wicked twin would fit the bill."

Fern shook her head, managed a smile. "No, he's an only child."

"Well, then, girl, just accept that, for whatever reason, he lost it with poor Rose, and now he's fastened up in a place where he can't hurt anyone else again, for a very long time."

Fern stood and hugged him. "Thank you. You've put my mind at rest."

"Good. Now let's get your bags and try and find a taxi for you before the weather worsens."

****

Richard Phelan rubbed his hands together in relish, looking forward to the next report by the man who called himself The Facilitator. His computer message app pinged, and he eagerly pressed the open button.

Facilitator: *Our friend is in hospital, Boss. What now?*

Mr. Brown: *Now we get him out. How bad was he injured?*

Facilitator: *Enough for surgery. The man must be damn sore. He'll not be running in the marathon any time soon.*

Mr. Brown: *Didn't I tell you he hadn't to be hurt too much? What the fuck were you thinking?*

Facilitator: *I wasn't the one that stuck him, Boss. The stupid asshole that did this had a touch of the over-*

zealous nature in helping our friend. But he should be okay and ready to return within a few days.

Mr. Brown: *Okay, I'll have another package for you at the usual spot, with instructions. I want our friend out of there, whatever it costs.*

Facilitator: *Okay, Mr. Brown. I'll be there.*

Richard Phelan swore as he turned off his internet connection. *Damn it all to hell!* Now he was going to have to do something about Slater, after all. He'd been so angry with the man that he'd slipped up and all but confessed in the message to conspiracy to have Alvarez assaulted and then freed from the hospital. He didn't think the police were that bright, but even they would be bright enough, if presented with copies of the texts and Slater's sworn statement, that he could be investigated at least. *And that would never do.*

He wouldn't put it past Slater to have made a deliberate effort to get him to make a damning statement. Perhaps the man was even hoarding the texts as a little something to guard against a rainy day. *Blackmail.* That a fool like Slater could even consider blackmailing a man like himself made Richard Phelan snort. But a sobering thought occurred. *What if Slater was recording all these conversations for the RCMP or some other interfering government agency?* What if he was already being set up? He couldn't discount that possibility. It wouldn't be beyond the little worm to try to trap him.

Mr. Slater's time was definitely limited.

****

The same blowsy blonde cashier was on the cash desk of the greasy spoon café when Slater sidled in out of the bitter December wind to collect the latest package from Mr. Brown. She grinned at him cheekily as she handed him the package, leaning into him and blowing a bubble with the chewing gum almost into his face.

He reared back, his nostrils full of a chemically created strawberry scent, nothing at all like real strawberries. The smell sickened his already queasy stomach. She always seemed to have a huge wad of the disgusting gum in her mouth. Slater wondered if it was the same wad, or if she changed it now and again. *Did she stick it to her bedpost overnight, like that old song his mom used to sing?*

Her sudden friendliness made him brave. "Who delivered this to you?" he asked, keeping his voice casual while staring at the pastry cabinet as if he were more concerned with choosing something to pacify his sweet tooth than really interested in her answer. He opened his right fist, letting her see the two twenty-dollar notes resting there. She palmed them with practiced ease.

"I dunno. I didn't see it dropped off," she said, then to his acute embarrassment, yelled, "Hey, Morty—did ya see who dropped off this big envelope for the fella here?"

Slater bit down on his lower lip, mortified, feeling as if every pair of eyes in the place was riveted to his back, every ear listening for the answer.

Morty, the cook, leaned out through the pass-through and looked Slater up and down, the kind of hard look you give someone when you really want to remember them. Slater's stomach grew even queasier.

"Just a kid—a pimply-faced brat who tried to get his hand into the candy display while he thought I

60

wasn't looking."

"The same kid who brought it in the last time?" Slater asked, guessing that his deduction was correct, and "Mr. Brown" was using kids to make deliveries for him.

Monty gave him a strange look. "Nah, last time it was an old woman. Poor old dear looked like she lived out on the streets, barely able to walk, and she dragged her damned shopping cart in here with her. And smell! If you talk to whoever's sending you those packages, tell him not to send either of them here again." And with a last hard look at Slater, the cook pulled his head back inside the opening and got back to banging pots and pans around.

Slater was sure his face was burning. He tucked the big envelope inside his coat and, avoiding the mocking eyes of the cashier, sure that everyone's gazes were on him, he fled from the restaurant.

But the other customers looked far too interested in wolfing down their food and getting ready for late shifts at work, or for a night out on the town, or even readying for a late-night walk home to a lonely, silent apartment, than paying attention to the goings-on at the counter.

All except one. The bearded older man, dressed in a shabby jacket nowhere near adequate for the season, hogged the corner seat same as the last time Slater entered the cafeteria. He sat alone at a table for two and fixed Slater with an intense stare throughout the encounter. Now he followed the Slater's progress through the window as he loped off down the street toward an unpretentious "Middle Canada" car parked at the sidewalk.

The car was parked close by under the convenient

light of a streetlamp and Richard Phelan smiled a wolfish smile as he memorized the registration plate number as Slater drove away. He was sure he could grease a few palms at the vehicle licensing bureau and find out just where Mr. Slater lived. If not, there were other avenues to follow, other private detectives with morals just as soiled as Slater's. Richard wiped droplets of coffee from his false beard, careful not to smudge the theatrical make-up which made him look older and grubby, and pushed aside the flash of anger that stabbed him.

It seemed Slater was as interested in identifying him as he'd been in learning more about Slater, the "Facilitator" he'd dealt with so far only online. *No longer a trustworthy servant, after all*. Slater would need to be dealt with quickly, once everything else was in place.

Richard sighed. *It was so hard to get good help these days.* And he grinned at the young waitress who came over to offer him a coffee refill on the cup he'd been nursing for the past hour or so. The grin made her startle and step back, suddenly deciding to bypass this dirty old man's table and move on to fill up the cups of the hot-bodied construction workers at the next table.

Seeing the effect he'd had on the young girl, Richard's smile turned into a malicious scowl. *How many years had people thought they could treat him like some sort of leper, some worthless nonentity? Well, if only they knew who he was! He had the money, the means, and the inclination to have the likes of that snotty bitch fawning over him—and that time would come.*

But first, there were a few loose ends to deal with,

like Slater. And that could wait until the one major payback he wanted—the deadliest Halloween prank of all time on Joel Alvarez!

Chapter Six

"Hey, officer, the nurses thought you'd like a coffee. You've been here at your post so long you must be dying of thirst!"

Propped up in bed, a neglected month-old magazine on his lap, Joel stared out of the window at the cold blue December skies while he daydreamed himself far away from this overheated hospital room with its smells of disinfectant and sickness. The young woman's voice pulled him from thoughts of a beach and rolling waves, and he turned to watch through his open doorway as the pretty little Candy Stripe volunteer walked down the hallway toward the Canada Corrections officer sitting outside Joel's private room, her neat little hips swaying.

"Well, now, ain't that just the sweetest thing," Officer Dan Meade said, and the girl blushed charmingly, the color on her cheeks enhanced by the light from a sparkling reindeer Christmas pin on her shirt. Meade took a moment to stretch his stiff limbs before reaching out and taking the hot beverage with a grateful smile.

"I'm not used to all this sitting around," he declared, watching her out of the corner of his eye. Joel figured the officer was looking to see if the girl—jailbait as she looked under sixteen—appreciated the muscles that rippled under his shirt as he flexed his biceps. No doubt he was gratified to see her looking at him, wide-eyed, but Joel averted his gaze. *Why, this was just a kid!* Sure, she was wearing one of the hospital volunteers' uniforms, but she had a school backpack on her shoulders, probably full of her homework.

Even so, she had a sexy walk and that cotton dress was tight across her chest—

Fuck, Alvarez, you're turning into a dirty old man.

"It must be very boring, sitting here all day, being on guard. I bet you're used to a lot of action," the girl said, batting her eyelashes and using double-entendre in that way that only a teenage girl can do and not get called out over.

"Yeah, the most exciting thing I've done all day is walk my prisoner to the bathroom and back."

"Ooh, I heard he's a murderer, a man who…who did terrible things to a pretty young woman and then killed her." The girl's breathless speech and innocent, coy phrases made Joel wince.

"Now, you don't have to be worried about anything, little girl," Joel heard Meade say, and pictured him taking a big swig of his coffee. Joel's mouth watered at the thought. *What he wouldn't give for a decent coffee!* "The likes of Alvarez aren't going to pick a fight with another man. Girls are his thing— girls who can't fight back."

"Ooooooh!" The Candy Striper squealed, daring a nervous glance towards Joel's room. "I'm so glad they sent someone like you to protect us! You know," she added, and even though she lowered her voice confidentially, Joel could still hear the atavistic excitement. "There was a prisoner here last year, they told me, and he managed to grab one of the nurses and he…he touched her and threatened her before they were able to get him down." She gave a delighted little shiver. "Well, I shouldn't keep you from your duty, should I?"

"I sure appreciate the gesture, anyway. You tell those nurses that I'm real grateful for their kindness."

"I'm sure they appreciate your being here. It makes us all uncomfortable to have someone like…like that man in here." The girl cast a quick glance at Joel, her look unreadable. "Let me take your cup. Maybe I'll be able to bring you another drink later?"

"That would be very nice." He handed her his empty cup, and Joel imagined him smiling wolfishly at the pretty blonde. The teenager blushed to the roots of her hair at the masculine growl Mead injected into his tone. "Maybe I'll see you around some time."

"Maybe you will," she murmured.

Not if I see you first. Joel was sure he lipread the words she muttered under her breath as she turned and walked away. All the way down the hallway, as though she was conscious of Meade's hot eyes on her, she wriggled her butt just the right amount to keep his attention focused until she was out of sight. Joel saw her pause at the end of the corridor and wondered as, after a quick glance behind her, she pushed the cup down into her backpack.

Puzzled and wary, Joel heard the sounds of gentle snoring from the corrections officer who should be standing guard. Shivers ran through him at the sudden realization that she'd fed the officer drugged coffee. *What the hell were her intentions? Was she some kind of feminist avenger, wanting the chance to kill a rapist and murderer as he lay helpless in the hospital bed?*

Joel wondered if he should shout for help and dismissed the thought. No one would be coming to his aid. Then his gut tightened as he saw the girl walking back towards his room. Pausing at the door, she gently slipped the key ring from the guard's belt, a task made more difficult by the latex gloves she was now wearing. Meade stirred, and she drew in a frightened gasp, smothering the little sound behind her hand. She waited several heart stopping seconds until his breathing had settled back into that deep, drug-induced rhythm, then completed her task of freeing the key.

Just what was she up to? Torn between calling for help and curiosity as to what the girl's intentions were, his hand strayed to the call button that lay beside him on the bed. His wrist was sore and chafed by the metal of the handcuffs that restrained him. He'd asked if they could be removed, but the officer on duty then had grinned and said no, the nurses would refuse to come into the room if he wasn't restrained. After all, they didn't want to risk the same fate that the last lady who'd consorted with him had met, did they?

He'd laughed heartily at his own bad joke, ignoring Joel's stony stare, which seemed to amuse him more. So what the hell was this little hospital volunteer doing, prancing right into his room as if she hadn't a fear in the world?

"You Alvarez?"

"Yeah. I'm surprised they let a little girl like you come into the room with a bad guy like me all alone," he said sarcastically, expecting to see the guard's ugly mug come around the door. He glanced again at the girl, puzzled by her expression. On closer inspection, she looked a bit too old to be your usual high school hospital volunteer.

An impression that she quickly built on as she plopped her bag down on the bed and began to pull out an oversized t-shirt, track pants, a sweater, hooded jacket, shoes and socks, and boxer shorts.

"I'm hoping these are the right size. The guy just gave me the bag and told me to get it in to you."

"For God's sake, woman, what are you doing?" Joel looked with longing at the clothing and noted the shiny silver key in her hand. The two things that would allow him to get to freedom without being noticed. Jogging down the high street, barefoot on the icy sidewalk with his ass hanging out of a backless blue cotton hospital gown and shiny handcuffs hanging like bling from his wrists would certainly turn heads and bring out cell phones.

"If the guard outside comes in, you'll be in real trouble. I don't know…"

"*Shut the fuck up*," she hissed. "The guard's out to sleep and will be for another half an hour or so. All I want from you is—well, two things."

"What are they?

"A promise you'll not harm me if I undo the handcuffs…"

"I've never harmed anyone. I wouldn't be starting with someone helping me—"

"Yeah, I know. The prisons are full of innocent guys."

Joel swallowed back a surge of anger. "You said two things."

"I'm going to undo your cuffs, then I'm going into your bathroom to change my clothes. I want you to get into this outfit as fast as you can and leave with me. But no funny stuff. And no trying to get out of here and leaving me, right?"

Joel nodded. Words failed him. For an awful moment, he wondered if this was some sort of test, a trap maybe. They could shoot an escaping prisoner, and no one would hold it against them...

Another glance at the sky outside and the rapidly fading light, the street sounds from below...the call of freedom. He realized he'd rather be shot dead trying to escape than to go back to that prison cell. "It's a deal," he said, heart pounding as he pushed back the bedclothes.

"Watch your modesty." The girl—woman—grinned as she cut her eyes to Joel's nakedness under the short gown. Joel glanced down, face burning as he realized his exposure and yanked the covers back up. She laughed as she moved to the side where his arm was cuffed.

"Don't worry. You don't have anything I haven't seen before." Her tongue poked between her lips as she concentrated on using the key to snap the handcuffs free. Joel rubbed his wrists, watching as she went into the bathroom. Was she going to use a cell phone, call the guard, the police, scream for help and get him killed?

What choice did he have? Risk a fast death as an escapee, or die a slow death in that stinking prison cell?

Pushing back the soft cotton hospital blanket, he swung his legs over the side of the bed and stood up so quickly that dizziness swam over him like a dark cloud, and he plopped back on the bed for a moment until it passed. Weakness from the blood loss, or was it just that he'd been lying down so long with nothing to do? He raised his arms above his head to pull on the sweatshirt, and pain raced up his ribcage and his back from the wounds that were healing.

"Just my luck for the stitches to be opened up. I can bleed to death in freedom," he thought wryly as he pulled on socks, boxer shorts, and sweatpants. The sweater was a little tight across the shoulders and biceps, the pants a little loose in the waist, but the jogging shoes fit to perfection. Under the clothing he found a baseball cap, and the peak was big enough to shadow his face while covering his crew cut hair, especially when he pulled the hoodie up over his head as well.

And it felt wonderful to wear civilian clothes again!

He whirled around as his erstwhile rescuer came out of the bathroom dressed in jeans and a cotton sweater, her hair now loosened from its ponytail. She, too, wore a baseball cap that shielded her face.

"Okay, now, pack whatever you have in the bag and put it over your shoulder. Let's get out of here before the shit hits the fan."

Joel threw the few personal items he had with him into the bag and moved towards the door. She stopped him with a raised pink-nailed hand, and cautiously opened the door to peer outside. "Wait a moment while I return the keys."

Joel's heart went into overdrive. *What if they were stopped now? Surely Meade would awaken as the girl tried to attach the keys to his belt?*

And then it was over, and she was back by his side,

a forefinger over her lips to indicate the need for silence.

"Okay, here's the deal—you and I walk through the corridors hand in hand, as if we're visitors. Any sign of trouble or if we're challenged, we duck into a room and make like we're looking for someone. Once we get out of here, we walk towards the bus stop, and that's it. I'll never see you again, and you'd better not try to find me. We go our own ways and forget we ever met."

"Okay." Joel nodded.

"Coast is clear. Try to look like a visitor. Out we go." She slipped her hand in his and pulled him through the door, past the sleeping Meade, who didn't so much as twitch as the man he was charged with guarding sloped out along the corridor and off towards the elevators and freedom.

****

They crossed the sprawling hospital car park and by the time they reached the street, Joel's wounds were aching, and his legs felt weak. A damp sensation underneath the hoodie told him the stab wound and surgical site underneath his ribs had started to bleed a little. He fought the light-headed sensation of physical weakness, feeling disorientated in the unaccustomed rush of people and traffic. The girl with him shook his arm impatiently, sending the further stabbing of pain along his chest and back.

"Pull your shit together, Alvarez," she muttered, all the while keeping a pleasant smile on her face. "Don't get people looking at us, or someone will be suspicious and remember you, be able to tell the cops which direction you took off in. And finger me, into the bargain."

"Okay, I'm okay, just a bit weak, that's all."

"Well, get over it. There's money in your hoodie pocket, and the address of a place where a room has been booked for you under the name Jackie Phelan. You'll find another change of clothes there. Then, my man, I suggest you lay low for a few days before getting the hell out of Dodge. They'll be expecting you to rabbit, but if you stay put it'll be harder for them to find you."

"Who are you? Why are you doing this?"

"Don't get all misty-eyed. I'm doing it because some guy gave me a shedload of money to do it. And unless I'm mistaken, some other guy had given him a nice slice of cash to arrange this. What I'm saying is, I don't have a clue who's interested in getting your ass out of jail, or why he wants to bother. Myself, I'd let a murdering scum like you rot in the pen, but I need the cash."

Joel was still taking in what she said when the girl seemed to vanish from his side like a mist. For a crazy moment, he thought maybe this was all in his imagination, but a sharp push in his side brought him back to reality. "Get off the fucking sidewalk, man. You're holding up traffic," a tall, skinny white guy growled as he shoved past Joel with unnecessary aggression. Joel swallowed back a caustic comment, glad that he still had the hood of the sweatshirt up over the baseball cap, which effectively hid most of his face. One thing prison had taught him how to do was bite back smart aleck comments and not draw attention to himself.

First order of the day was to get out of this area

without attracting any notice. He walked like a man who knew where he was going, almost relishing the pain it caused him, because he was free!

Free—until they catch you. And won't they just be pissed with you when they do?

The thought brought Joel up short. He considered walking back to the hospital and giving himself up. Then he thought of Glory Jordan. His lawyer would help him surrender and see that he wasn't ill-treated. At least while she was around. He thought of the beefy fists of the brutal guard Meade, and his heart quailed. A few blows around the site of his wounds and it would probably be curtains for Joel Alvarez. Or was that Jackie Phelan? His mind snagged on the unusual name, but no matter how he scoured his brain he couldn't remember where he'd seen the name before.

He tucked his chilled hands inside the hoodie pockets, his fingers finding a wad of notes there. Looking up, he realized he was standing in front of a small restaurant and his belly was responding with a rumble to the delicious smells coming from inside the brightly lit and crowded premises. *Why not go in for a meal? It might be the last dinner he'd enjoy for a while if he was caught, sort of like a condemned man's last supper.* Joel grinned bitterly as he walked into the warmth of the café.

The perky young girl working as a hostess grinned back and led him to a small table away from the windows. He was happy with the cramped space. It had a fine view of the main entrance and was right by the kitchen doors if he needed to make a quick exit.

Already I'm thinking like a hunted man, Joel thought, stepping aside to allow a grubby looking, bearded older man brush past him. Right then he heard the sirens of police cars heading toward the hospital. The sound made his heart thump and ruined his appetite.

****

"How the hell could this happen?" Detective John Bamber demanded of the guard on duty outside Joel Alvarez' empty room.

Corrections Officer Meade stood up as straight as he was able, given the aftereffects of the sedative still swirling in his system with the drugged coffee. His face was so flushed and his breath so harsh that Bamber would have feared the man was about to stroke out if he hadn't been too furious with him to be concerned about his wellbeing.

"I don't know. It must have been the drink. That Candy Striper brought me a coffee. But who'd have thought a little girl like that—"

"You're a court officer. You should have thought. You're trained to suspect people."

"But she just said—a little candy-striper, looked about sixteen—she just said the nurses all thought I could use a drink, help me keep awake, like, while I was guarding."

"While you fucking slept and let a convicted rapist and murderer walk out of this hospital, let him out like a fox in a hen run," Bamber snarled, and Officer Meade's face went from red to white. He muttered more excuses, but Bamber just turned his back, growling at one of the uniforms present, "Check Meade's story with the nurses, and get the hospital closed circuit video tapes, see if you can identify this clever 'little candy-striper' who outwitted our big, strong officer here."

The uniform risked a smirk at Meade's expense before snapping a crisp "Yes, sir" and taking off toward the nurses' station.

"What's going on here? Where's my client?"

Bamber rolled his eyes and cursed again. He didn't need to turn around to know that Glory Jordan was right behind him and no doubt out for blood. The woman always seemed to show up when he was displaying his less than best side. *Or maybe she brought out his less than best side.*

Knowing damned well that he was being unfair, even untruthful, he pasted as pleasant a look as he could muster on his face and turned to face the lawyer who'd defended the now missing Joel Alvarez.

"I was kind of hoping that you'd be able to shed some light on the question of Mr. Alvarez's whereabouts."

Glory raised an eyebrow. On most women, the gesture would be sexy. On Glory it was both sexy and intimidating. Bamber swallowed.

"I assumed my client was under the care of the hospital, possibly with one of your delightful officers present to ensure he came to no harm."

"Well, no, you see, Alvarez seems to have taken himself off for a little walk, and I was expecting he'd have taken himself off right to you. Being as how you're probably the only person on the planet who has any sympathy for the rapist/murderer."

Score one for Bamber. He saw her face tighten and enjoyed a flare of satisfaction that faded at the chilling look on her face. Glory made a big performance of turning out her jacket pockets, opening her bag and peering inside. "Nope, Detective Bamber, I'm afraid my client doesn't seem to be anywhere in my vicinity. Of course, if he were, I'd have made damned sure to keep closer tabs on him than your officers obviously have. So, are we through with the blame game charade, and can you now tell me just what happened to my client?"

"Why are you here?"

She scowled at him. "No one from the prison or police department saw fit to inform me until this morning that Joel had been attacked and suffered serious wounds while in custody. I found a message on my office answering machine this afternoon when I finished in court. Obviously, no one thought it important enough to contact me on my cell phone."

Bamber winced. She should have been told as a priority, and also informed of Alvarez' escape. He vowed some other minion besides Meade was going to have a strip or two torn off today.

But the first priority had to be finding Alvarez and getting the killer off the streets before he found another victim. He didn't risk repeating those thoughts in that way to Glory, however. Instead, he walked briskly towards the elevator and wasn't surprised that she hurried to keep up with him. There was an elevator car being held for police use by a uniformed officer, and Glory followed Bamber inside without preamble.

"I think you'll agree that, as Joel's legal representative, I have the right to know what has happened to my client while he is in police custody. He has already been wounded while in the care of Corrections Canada, and I can assure you, there'll be questions asked about that. What now?"

Bamber paused to look at the pretty young lawyer, her face serious. He had difficulty correlating the obviously smart and moral woman this was with her predilection for representing and even protecting hardened criminals and murderers. It put them on opposite sides, and this bothered him for reasons he wasn't willing to examine at that moment.

Bamber gave her the basic facts, quickly bringing her up to date with the events of the last forty-eight hours, and again asked if she had any idea where Joel Alvarez might have fled.

She was silent so long he thought she wasn't going to answer. At last, she said, "I'm sorry. This is a bit of a shock. I would never have expected Joel to do something this foolish."

So it was Joel now, was it? Bamber wanted to ask if she was on first name terms with all her clients or just the handsome murderer? He bit the words back, knowing he was being stupid. *Or jealous.*

Now where did that thought come from?

"I have no idea where he would have gone, Detective Bamber. He has no living relatives, and all his friends seem to be his colleagues at the fire department. I doubt any of them would be happy to harbor a man who has been convicted of murder, even if he was once a friend or co-worker."

"The fire chief who testified at the trial? He seemed to have a lot of faith in Joel, or at least in his experience working with the man. Perhaps he wasn't totally convinced that his boy's a killer, not a hero."

Glory gave him a sharp look but didn't rise to the bait. Instead, she said mildly, "Yes, Chief Warner always had a very high opinion of Joel, but he's also a conventional man who believes that justice goes hand in hand with law and order."

Bamber wanted to ask her if she didn't believe that was the case, but wisely didn't. He knew she'd been around the block a few times and, like himself, had witnessed occasional miscarriages of justice in her time.

"Do you believe in your client's innocence, Ms. Jordan?"

Glory cast a surprised glance his way. "I've defended some men who I've had doubts about, Detective Bamber. Joel Alvarez was never one of them."

"Well, you know the drill. It would be way better for your client to turn himself in, and I'm sure you'll advise him of that if he contacts you."

Glory was silent for a telling second before she answered. "Of course, detective, that would be my duty as an officer of the court." And she turned and walked away without a backward glance.

****

Fern had had a long stint in the trauma unit at the hospital and looked forward to a quiet evening with a good book and possibly a glass of wine. She'd stopped in to check on things in the hospital after her return flight from New York, but her timing was bad. A traffic accident had brought in two critically injured patients, and she'd been needed in the struggle to save their lives. The small, curtained area of the ER had reeked of sour booze from the breath of the young man who'd been driving the car that had ploughed into a highway bridge abutment.

Her eyes filled with tears of sorrow and anger. They'd managed to save the life of the drunk driver, but the young girl in the car with him had suffered horrendous injuries and was beyond their help. Life is so unfair, she thought, and momentarily her sister's face rose on her closed eyelids. That someone so full of life and promise, with many years ahead of them, like the young girl and like her sister, should have their lives cut short, while selfish, wicked men like the drunk driver and like her sister's killer should continue to draw breath and live in anticipation of enjoying the rest of their lives, was unfathomable.

She shook her head. Maybe it was unfair to put that stupid young drunk driver in the same category as Joel Alvarez, the vicious killer. After all, while the young guy should have been aware of the danger of drinking and driving, he hadn't deliberately set out to kill his girlfriend. *Somehow, though, the end result was the same—an innocent life tragically cut short, and grieving families and friends left devastated.*

Then her cell phone buzzed and, weary as she was, she whispered a little prayer that it wasn't a call back to the emergency department. But the call was from the O.P.P. detective, Bamber, the man who'd built the case against Joel Alvarez, and his words shocked Fern to the core.

"Joel has escaped? You let that monster get away?"

"He was attacked by another inmate and hospitalized. Seems someone helped him leave the hospital by drugging the prison guard who was supposed to be keeping him there." There was no mistaking the anger and frustration in the officer's voice, but that was nothing to the rage and heart-thumping fear that filled Fern.

"Alvarez was here, at this hospital? And no one

told me—no one warned me?"

Bamber swore under his breath. "We understood you were away at a conference and couldn't be reached. Plus, there were security issues, and we had done everything possible to shield you and the rest of the hospital staff, except for those treating him, from the knowledge of Álvarez' whereabouts."

"Well, it seems like *everything* hasn't been enough." Fern's voice shook as she snapped back.

"The reason I am calling you now is just to ask you to take extra precautions. We don't believe for a moment that Alvarez would come near you, and I'll have a car pass your home on frequent patrol. He's sure to be as far away as he can get, probably heading for the States to try and start a new life there.

"In the meantime, is there anyone you can stay with? Or perhaps you could take some vacation time?"

Fern gave a hollow laugh. "I'm an emergency room doctor, Detective Bamber. We're short staffed, and I can't take off on vacation just because you've lost a dangerous murderer."

"We didn't lose... Okay, I understand how upset and angry you must be, Ms. Adams."

"You have no idea. And it's Dr. Adams."

Bamber took a deep breath, readying himself for a pretty explosive response to his next question.

"Where were you, Dr. Adams, this afternoon between the hours of three and six p.m.?"

The explosion didn't come. Instead, he was shocked to hear Fern's peals of laughter.

When she'd taken a deep breath, she replied, "I was on a plane travelling from New York to Toronto after a medical conference. Then I was on the road driving back to Primrose Hill from Toronto Lester Pearson Airport. I'd stopped at the hospital to check on things on my way home and got into helping with the casualties from that accident on the 417." She paused for a moment before adding, "Detective Bamber, if I had anything to do that Alvarez' escape, I can assure you you'd never find any proof, or the body."

Bamber swallowed his irritation. "Well, take extra precautions, and keep your cell phone with the emergency number and my own number with you at all times. You'll be informed immediately if there is any news."

Fern jabbed the button to end the call, her heart thumping like a wild animal in her chest. A movement at the edge of the car park caught her attention, and her breath stopped. *How could he be here?* Had her exhausted mind conjured him up as an illusion, or was Joel Alvarez actually lurking beneath the row of trees that sheltered the car park?

"Dr. Adams? Fern? Are you okay? Goodness, you're shaking!" Jennie Oliver, ER department head, stopped beside her.

"Over there...no, don't look, don't be obvious. Under the trees near the barrier. It's Joel Alvarez. I'm sure it is!"

Jennie knew at once who Joel Alvarez was. She'd followed the trial and tried to offer what comfort she could to Fern. Now she slid her eyes to the spot Fern had indicated, then shook her head, her expression sad. "Fern, hon, there's no one there. And even if there was, it couldn't be that brute."

"No. I know I saw him!" Fern whirled around to study the spot under the trees. Her heart was thumping so loud she was sure Jennie could hear it. The car park was empty of human life. "I don't understand. I saw him there. You know he escaped, don't you?"

Jennie sighed. "I heard just as I was coming off shift. I gather you have just heard, too? I am so sorry, Fern. I know that bastard was under lock and key, with an armed guard sitting right outside his door. But apparently no one thought a little Candy Striper would drug the guard and set him free."

"That's what happened? A hospital volunteer, one of the kids who come in to help out, is who got Alvarez out of the hospital?"

"That's what they're saying, but I expect there's much more to it than that." Jennie sighed and put her arm around Fern. "Listen, I know how much of a shock this must be to you and, while everyone expects that Alvarez will have taken off for parts unknown, you must still be anxious. Why don't you come over and stay with me for a day or two? I have lots of room since Joey and Freda left for college."

Fern thanked her. "That's a lovely invitation, but this murdering skunk has turned my life upside down one time too many. I'm going home. And if he shows his face, well, I've got my dad's gun to greet him with."

****

Richard Phelan hadn't been able to resist the temptation to see for himself that the plot was unfolding as he'd intended. He'd been the puppet master, pulling the strings that got Joel Alvarez out of jail, and now it was up to Alvarez what he did with his newfound freedom. He wasn't going to have long to enjoy it, anyway.

He waved away the waitress at the restaurant,

saying he'd changed his mind about eating there after all. He'd already brushed past Alvarez, close enough to touch the man, and was surprised that his hatred hadn't sent obvious shivers of alarm through his victim.

The man didn't know enough to be hyper aware of his surroundings. How long would he survive when law enforcement officers from the entire province, and soon from the entire country, would be hunting him?

Phelan smiled, but there was no warmth in it. Instead, it was the cruel smile of a hunting cat when the cornered mouse was frantically trying to escape its fate.

Chapter Seven

"So, where would Alvarez run to?" Detective Bamber leaned back in the creaky office chair, his feet resting on the edge of his desk. His new partner, Lee Groves, was perched on the desk itself. Groves still shone with the eagerness of the newly promoted young detective, his eyes lighting with anticipation at every new turn of events. His attitude irritated Bamber, reminding him of the mossy velvet that covers the antlers of a deer or moose as they grow. The stuff eventually itches and irritates the animal so much it rubs itself against a tree or anything else it can find in order to rid itself of the covering and let the hard new horn shine through.

In this case, Groves' eagerness was annoying Bamber to the point of total exasperation. *Was I ever this young and enthusiastic?* he wondered.

"Has anyone notified the victim's sister? What was her name?" OPP Sergeant Dave Lorimar, officer in charge of the Primrose Hill station, flicked through the file folder on his lap. "Fern—that's it, Fern Adams. Her sister Rose was Alvarez' victim."

"Yes, I called her," Bamber assured him. "She'd just arrived back from a conference in New York, and she wasn't impressed either with me asking where she'd been or with our mislaying the man who'd murdered her sister."

"Their mother must have been a keen gardener—Fern, Rose," Groves jested, but his grin faded under the glares of the two older officers.

"Do you think it's possible Alvarez set this whole thing up?" Lorimar said.

"What? Had some asshole almost rip out his guts just so that he could go to hospital? Taking a bit of a chance, really. It would have been a fine balancing act to get the injury serious enough to be taken to the county hospital rather than treated in jail, and yet not serious enough to cause him to be incapacitated so much that he couldn't walk out of the hospital after a few days.

"Or be taken out feet first," Groves interjected.

Lorimar rolled his eyes. "According to Alvarez's cell mate, a mousy little guy by the name of Jack Godsell, Alvarez had often said he'd rather be dead than spend the next twenty-five to life in jail. So maybe it was worth the risk to him."

"They had to do some emergency surgery, anyway. As it was, the doc there said it was touch and go that he hadn't lost a kidney or had a punctured lung." Bamber chewed the inside of his cheek for a moment, wishing to hell that he could have a cigarette. He cursed Joel Alvarez for being the stress test that had him wanting nicotine after seventy-five smoke free days. "It certainly looks as though it was a setup somewhere along the line. The so-called Candy Striper volunteer wasn't known to any of the hospital staff, but she was smart enough to bring along a change of clothes to change her appearance and leave the hospital with Alvarez. We have a couple who resembles them on the surveillance tapes from the hospital—they look like any young couple visiting someone in hospital, right down to the anxious frowns. And she'd brought in clothes for Alvarez, but I've not seen any mention of a girlfriend in any of the files."

"Yeah, according to the files, Alvarez has no relatives living, and no close friends left. Looks like the fire department was his life and, once he was convicted, he was thrown out of the club. Guys like that, who put their lives on the line, don't want any part of scum like Alvarez once he's shown his true colors. So, who the hell would have been there for him and set this up?" Lorimar commented.

"Well, the little blonde obviously played a big part in all this. Meade, the officer standing guard, swears he'd recognize her if he saw her again. Could she be one of the hangers-on, you know, the weirdos who target prisoners like Alvarez, write to them, make offers of marriage and all that stuff?" Groves interjected.

"Good thought. Check and see if Alvarez was receiving any letters from anyone," Lorimar said.

Groves preened at the slight praise and disappeared into the outer office to his own desk.

While he was gone, Lorimar turned to Bamber. "Keep an eye on that guy, the corrections officer—Meade? Seems a bit like a loose cannon. He was telling some of the guys that he's going to go out and find that woman, even if it kills him."

Bamber cursed, swinging his feet off the desk and sitting up. "We don't know who we're dealing with, but whoever it is has plenty of money and good connections with the criminal element to be able to summon up this kind of help. Criminals don't do things like helping a prisoner escape from the goodness their hearts. Meade's running the risk of getting himself hurt or compromising the investigation by harassing a witness when we finally find the candy-striper."

Groves came back in, carrying a file folder. "According to the prison, the only letters he got were from his lawyer, Glory…er, Glory something or another. She was his only visitor, and she turned up only once or twice while they were setting up an appeal hearing."

"So, the lawyer is the only one who's bothered with the poor creep all this time? You know, some women do get a hard-on for guys like Alvarez. Maybe it's time you had another chat with little Glory whatever-her-name-is?" Lorimar said.

Bamber wondered why it was that the disrespectful reference to Glory irritated him so much. He also wondered why someone like Alvarez, who painted himself as a straight arrow, would risk the penalties for a prison break when he had could be granted an appeal hearing.

****

Fern struggled under the weight of parcels and a bag of groceries as she pushed through the ice-rimed mud of her driveway and the chill winter wind from her car to the front door of the house that was all that was left of the family farm. Their parents had left it to her and Rose, but now it was just hers alone. Funnily enough, Fern had always loved the house, while butterfly Rose had lived for the day when she could take her own place in the big city. Her parents had often joked that the only thing that made Rose buckle down and study at her academic subjects in high school was her longing to get into college at Queen's University in

Kingston.

Rose had got into the fine arts degree program, announcing to all who cared to listen that she was launched at last. "Look out world—here I come!" she'd yelled gleefully when the acceptance letter had arrived. Rose was going to get her degree and take the music and acting communities by storm.

Their parents had been so thrilled that their butterfly child seemed to have found a direction at last that they lavished all their praise and most of their cash on Rose. By the time Fern made it through the entrance exams and into a medical program, they were pretty much worn out and broke. Fern had to struggle to get by, working two part-time jobs to supplement her government education loan and grants.

Ironically, no one was surprised when Rose dropped out of college midway through her second year. "You have to show the world what you've got, and that means getting out and strutting your stuff. University is suffocating my talent," she told her skeptical family. While she waited for her path to glamor and stardom to open up, Rose spent her time waitressing in some seedy bars and clubs, working on the occasional cruise ship assignment, working at the garden center, and snatching any opportunity to take the spotlight and sing.

Sometimes, exhausted and with an essay on deadline, Fern had admitted to herself that she had seriously resented Rose, both her butterfly attitude and the way her path had been smoothed by parental cash and encouragement. And that still prickled at her conscience, particularly now that Rose was gone. Dead. Her sister would never demand her share of the family homestead. The house Fern had loved and wanted was now all hers. It was a bittersweet thought.

Her sister would never again dazzle and steal one of Fern's boyfriends. Joel Alvarez had been the last, and Rose had died for it.

Looking up at the century-old house through the tears that stung her eyes, Fern thought she could hear Rose laughing somewhere in the ether. Rose had always teased her, playing on her love of the house, saying she wondered how Fern would raise the money to pay Rose off for her share of this valuable piece of real estate. Her share of a near ruin. The house had stood empty for several years after their parents died and now needed what realtors called, tongue in cheek, "TLC."

Tender Loving Care. She could use some of that herself.

Somehow it seemed there was never enough time or money to finish even the smaller jobs on the house. She didn't want to even think of the big stuff, like a new roof, for example, or updating the leaky, cranky plumbing in the bathrooms and the kitchen that was so old-fashioned it was now very fashionable, according to the glossy magazines.

What I need is a real handyman—for me as well as the house! Fern was only half joking. She would love to have someone to share this house with, to turn it once more into the warm, loving family home she remembered from her childhood.

Although she realized that childhood memories are often flawed....

Out of nowhere she thought of Joel Alvarez again, the warmth of his smile when she first met him, the witty stories he told over dinner, the way their hands had met as they walked down the street together…the way she'd hoped that maybe they could be something more.

Vomit rose up in her throat as she remembered how much she'd enjoyed his company. In her mind's eye, she could still see his pale, handsome face when the verdict was read, the haunted dark rings around his eyes and the stark, harsh points of his cheekbones registering shock and pain.

As well he might. But why was she thinking of him all of a sudden? Especially in the context of wanting a home and family. She chewed her lip. After a couple of dates, Joel had had her daydreaming that he could be The One. Now he'd soured her of all men forever. His brutal murder of the one person Fern had left to love meant she was all alone in the world. Pain arced through her hand, and she realized she was standing with her door key pressed into her palm so hard it had drawn blood.

Dear God, what was she thinking?

She hoisted the box of groceries she was carrying onto one hip as she balanced her purse and a cloth bag filled with fruit and other items so she could insert the key in the door. The rain clouds that had been filling the sky all day finally started to pelt cold spears of ice onto her head as she struggled with the recalcitrant lock. It would probably turn to snow or worse, freezing drizzle, before morning.

Inside the house the telephone rang, its tone loud and insistent. The shrilling of the phone made her hurry and, as her father always said, *"Haste makes waste."* She dropped the box of groceries on the front step and rushed into the house in time to hear the telephone answering machine peep to signal the end of a message.

Should she listen to the message or return and collect her groceries from the front step? Messages usually fell into two categories—friends calling for a chat, or her hospital admin calling to ask her to come in, change shifts, or update a patient's treatment. If it were urgent, though, they'd have called her on her cell phone. Fern sighed.

She couldn't ignore the call, just in case. Wearily she pressed the play button.

"Dr. Adams? This is detective John Bamber of the OPP. Just checking on you and letting you know a patrol car will be keeping an eye on your home. Dr. Adams—" The man's voice was cut off as the old-fashioned answering machine her parents had hooked up to the telephone years ago cut the call off abruptly as its recording tape ended.

Listening to the detective's words, her heart seemed to leap into her throat. Had there been a sighting of Alvarez in the Primrose Hill area? Was that why the detective sounded so anxious? Her hand reached for the telephone, intending to call Detective Bamber back. But her front door still stood open letting a wicked draft into the house, and her ice cream and other groceries were no doubt defrosting on the front step in the rain. She'd bring them in, secure the front door, and then call Detective Bamber back.

She turned around towards the door in time to see a hooded figure step inside the hallway, startling her. He clutched the box of groceries, and she automatically responded to his thrusting the box towards her by taking it and stepping backwards. He swiftly followed, slipping uninvited into the hallway and slamming the door behind him, blocking her exit.

That's when she got a good look at his face—the very face she'd been thinking about only minutes before. *Joel Alvarez!*

"You! How dare you come here! Get out of my home!" Fury made her brave at the idea this murdering piece of trash should invade the sanctity of her home.

"I have to talk to you," he said, his eyes glittering in the dim light from the hallway bulb. "I need to know why…"

But Fern wasn't interested in his questions. Throwing the box back at him, she whipped around and ran, heading towards the back kitchen and the door leading out into the yard. *Her car keys. Where the hell were her car keys?* Too late, she realized she'd left them on the keyring in her front door lock as she rushed to answer the phone.

She stumbled on the doormat in the hallway, only too aware of the harsh shout behind her and the pounding of footsteps on worn linoleum as Joel Alvarez gave hot pursuit. Risking a glance over her shoulder, she saw him closing in only a few feet behind her. He clutched his side as though in pain, and their eyes met along the length of the hallway. For a moment they held, frozen in place, their glances taking each other's measure.

Was that beseeching that she saw in his eyes? No, she'd been fooled once by him, she wasn't going to let that happen again. She tore her look away from his and swirled around to make a frantic grab for the kitchen door handle. Her fingers were inches from the antique brass doorknob—inches to safety! In her clumsy headlong rush, the welcome mat slipped beneath her feet on the slippery floor, and she stumbled. Her fingers brushed against the cold metal but couldn't get a grip, and she hit her head on the floor as she fell.

And that slip was all Joel Alvarez needed. He sprang along the corridor and grabbed her, his hand going over her mouth as he roughly pulled her against him. "Don't start screaming—I don't want to hurt you," he snarled in her ear as he pulled her to her feet.

Joel winced at the pain that swamped him when he'd grappled with Fern. The stitches that had been seeping were now pulling apart, and he felt the warmth of his own blood sticky on his stomach and the small of his back. But he'd couldn't let Fern escape him before he got the answers he needed from her. If he had to face her across a courtroom, or even a police interrogation room, she'd cling to the story she'd told during the trial.

Slowly, awareness of the warmth of her softness against him registered through his confusion. He remembered other times, a thousand years ago it seemed, he had held her like this. Held her and wanted more, much more. Her hair still smelled of lemons and rain, clean and fresh, and he inhaled deeply so it invaded his nostrils as if it could push out the stale piss scent of prison.

His hand slid of its own accord over the smooth warm flesh of her stomach to rest on the soft mound of her breast, his fingers briefly cupping her before the reality of what he was doing hit him. Repulsed by his own behavior, he pulled his hand away as if burned. All the same, he held tightly to his prisoner and pulled her down the hallway that led back to the kitchen.

"I'd hoped we could just sit and talk," he said,

shoving her down onto a chair and pulling the cord out of his hooded jacket.

Fern's eyes widened as she saw the cord wrapped on his strong, pale fingers, and she felt the blood drain from her cheeks as she struggled with light-headedness. Once she'd thought there could be something between herself and Joel, and her flesh still remembered the warm thrill of the attraction between them.

But that died along with her sister the night Joel proved himself a monster. Moments before, when that same hand swept over her breast, she'd felt a thrill of fear and—something else. Something that shamed her. Desire. She didn't want to examine that, not when the man in front of her stood with his eyes glittering wildly out of a flushed face.

She thinks I'm going to kill her with this cord, strangle her! Joel's blood ran cold at the idea that this woman, any woman, could possibly think that of him. He'd known in his heart he could never hurt a woman, let alone someone like Fern. Yet he remembered times in his cell at the jail when he'd imagined hurting her, forcing the truth from her...

Have I become the monster they said I am?

Shaking his head to dislodge the thought, Joel moved quickly. He dropped the cord and grabbed her arm, pushing her ahead of him towards the other end of the open plan room. "I'm sorry to have to do this," he muttered against her ear. "You didn't leave me much choice."

Fern stumbled as he pushed her, too shocked to even struggle. *Was he going to bind her, rape, and torture her, like he'd done with her sister? Is this how it started with Rose, the rope, and the blame, and then....*

Fern closed her eyes, speaking around the nausea that rose in her throat.

"Like my sister didn't leave you much choice, either? Like she forced you to rape her and slit her throat?" She whirled to glare into her attacker's eyes, fighting to drag strength from her anger to cover her fear.

Using the last of his rapidly ebbing strength, Joel pushed her down on the loveseat as he recognized the fear that flared in her eyes, and he was ashamed. He'd been raised to respect women, and he'd never raised his hand to one in his life.

But this wasn't just any woman, he told himself, hardening his heart against her. This woman had perjured herself to steal his freedom and robbed him of his life.

She held the key to everything that had happened. And he intended to make her confess.

Whatever it took.

"I told you I just wanted to talk."

"Yeah, did you talk to Rose? Did you explain how it was her fault as she begged you for her life?"

"I never even met your sister, except when you introduced us. I don't know—"

"Liar!" Fern threw herself forward, using her feet for leverage, catching him squarely in the chest with both hands. Her movement sent her sprawling onto the floor but as she fell, she had the satisfaction of Alvarez' cry of pain and muttered curse words. Almost in slow motion, she saw from the corner of her eye that he was folding up, buckling in the middle, clutching his side and falling backward to slide down the wall behind him.

Joel Alvarez lay sprawled against the kitchen wall, pale, still, and silent.

Icy cold shock ran through her body and dizziness clouded her sight. Cursing herself for moments lost, she pushed to her feet and stepped stealthily past Alvarez' slumped form. She had to get to the kitchen, get her father's shotgun.

Still as death...*good lord, was he dead?* Her breath caught in her throat as she saw the ruby red of fresh blood that stained the front of the shirt he wore. Unable to deny her doctor's instincts, she stumbled forward and fell to her knees alongside him.

Her breath hitched again. All these months she had believed Joel Alvarez was a monster, yet as he lay there, pale and bleeding, she was taken by surprise as the burgeoning feelings she had felt for him when they'd first met blossomed again. There had been a very real attraction between them—until he'd chosen to date her sister behind her back, and then...then he murdered Rose.

It should have been me! The guilt tore through her again and again. She had brought this man into their lives, she had dated him, a stranger in town, a man she knew nothing about. She should have been the one he killed. Rose should still be living her butterfly life...

It must be the shock talking. How could she even think he was attractive? Cramps gripped her stomach, and she fought to hold back vomit. Shaking her head to rid herself of a line of thought that appalled her, she yo-yoed between wanting to run and get her father's shotgun from the hall closet and the compulsion to staunch the bleeding and save a life.

The life of the man who had robbed her sister of

hers.

What if you get the gun, and he gets it away from you?

Well, in that case, at least being shot would be a faster way of dying than having my throat slit and bleeding out...like Rose.

How will you live with yourself if you let him bleed to death, here in your family home?

It's no more than he deserves...

For the first time in her life, Fern considered taking a life rather than saving one. No one would blame her if she let him bleed to death...or even blasted him with the shotgun to help him on his way. After all, he'd broken into her home, terrorized her...

Then Joel Alvarez groaned in pain, and Fern knew she didn't have it in her to take a life – or let him die.

Chapter Eight

Richard Phelan couldn't wait to get to his computer and see if the Facilitator had carried out his instructions, and hopefully, the low-lifes he'd hired to do the work managed to keep their end of the bargain. He fumed, remembering how that idiot of a boss of his at the car detailing business, the cretin with the low IQ and company director father, had kept him late rabbiting on and on about commitment to the job and giving a hundred and ten percent to customer service. *If he had his way, he'd do customer service with a semi-automatic weapon.*

Richard smiled as he imagined the shocked looks on the faces of all those macho rich boys whose cars he was paid little more than minimum wage to detail if he were to pull out such a weapon and point it right at the spot where their brains oughtta have been.

Someday soon he was going to show them all. One day soon.

A gentle ding from his computer brought him out of that satisfying fantasy. His email account had opened, and there was a message from The Facilitator. *Shit, that silly name was beginning to irritate him more and more. Yes, the private eye's days were numbered. Add another one to the "To Kill" list.*

The mean smile grew even wider as he read the opening paragraph of The Facilitator's post.

The Facilitator: *Our friend is out of hospital!*

Of course, he knew that—he'd witnessed the man's escape by watching in the hospital car park and tailing him to the restaurant. There'd been an added bonus of seeing Fern Adams. *My, that was one delectable little morsel! Not as showy as her sister, but he'd bet there were hidden depths a man could explore…*

Richard pulled himself out of that pleasant daydream. Now he was sure that the getaway had been clean, and Joel was now a free man. *Not for long.* Besides being hunted by law enforcement across the province, the bastard was now a sitting duck for whatever new nasty trick Richard wanted to play on him. He'd promised long ago he would make this man suffer for what had been done to him. Others had thought of Joel as a hero, but Richard had known better, and now he'd shown the rest of the world.

The smile faded when he got to the end of the private investigator's message. *The fool had lost Alvarez after he'd left the hospital? How was that possible?*

Furious, he started typing, his fingers pounding out his rage on the keyboard and wishing it was The Facilitator's face.

Mr. Brown: *What the hell? Did you not use the GPS device we agreed upon?*

He hit SEND so hard that the keyboard danced across the desk, over its edge, and came to a rattling halt on the floor. Richard picked it up and put it back on the desk, tested to be sure it wasn't broken, then grabbed a beer from the tiny, ancient refrigerator that went with the apartment rental. The appliance was probably as old as the scruffy slum of a building that had been split into tiny living areas for people who couldn't afford any better. Or were one step away from being homeless. Richard passed a disgusted look around the place, with its dirty walls and sagging floors, and comforted himself with the thought that soon, very soon, he'd be living in a much more luxurious accommodation, somewhere with a warm climate and an ocean view…

Then he shook himself out of that delicious daydream. *Time to get back on track!* He glanced back repeatedly at the screen to check for a reply to his post as he paced up and down the length of small room he'd been renting ever since Mama died.

Mama. Who'd loved Joel Alvarez. Mama. Who claimed he'd broken her heart?

Where the hell was Alvarez?

****

Despite the little voice in her head that was screaming at her to *Run! Run!* Fern stood on the cold linoleum floor and hesitated. In seconds she could be out of the door, running for her life to her car where lay her cell phone and salvation. She could lock the car doors, call the police, and within minutes cruisers and armed uniformed men would be swarming over the house. Paramedics would treat him, and the responsibility—and the abhorrent temptation—would be off her shoulders. Joel Alvarez would be back in custody and Fern would be safe.

Inside her head, as the doctor whose passionate belief in her dedication to healing the sick and the frightened woman who wanted to flee warred with each other. Self-preservation finally won out. As she tiptoed past the prone body, Joel moaned, the sound almost sad.

Fern's mind flashed back to the look he had given her earlier, the one that had been almost beseeching.

Joel moaned again, obviously in pain, and the bloom of watery blood grew on his stomach. Images of her dead sister lying in her own blood, swamped Fern's mind, and a murderous rage rose within her. *This man deserved to suffer and die for what he had done to Rose.*

She looked at him lying helpless at her feet. *I could do what the so-called justice system won't. I could mete out the justice he deserves. I could avenge my sister. Blood for blood.*

The very savagery of her own thoughts shocked her back to sanity.

Trembling, she struggled with the images that rushed through her mind. *I'm a trained and experienced doctor. And a human being. One who took an oath in which she promised to recognize the special value of human life. Did her Hippocratic Oath extend to healing her sister's killer?*

And here she was, considering the cold-blooded murder of a man who was in such pain, perhaps dying. Could she just stand back and let someone die when her own medical expertise might save his life?

Not even if he was a convicted killer, the monster who raped and murdered your sister? You could just leave him, let him die. No one would blame you. Say you panicked, tried to save him, but couldn't.

Vomit rose in her throat, and she rushed to the small powder room off the kitchen and threw up, retching until her stomach was empty and her head pounded. It was over in minutes, and she dragged herself to her feet to splash cold water on her burning face. The image that stared back at her, wild-eyed, from the mirror was someone she didn't know. *A woman, a trained doctor, who had actually considered taking the life of another human being.*

Fern swallowed hard, shame swamping her even while the sharp voice of hatred taunted her, asking why it would be wrong to dispatch a man who had committed such evil.

It took all her self-control not to hammer her fists on the glass, obliterating the image of this savage self.

Back in the kitchen, so familiar and yet now seeming changed, Fern grabbed the big carving knife from the wooden block near the stove. She slipped back into professional mode. She'd see what could be done for Alvarez. It was her duty as a doctor, but if he made one false move, she'd carve him with no more compunction than chopping up salad vegetables.

She knelt beside the unconscious man and slapped him—hard. Much harder than necessary and was surprised at how little satisfaction the small vicious act gave her.

"Come on, Joel, let's look at you. I want you well enough to be dragged back to jail for another twenty some odd years of misery," she gritted through her teeth as she pulled his body down into a prone position. Yanking off her jacket, she folded it so that it was beneath his shoulders, letting his head fall gently back to be below his heart. This would help slow the bleeding. Then she pulled up his shirt to expose the pale but taut muscled skin of his belly.

As a doctor, she had handled many men, in many very personal ways as part of their treatment, but never before had it felt so…intimate.

Her fingers touched warm flesh, brushed against the fine mat of chest hair, and Fern gasped. Not so long ago, she'd warmed to the heat of his flesh and the beating of his heart when he'd held her. But that was before everything that had happened.

Before she knew what evil lurked in that heart. Now she told herself all she could feel was hatred…

Stupid cow, just do what you need to do and get this over with.

"Then you can wave him off in a police cruiser," she muttered.

"No, no…no police." The hoarse words startled her. She didn't think this man had enough strength left in him to speak. Did he have enough left to grab her? Were those hands still strong enough, still evil enough, to choke the life out of her?

One of those hands came up and clasped hers tightly, and she saw again that beseeching look in his eyes. "Don't…call…police. Didn't come here…to…hurt you."

"Sure, you didn't, you bastard. You're sick enough to think that tying a woman up is chivalrous behavior."

"Didn't tie you…Needed…you to talk…talk to me."

"The only words I want to say to you right now are unprofessional and very, very rude. Now shut the fuck up and let me look at where this blood is coming from."

Fern cast a professional eye over Joel's flat stomach and the grim slash of the surgical repair under his ribs, raising him slightly to see the wound caused by a primitive shiv in the prison. "Well, it looks like someone likes you just as much as I do," she muttered. "But he had the guts to do something about it."

"You're nothing…nothing like the thug who…stabbed me,"

"Doesn't mean to say I wouldn't like to take this big old kitchen knife to you and carve you like the Thanksgiving turkey," she said, holding up the knife in front of Joel's face. He went even paler than she would have credited a person could. His dark eyes now burned in an almost white face.

"I need to clean the wound and check that the stitches haven't come completely adrift. Was this the only wound?"

Joel managed a slight shake of his head. "In my back, as well," he murmured, his voice so low that she had to bend her face near him to hear.

Fern walked on her knees to the far kitchen cupboard and pulled out a first aid kit, returning to her patient. "This is going to sting," she warned as she poured hydrogen peroxide onto Joel's belly and watched in satisfaction as his eyes went wide in shock and pain. Then she set about cleaning the wound.

"Looks like you're in luck. The stitches are pulled, but they've held, and there doesn't seem to be much infection. I'm going to finish cleaning this, check the wound in your back, then put a bandage on to keep it clean and mop up any leakage. You just lie back there and don't make any sudden moves. That would be really bad for your health."

"Look, I'm unarmed. Like I said, I only came here to talk to you, to get some answers."

"Yeah, like you wanted answers from my sister, you sick bastard."

Joel lay back and closed his eyes. There wasn't really anything more he could say.

Chapter Nine

Joel was dreaming of a smooth, warm body, his hands roaming silky soft skin, the lemony scent of a woman's hair in his nostrils—and came awake groggily to realize his hands were tied and the wounds beneath his rib cage front and back hurt like the blazes. In fact, his whole body hurt, and he would have given whatever future he had to just sink back into his dream. Forever.

"Try to stay awake now, Joel. It's important that you keep conscious and keep still as much as you can. Your wounds are bleeding again."

And there she was, the woman in his dream. But he'd had other dreams about this woman, dreams in which he faced her down and forced her to tell him why she'd destroyed his life.

He struggled to get to a sitting position, already surveying the room for a means of escape. His bound hands made him clumsy, and weakness sent the room spinning before his eyes. But his senses were sharp enough to see this woman would have no more mercy on him now than she'd had when she'd delivered her evidence at his trial and damned him to purgatory. He'd come here to find answers, intending to ask her to sit down with him and talk, try to shame her into telling the truth.

It hadn't worked out that way, and he blamed himself partly. *What had he been thinking? That he* could appear on her doorstep, the helpful friend helping with her groceries, and she'd welcome him into her home? Offer him tea and cookies and pour her heart out to him?

His desperate reactions—chasing her and dragging her back into the family room, pulling the cord from his jacket with the impulsive thought of tying her up until she listened—would have been enough to send any red-blooded woman into a panic. And a woman who'd experienced what she had...

But was her reaction that of a woman frightened at the intrusion of a man she believed to be a brutal psychotic killer? Or was it that of a woman afraid to be caught out in her lies?

He saw she'd reacted with fear, certainly. Fear of him? Or fear of whoever had set her up to make sure Joel was convicted and went to jail? The latter seemed the most likely answer, given that she had taken advantage of his weakened physical state to attack him. Now he lay at her mercy, trussed and helpless before her carving knife.

****

Richard Phelan finally had his answer. That fool Facilitator had slipped a miniaturized GPS chip into the pocket of the hoodie that the woman had taken to the hospital for Alvarez. Then something had happened to block the signal. Maybe Alvarez was around some heavy voltage electrical equipment, whatever. The problem seemed to be solved, anyway, and Alvarez was on the move. The Facilitator was now following the signal in person, and pretty soon Richard would know where his quarry had gone to ground

So far, all was according to plan. Richard couldn't

wait for the next step.

****

"How do you do it?" Bamber asked suddenly.

"Do what?"

They were sitting in Glory Jordan's office, a surprisingly austere room, the large practical desk and credenza softened by deep rich red woods, an antique Persian rug in muted colors, and a jungle of green plants.

"How do you go on, day after day, dealing with liars and cheats, with violent men, with the aftermath of crimes so god-awful most of us can't sleep at night?"

"Well, I could ask you the same question. Don't cops go through this, too?" She watched as Bamber flinched, and she knew her words had hit the mark. "But I suppose you'd say that you're on the side of the angels, while I'm facilitating evil men going free? For one thing, our Canadian justice system says that everyone is entitled to the best defense. And I only defend people I believe are innocent. Or at least, the evidence says they may be."

"And I asked you this before—do you really believe Joel Alvarez is innocent?"

She paused, tapping a pencil against her teeth, knowing her answer could well affect the way the police treated Joel when he was recaptured, as she was sure he would be.

Bamber watched the yellow shaft of pencil, mesmerized as it butted against the ivory white. When she looked directly into his eyes, there was a softening in his gut as if he'd just experienced an unexpected kindness. Truth shone from Glory's dark eyes, and Bamber immediately knew that she believed in what she was saying.

"When Joel Alvarez came to me, it looked like an open and shut case. Then I started to ask myself, why would a man with Alvarez' record kill like this? It's unusual for someone to live the kind of life he has, and then out of the blue just up and kill. Not just a spur of the moment kind of killing, like something done in a rage. You know, as well as I do, that good men sometimes do terrible things when they're out of control. Usually, they're the ones who turn themselves in, or they break down quickly when the police close in on them, and they're desperate to confess and get the burden of guilt off their shoulders.

"I expected Alvarez would be like that, that we'd have to find a reason for his actions. Then I saw the crime scene photos and read the statements, and I knew that this crime was totally out of character. This killer was deliberate—cruel and calculating. He displayed the naked, brutalized body for the world to see. It wasn't a spur of the moment crime of passion or rage, despite the sexual component. Joel continued to declare his innocence even when he was offered a deal if he pled guilty. Usually, the guilty ones grab any deal they can get. It gives them a kick to think they're bucking the system by not paying the full price for their crime."

Bamber nodded. Like many cops, he hated letting the guilty escape with a plea bargain or deal; yet sometimes it was the only way to obtain necessary intelligence or get a conviction to take a brutal animal off the streets for even a short time. Still, it went against the grain...he became aware that Glory was speaking again, her fair hair turned to a halo by the sun through the broad uncovered window behind her.

"Fern Adams admitted that she had dated Joel several times, but that she had not known he'd met up with her sister and was dating her while Fern was away at a medical conference in Boston." Glory gave a wry smile. "If she hadn't had two hundred delegates to say she was at the conference, I'd have played the 'woman scorned' card. And even though the witnesses said he'd dated Rose Adams at least once, Joel knew absolutely nothing about the woman. He didn't even know the town well enough to know where she lived when I prodded him with a few innocent-seeming questions. If it wasn't for Fern Adams' statement that she saw Joel there when she dropped by her sister's place the evening of her return to Primrose Hill—"

"What about the bartender and the bar patrons who saw him with Rose? And then there's a little thing called DNA," Bamber interjected.

Glory rubbed her forehead wearily. "Yeah, the witnesses and the DNA. I can't explain that. My reaction was at one point Alvarez had been in some sort of fugue state and didn't remember what he'd done, had lost several days of his life. That's the only way I can explain how the man came to be so convincingly innocent."

"But psych evaluations didn't hold up on that."

"No, but they also didn't offer any indicators of personality disorders that you might expect if someone with Joel's background suddenly turned into a killer. Men who kill like this usually work up to it. They start with small acts of cruelty, then move on to stalking, harassment, rape—with steadily increasing violence until they hit the big time of murder.

"There should be some record of complaints,

maybe to the local police in Toronto, maybe to the fire chief in charge of Alvarez' workstation. Gossip among his friends or acquaintances, at the very least. But this man's squeaky clean. Joel Alvarez is a bone fide hero. You saw the newspaper reports about his actions in saving the life of a pregnant woman in a house fire."

"Yeah, it's hard to reconcile the glowing tributes to the hero with the actions of a deranged killer," Bamber admitted.

Glory narrowed her eyes at him, then seeing he wasn't being sarcastic, she offered him a smile that lit up the room.

The steady *click clack* of the secretary's keyboard in the outer office was the only sound in the elongated silence that followed. Then Bamber grinned.

"So, Counselor, how do you do it?"

"Probably the same way you do, detective. How do you cope with the horror of it all?"

"Me? I go home, take my dog for a run, and then sit around in my underwear with my good buddy Jack Daniels until I can't see the victims' bodies anymore when I close my eyes."

Glory frowned, then smiled. "Well, I've got a little place up north of Kingston, a family cottage really, with no telephone or internet connection. I go there and let the woods and the lake wash the nastiness out of my mind."

"Sounds nice."

"Well, maybe some time when all this is sorted, I'll invite you up for a barbecue."

For some reason, her words brightened his day. "It's a deal."

As he stepped back out onto the street from Glory's

office, Bamber realized he suddenly felt happier than he had for a long time. *So where did that come from?* he wondered, but deep inside he had a pretty good idea what—or who—was responsible for the warm glow he felt.

****

He had to stop her from making that phone call. One word from her, and the police would be all over him like white on rice and, if he survived, he'd be back in jail. Maybe even facing further charges that would put an end to any hope of parole forever.

He'd rather die.

Here he was, trussed up like a barbecue pig, aching from the wounds she'd just redressed. Why that act of kindness, he wondered? Hell, yes—she wanted him well enough to return to jail and to spend the rest of his life in that hell hole. What had he done to make this woman hate him this much?

You killed her sister. Was it a voice in his head, or for real? Joel knew he was getting feverish. His skin was burning, his head pounded, and there was this peculiar feeling of unreality, of floating…maybe he could just float away from everything.

The sharp ding of the telephone receiver being lifted jerked him back to reality. Fever or not, he had to stop her using that phone.

"If you love your sister so much, how can you stand for her killer to go free?"

Fern swirled around to face him, the deadly looking chef's knife glittering almost as brightly in the kitchen light as the pain and hatred in her eyes. "I'm calling the police and turning you in. That way I'll know that Rose's killer is being punished." The vitriol in her tone made him shiver.

"But what if you're wrong? What if I'm telling the truth? Somewhere out there is another man, one who may look a bit like me, enough to confuse you on a dark stairwell. And that man is a stone-cold killer who'll go free, enjoying life—and probably looking for his next victim."

She stood statue still for long moments, glaring at him. Joel tried to read her face, the stiffness of her stance, but couldn't divine whether she was listening to his words or deaf to anything but the guilt she believed was his.

Then Fern advanced towards him, the knife raised high above her head, and Joel closed his eyes.

****

"Hey, Molly! Look at this good quality jacket here! That nice young man who was in earlier must have just left it behind in the donation box." Brenda Dawson was the manager of the Community Closet, a thrift store not too far from the Primrose Hill Community Hospital Joel had so recently left.

The store was also the provider of the previously owned, "gently used" hoodie and change of clothes that Joel had purchased to take him one step farther from being identified. He'd dumped the hoodie that he'd been given by Little Miss Candy Striper into the donation bin as he left the store just in case anyone should recognize it and unknowingly also left behind the GPS chip that The Facilitator had slipped into his pocket.

"Well, jeez, what do you know! It's almost new. Wonder why he'd buy an old one and leave this one behind?" Molly said, her brow furrowed as she set down the armload of used and musty-smelling clothing she was sorting and paused to examine the hoodie.

"You know, this would just fit our Marylyn's boyfriend to a T. Lord knows, he could use some decent clothing. He always looks like he sleeps rough."

"She still seeing him, then?" Brenda said sympathetically. She often wondered how Molly managed to raise six kids on her own, work full time for the pittance the store paid, and still be cheerful and kind. "Look, love, why don't you take it for him, then? It's not been put on our books, and besides, with what they pay here, we all should have a bit of a bonus now and again."

Molly didn't need telling twice. She shoved the nearly new hoodie into her bag and looked forward to giving it to her daughter for her boyfriend. It would perhaps be a peace-offering after the blazing row they'd had over him last night.

****

Twenty-four hours had passed since Joel Alvarez had left the jail, and the GPS chip should have been tracking him. The Facilitator was in a panic. How could the man have found the chip and deactivated it? If that bitch he'd hired to play Candy Striper and get Alvarez out of jail had ratted on him…The private detective took a deep breath. The woman hadn't known about the tracking device and wasn't bright enough to know what it was, anyway.

He was beginning to sweat, imagining the wrath of his client, Mr. Brown, if he admitted what happened, when suddenly his ass was saved as the chip began to transmit. An hour later, he was following the GPS signal, but his relief started to slide away. Joel Alvarez was disappearing into a tough neighborhood, and the Facilitator wasn't at all happy to go unarmed into this rabbit warren of public housing and dark alleyways. He'd had to leave his car behind on the downtown street where he'd picked up the GPS signal, and he'd surely have a fat parking fine or, worse, his car would be towed away. Even worse, parking authority paperwork would put him on the spot if anything went wrong.

And the girl. Thinking about that hard-faced young woman, his stomach ulcer began to burn. She was probably a junkie, that's why she was willing to walk on the wild side, and junkies were notoriously unreliable.

But she did well getting Joel out of the hospital, and right under the nose of that corrections officer, too! He felt a bit better as he thought about how successful his plan had been. Until now. It had all gone well. Although these days, he never quite lost that feeling of insecurity, of waiting for the axe to fall on his neck. An axe no doubt wielded by that cold-blooded bastard. The Facilitator twitched his shoulders, trying to relieve the tension there. He thought about the waitress and the cook at the restaurant, the Candy Striper wannabe, the medley of oddballs he'd had to go through to find the right resources to get this job done. The more people who were involved in an operation, the more likely it was to be screwed up.

He wished he'd never gotten involved with Mr. Brown, despite the money that had flowed so easily from the case. He'd been raised a Presbyterian, and he knew that someday there'd be a reckoning.

He'd better make sure he got Mr. Brown before

Mr. Brown got him.

****

Richard Phelan kept busy on the computer, doing his banking. Every two or three days he sent $9,900 to a secret bank account in the Cayman Islands. He'd been assured by a financial advisor, who'd charged him elegantly for the information, that if he kept his withdrawal and deposits under $10,000 he wouldn't come under scrutiny from Revenue Canada or any other government agency.

The same advisor assured him that once his cash arrived in the Caymans, no one could trace it or him, or freeze the account. Which was exactly what he needed. In about two months from now he should have all the cash from his big lottery win stashed safely away.

He blessed the day he bought that lottery ticket. Without that spur of the moment event, he'd never have found Joel Alvarez, nor would he have had the money to make the man pay him back for all he'd suffered.

Richard smiled to himself as he pressed SEND and sent another payment flying through cyberspace. Soon he'd be off to some tropical island paradise with no extradition, and Joel Alvarez would be—well, alive or dead, he'd be in hell.

Richard's face split into a grin that would have disturbed even the most hardened onlooker.

****

The Facilitator was getting unhappier with every passing minute. He'd had a hard time keeping up with his quarry, who moved swiftly on foot down streets of shabby houses that had been converted into cheap flats and a couple of neglected-looking low-rise apartment buildings. The area seemed almost deserted, as areas like this often were when dusk fell, and the ordinary working folk surrendered the streets to the dealers, the drunks, and the muggers.

He didn't like being down here at all, feeling vulnerable in his suit and tie and good quality overcoat. He knew he looked like a mark for any of the marauding lowlifes that might catch a glimpse of him, and he wasn't carrying his handgun. He smiled a sour smile. He was a law-abiding citizen and wasn't going to carry a weapon without a carry permit, something that was well-nigh impossible for an ordinary citizen to acquire in Canada. At least, to acquire legally. When this was over, he was going to inquire into other means. Or he simply wouldn't take on any more jobs like this.

When this was over, he was going to spend the winter somewhere warm, cheap, and safe from the prying inquiries of law and order that might follow if any of the amateurs he'd had to deal with got scared and decided to blab.

Oh, shit! He'd been so deep in his own anxieties that he'd lost sight of Alvarez! *Where the fuck had the man gone?* He checked the cell phone which should have had a little blinking red light to show where the tracking device was. And where the device was, Alvarez should also be. But oh, hell, he'd lost the connection! There was no cell phone reception down here! Furious, he threw the cell against the wall of the grubby alley he found himself in. These little streets were like a maze from Dante's Inferno. Slater, the Facilitator stood silently for a moment, listening to the night sounds that echoed around him. The area seemed deserted—the night quiet. Straining to hear, he picked up the sound of footsteps around the corner and hurried forward as silently as he could to peer into the gloom. Yes! There was someone, a tall man in a hooded sweatshirt, limping a bit. *Alvarez!*

Finally, he had his quarry in his sights. He flattened himself against the wall, intending to pick up his phone while staying invisible in the dim light. From the echoing sound of footsteps, The Facilitator guessed that Alvarez had slipped down a dark alley, and he smiled in satisfaction. It looked as though Alvarez was going to ground in one of these scruffy apartment blocks. But he had to be sure, so he waited a moment or two and then slipped into the alley after him. He probably should have been a bit more cautious, but he knew how badly injured Alvarez was. If the man should spot him, he'd either lie his way out of it or pretend to be a mugger himself. Alvarez was probably weak as a kitten from the injuries, the blood loss, and the drugs after his stay in hospital. Probably in pain, too, since to Slater's knowledge, the man was operating without the pain killers he probably badly needed.

God, this alley stank! Rotten foods, piss, and something more... he didn't want to think what the something more odors might be. He stepped farther into the inky darkness of the alley and bent to pick up the phone he'd hurled at the wall, and seemingly out of nowhere a hand grabbed him around the neck from behind.

"Who the hell are you?" a gruff voice whispered in his ear, accompanied by the fetid breath of a long-time drug user.

"What d-d'you mean?" The Facilitator gasped out. He could barely get enough breath to speak, and his heart pounded so hard at the unexpected assault that he thought he'd have a heart attack.

"I said, are you following me? Are you a pig?" The arm loosened a little, just enough to let him speak.

Slater struggled for breath, horribly aware that he'd been afraid enough to dribble pee down his pants leg at the sudden realization that his assailant wasn't Alvarez. *Pull yourself together, man,* he told himself. "No, of course not. Why would I follow you?"

"I dunno. Maybe you fancy me. Is that it? Are you a ponce looking for a good time?" The voice was softer now. The Facilitator thought maybe this was his only chance to get out unscathed. He'd go along with the fiction, then pretend to lose his nerve at the last minute, hand this man a few notes, and get away.

"Yes, maybe I am. How would you feel about that? I have money…"

The laugh that followed sent shivers up and down Slater's spine. He'd thought he was a hard man, but he'd nothing on the man who held him in a cruel grip. And he knew with appalling clarity that he'd just made a terrible mistake.

"Oh, yeah, I know the likes of you. Looking for a bit of rough, for a boy with a sweet ass who'll give you what your nice, respectable wife won't. Well, you followed the wrong sucker there, my man."

And then The Facilitator lost his footing as he was pushed hard down onto the filthy concrete. As his head bounced on the slimy ground, he just had a chance to see the man's face and take in the vicious grin of a thug who enjoyed what he was doing. And then his world turned purple and hazy with pain as the first kick landed on his stomach. And then the next kick hit his balls and he retched uncontrollably as blackness claimed him.

****

Fern Adams was in a private hell of her own. She'd caught sight of herself in a mirror over the kitchen table but hadn't recognized herself. The woman in the mirror looked nothing like Dr. Fern Adams—not with the contorted expression of rage on her face, the knife raised high in her hands, and the madness shining in her eyes.

With a few simple words, Joel Alvarez had destroyed Fern's belief in herself as a good, rational human being who believed in the law. He'd said, "*If you love your sister so much, how can you stand for her killer to go free?*" And suddenly good girl, responsible citizen, dedicated doctor Fern Adams had been filled again with the lust to kill.

But the tiny voice of reason, the good person she thought she was, struggled to get through the desire to plunge the knife over and over into Alvarez' helpless body. The voice asked, "*But what if he really is innocent?*"

And the ages-old argument against capital punishment got through to Fern, but not before she stood over Joel. He held her gaze, his eyes clear and unafraid even as his body trembled and tried to cringe back out of range of her knife. It was that look, the same look she'd seen in the courtroom, that undid her.

It was the look of an innocent man.

Fern collapsed to her knees on the floor, the knife falling from her hands, and she covered her face and wept. Out of the corner of her eye, between her fingers covering her face, Fern saw Alvarez' bound hands reach out. She'd left herself helpless when she dropped the knife. What if her instincts were wrong? Was he going to grab it and kill her as he'd killed her sister?

Suddenly Fern didn't care. Live or die, it was all the same to her in that moment. Because what if that look Joel gave her, the look of an innocent man, what if it was genuine?

That meant her testimony had sentenced him to a nightmare. But how could that be? She'd seen him with her own eyes.

Her body shook with shock as her prisoner ignored the knife and, with his hands bound clumsily together, patted her gently on the shoulder, offering her comfort when he could have taken the opportunity to free himself.

At that point Fern's mind opened, just a crack, to the possibility that Joel Alvarez was telling the truth. Her mind strayed back to the dates they'd had, the long talks about anything and everything, the Sunday afternoon walks in the lakeside park, the laughter they'd shared watching children playing. She remembered him throwing a ball for a scruffy dog, over and over again, until the dog was tired out and they were laughing as the pooch lay down at their feet for a nap.

She was startled out of her fugue by the insistent ringing of the telephone. The answering machine picked up finally, and she heard the voice of Detective John Bamber asking her to return his call as soon as possible. "I don't wish to alarm you, but there have been no sightings of Alvarez, so please continue to…"

She managed to grab the receiver before he finished speaking.

"Detective Bamber? It's Fern Adams. Thank you for calling back. The tape on my answering machine ran out. You say Joel Alvarez has disappeared? Evaded all the people looking for him? How can that be?" The fear in her voice wasn't an act.

"I must apologize. You should have been kept in the loop of our investigations. Truth is, I'm afraid to say, that there've been no sightings of the man…but he can't hide forever, not in his condition, so please don't worry. The good news is that he's probably left the area, that's why no-one has seen hide nor hair of him. Just keep your doors locked and remember Alvarez was seriously injured in an altercation with another prisoner. That's why he was taken to Primrose Hill Hospital for treatment in a secure area."

"Obviously, it wasn't that secure, if he was able to walk out!" Fern snapped. "I had to find out he'd even been in the hospital from one of my colleagues when I returned to Primrose Hill."

"You weren't informed by the hospital administration?"

"No, I'd been away for a couple of days and only called back in for an emergency RTA. I must have missed all the excitement." Fern's voice dripped sarcasm.

Bamber ignored it. In his book, Fern had every reason to be angry. "Now, we have no reason to believe that he will go anywhere near you. The man is not fit medically to travel, but like all escaped prisoners, he likely wants to put as much distance as possible between himself and the penitentiary. All the same, it would be wise if you were to take extra precautions for your own security in the next few days. Keep your doors locked, take care going to your vehicle, and so on. And please, call me back or any other officer if at any time you have concerns."

"Yes, I'll take your advice and be more careful about security," Fern raised her eyebrows as she looked over at Joel and continued with her lie. "But...but you don't think the man would try to find me, do you?"

"No, not at all. I think he'll be like most escaped cons and try to get as far away from Primrose Hill as he possibly can. He can set himself up somewhere else, probably another province, where he might not be recognized."

"Oh, I'm sure you're right..." Fern's voice trailed off. *Should she tell him? Should she hand Joel over to the authorities and let them carry the burden of proving whether he's guilty or not? But really, hadn't he already been tried and found guilty? And wasn't it her evidence that convicted him?*

Fern struggled with her conscience when Bamber asked, "Ms. Adams? Are you okay? Your voice sounds very shaky."

"What? Oh, I'm really shaken by all this. How could something like this happen?" *Should she tell? Should she hand Joel over to the police? And then...how would she ever know for sure that he is guilty?*

Damn the man for raising that doubt in her mind!

"I'm so sorry about this. Alvarez is in bad shape and the only way he could have escaped is with outside intervention. We're following a number of leads, and we're sure we'll find his accomplices and get him back behind bars in short order. Officers from other provinces, as well as over the border with the U.S., are on alert for the escaped prisoner. I can understand you being upset, though. Is there anyone you could perhaps go and stay until this is over?"

The detective had inadvertently given her an idea. "Thank you, I'll think about that. Again, thank you for calling."

"You're welcome. Again, my apologies. Do let the police know if you do decide to leave home, and where you'll be located."

"I will, for sure. Detective Bamber?"

"Yes, Ms. Adams?"

"Do you think Alvarez really was guilty? Is it possible there was any mistake?"

The silence that filled the air between them accused her. She heard Bamber sigh. "Ms. Adams, do you have any reason to believe Alvarez is innocent?"

It was her turn for silence. She swallowed over the lump in her throat, looking over her shoulder to see Alvarez still slumped against the wall, his eyes closed. "I know I saw him leaving my sister's apartment. I can't deny the evidence of my own eyes. But I knew him, dated him for a while, and I'd never have dreamt…He has always insisted he was innocent, and since the trial I've wondered…well, what if he's telling the truth and my sister's killer is walking around, enjoying his life? Maybe thinking of another victim at this very moment?"

"Ma'am, the evidence was pretty damning—not just your testimony but that of the forensics experts, too. Other witnesses also put Alvarez in the company of your sister, and he could not come up with a tenable alibi."

Fern exhaled a long breath. "Thank you for the reassurance, Detective Bamber. I'll be sure to be in touch if I go away or if I see anything around here that makes me anxious." And on that lie, Fern replaced the telephone receiver and went to kneel beside Joel to take his temperature. The man was burning up with fever.

Even so, he struggled to speak through dry lips. "Thank you." And then he lost consciousness.

Leaving Fern to wonder just what the hell she had just done.

Chapter Ten

"What the fuck!" Glory glared in amazement at the woman sitting across the desk from her. Dr. Fern Adams looked perfectly calm, but she'd just dropped a bombshell on Joel Alvarez' lawyer.

"Do you mean to tell me Joel is at your home, unconscious—maybe even dead, and you have done nothing to help him?" Glory was having trouble not yelling at the top of her lungs at the other woman. "For God's sake, Dr. Adams, were you allowing him to suffer and die by default? Is that why you didn't call the police the moment you saw who was at your door?"

Fern shrugged. "That's kind of a long story, involving a chase through my house and being tossed onto a chair in my living room...but I have fixed his stitches and—"

"Jeez, woman, are you quite insane?" Glory spluttered. She leapt up from her chair, grabbing her briefcase and cell phone, and moving towards the office door. As she pulled her jacket from a hook, she turned to Fern with a dark look. "If anything has happened since you left my client, injured, in need of urgent medical care, and all alone, I swear to God I'll see you pay dearly, to the full extent of the law. Come on now."

Fern sat quite still. "No." She refused to meet Glory's eyes.

"What!"

"I want you to help me hide Joel, to find a place I can take him until he's recovered."

Shaking her head, Glory dropped her coat and returned to face Fern across her desk, the air sizzling with distrust between them.

"If what you're saying is the truth—"

"It is."

"Why?" Fern Adams' utter calm brought Glory's temper to boiling point. "And why would Joel Alvarez come to you? I'd have thought you'd be the last person in the world he'd turn to, given you were the one who sent him to jail in the first place." In truth, Glory was a bit annoyed that her client might have sought help from Fern Adams rather than herself. If, indeed, she could believe what the pale-faced woman standing in front of her was saying.

Fern hesitated. Joel's defense lawyer was the only person she could trust, but that trust was flimsy. "He...he says he wanted me to tell him why I testified against him. I...I was afraid he'd hurt me, and I tried to run away. Joel grabbed me but I got loose, and I head butted him in the stomach. He collapsed against the wall, and there was all this blood—"

"Yes, I understand he was seriously wounded in a prison assault." *So, it's Joel, is it? On first name terms with the man you believe killed your sister?* Glory's eyes narrowed in mistrust.

The thought must have telegraphed itself to Fern because she asked, "Why don't you trust me? I'm telling the truth!"

"Well, now, Ms. Adams...Dr. Adams. I happen to believe in my client's innocence. Because of that, I have to consider any testimony or evidence against him to be a lie. Your testimony led police to Joel, led to the DNA testing, led to his conviction. Therefore, if he's innocent, as I believe, then you're lying. How can I trust you when your lies put an innocent man in jail for twenty-five years?"

Fern flinched under the other woman's hard glare, but she refused to back down. She thought of the man now lying on her living room sofa, his face flushed from fever but his breathing strong and steady.

"I wasn't lying when I said I saw Joel running away from my sister's apartment, and that he had blood on his clothes. I'll never forget that. But Joel claims he didn't kill Rose. And if he's telling the truth, if somehow there's some missing piece of the jigsaw that proves he's innocent, then I want to find it."

"Why? You were all gung-ho to get my client slung into jail for the rest of his natural life. Now you want to prove his innocence all of a sudden?" Glory's voice dripped disbelief.

Fern dragged in a deep breath. "No, that's not it. I still believe he's as guilty as sin. But what I can't live with is he has always claimed innocence, and then it was something he said. He asked me how I would feel if he was innocent and the man who murdered Rose was going Scot free? Because if Joel *is* innocent, then the real killer is still out there enjoying his life." She spat the words. "My sister is rotting in the cemetery, and her killer may be sitting in the sunshine, watching the pretty women going by and picking his next victim. And I can't live with that."

Glory worried her bottom lip with her teeth. "And if he can't prove he didn't kill your sister? Then what?"

Fern hesitated. If she told Glory what she really

intended…

But the other woman could read her expression. "You're not thinking of meting out your own form of justice, are you?"

Fern sniffed. "Of course not. I'm a doctor, after all. I'm sworn to try to save lives."

Right then and there, she saw the change. Glory believed her. But that belief was limited. Even so, the attorney's face softened, and she moved back to her chair. "We need to talk."

****

Detective Bamber rubbed gritty eyes and tried again to read and make sense out of the stack of reports on his desk. He couldn't remember the last time he'd been able to snatch more than a couple of hours' sleep. Primrose Hill seemed to have its own personal crime wave going on right now. He'd not been able to keep up with the workload, not since Joel Alvarez had escaped, in fact.

And Alvarez wasn't his only case. Just this morning he'd been assigned a case where a man in his fifties had been found kicked and beaten almost to death in a filthy alleyway in Primrose Hill.

There's about as much chance of finding out who did this as there is of my winning Saturday night's lottery, he thought bitterly to himself. *What was happening to this town?* Once a prosperous rural farming area, the crime rate now seemed to resemble gang territory in Toronto.

Tossing the file aside onto the others on his desk: the usual missing persons, a domestic that led to bloodshed, and a drug turf assault and battery. He tipped his chair back, put his feet on the desk, and closed his eyes. He called this his thinking pose, although power nap was another phrase for it. Either way, all his colleagues knew this wasn't a good time to interrupt. All, that is, except for Lee Groves.

****

Fern rushed back to her house, wondering if Joel Alvarez would still be there, or would he have made good his escape? *Or, dear God, what if he'd died from blood loss...Would that make her guilty of failing to provide care?* And she'd always feel morally guilty, because of her vows as a healer, but also if Joel died, she'd never know for sure if he was an innocent man or a coldblooded killer.

She had been so sure of herself when she talked with Glory, but on the journey back to the old farmhouse, her doubts had returned. Joel's defense attorney certainly seemed sure of her client's innocence, but she couldn't add anything except a gut feeling and some vague story of a letter that may or may not have mentioned some distant relative of Joel's mother. No evidence to back that up. Just as Joel had no alibi, no way of explaining how she could have seen him rushing away from Rose's apartment, his face, hands, and clothing stained with blood.

He claimed it never happened, but she had to believe the evidence of the barista and customers who swore Joel and Rose had been together in the bar the afternoon that Rose died. Then there was the damning DNA evidence, and that couldn't lie. She remembered Dr. Kyle Witburg's assertion that the only explanation that Joel was innocent could be that he had a twin. An identical twin. But all indications said he had none. No relatives at all, living or dead. Most of all, she had to believe the evidence of her own eyes. How could she trust a man she'd seen covered in her sister's blood? And yet— was it really doubt that niggled at her? There could be no doubt about his guilt. But Joel's question, *"If you love your sister so much, how can you stand for her killer to go free?"* had hit a nerve and she couldn't rest until she was sure, once and for all. And then she'd move heaven and earth to pack his murdering ass back to prison to rot.

Or maybe she'd just do what the courts could not do. Take justice into her own hands. For Rose.

Her resolve weakened as she entered her home, wondering if Joel was now lurking, armed with one of her own kitchen knives, ready to fulfill some psychotic fantasy of his own. For the man was surely mad.

Fern shivered.

The house was quiet. Alvarez should have recovered now. She'd dosed him up well with pain killers which had made him sleepy, but she'd been gone longer than she expected because of her detour to purchase some protection for herself. Taser guns, she was told, were very effective. The effect of the drugs would have worn off by now. He could be waiting for her, ready to slit her throat as he'd done to Rose. And maybe other women before. The books and experts all seemed to agree that killers like the man who had killed Rose had done the deed before. They predicated their belief on the confidence shown, the organization, and the sheer brutality.

Fern shivered again. For a moment, she considered turning tail, calling the police, and washing her hands of the whole thing.

But a wee, small voice in the back of her mind

stopped her. It sounded like her conscience. Joel had planted the seeds of doubt in her mind, a mind she realized was receptive because, whether she wanted to admit it or not, she already had reservations about his guilt. *Maybe it's wishful thinking. I have to find out once and for all if he really was my sister's killer, or did some monster still roam the streets, free to go on killing?*

Fern swallowed over the ball of fear in her throat. She simultaneously turned the key in the door and grasped the handle of the Taser gun that nestled in her jacket pocket. The store assistant had assured her, with a mocking smile, that it was all charged up and ready to zap anyone who got in her way.

Filled with false confidence now, she pushed the door open and stepped inside. The familiar sounds and odors came to her—the scent of pine paneling in the dining room, rose scent from the crystal bowl of potpourri in the hallway, new paint from the work she'd been doing on the spare bedroom. And the reassuring hum of the refrigerator, the tick, tick of the grandmother clock on the wall in the den...

No madman leaping out at her.

Maybe he'd taken the opportunity to walk out before she came home, expecting her to bring a posse of police officers with her. *Which is exactly what any sane person in her position would have done.*

Swallowing back her fear, Fern stepped quietly towards the den where she'd left Joel on a pull-out couch, blankets wrapped tightly around him to ward off the chill of shock that had wracked his wounded body.

She let out a deep breath of relief but didn't let go of the Taser handle even though it was now sweaty from her frightened grip. Joel lay curled on his side, almost exactly as she'd left him, one muscular arm flung out over the colorful antique quilt.

He was so silent. So still. *Surely the noise of her entrance should have woken him?* It was hard to breathe around the pounding of her heart. The man had not been in good shape when she'd left him. He should really have been returned to a hospital. What if he had been injured worse than she thought?

What if Joel Alvarez had died while she was meeting with Glory Jordan?

Tears sprang to her eyes, and she drew in a ragged breath. *If he's dead, I'll never know for sure who killed my sister!* Surely that was the only reason she could barely force her feet forward to look for his pulse? Nothing to do with the fact that she'd dated him once before the world went crazy. Dated him and had such hopes...

She forced herself, step by step, across the room to where Joel lay, so pale and still. Dread squeezed her heart and fogged her vision, and she startled when Joel shivered, struggling to rise to the surface of the dream that encapsulated him. She heard his ragged intake of breath.

At least he was still alive. Whether that was a good thing remained to be seen.

****

It felt like he'd barely closed his eyes before the phone on his nightstand was shrilling. Bamber came bolt awake and grabbed the instrument, barking his name into it.

"I found her! I found the bitch that tricked me!" Officer Dan Meade's voice came triumphantly over the telephone.

"Slow down there and tell me what you're talking about!"

"The fake Candy Striper who helped Alvarez escape from the hospital. I told you I'd know her anywhere? Well, I've been out and about every night, hunting around the places where lowlifes like her would hang out. And I found her. I'm watching her this minute."

Bamber sat up, rolling his eyes when he saw the time on the bedside clock. "Where are you?" he asked Meade as he thrust his legs into jeans and pulled on a soft cotton sweater.

"I'm at a bar called Napoleon's Bower, in Napanee. Do you want me to bring her in?"

"On what grounds? Imitating a hospital volunteer? Do I have to remind you that you aren't a police officer?"

"No, dammit. Assaulting a law officer. Interfering with the law. Helping a convicted killer to escape. Take your pick. Do I have to remind *you* that I was in charge of Alvarez while he was at the hospital? He's my prisoner, my responsibility."

Bamber bit down on a harsh response. The man was a corrections officer. He had been in charge of Alvarez, and he was working to help the police. Now was not the time for confrontation. Still, he could hardly keep the sarcasm out of his tone as he replied. "Are you alone? Do you have backup?" The woman who'd tricked the officer looked to be about one-hundred pounds soaking wet on the grainy hospital surveillance tape, just a girl in her teens, compared to Meade's brawny two-hundred seventy-five pounds.

"No, just me. I could call one of the women officers from Napanee. I wouldn't want this tricky little thing claiming I'd done anything improper. She looks like butter wouldn't melt in her mouth, and about sixteen years old."

"Okay, that's good thinking, officer. Get a female officer to meet you outside the bar. I'll be with you in twenty minutes."

"Right you are, sir."

"And Meade—don't do anything to fuck this up."

Twenty-five minutes later Bamber studied the hard-faced girl who sat across from him and Meade in the darkened booth of the working-class bar where the corrections officer had tracked her to earth. A female uniformed officer stood beside them, her expression bored. The girl was pale, and looked to be in her early twenties, not the young person they'd thought from her appearance on the hospital security tapes. Even though she was obviously frightened, defiance oozed from every pore of her body. This was a woman who had never had good dealings with authority figures and had developed her own way of dealing with them.

Total, lip-thinned, insolent silence.

But Bamber had dealt with many people like her, and she wasn't going to fob them off with this rebel act. Although as she blew cigarette smoke into his face, he wished he'd let a uniformed officer arrest her and drag her sweet little rear downtown. *What he wouldn't give for a cigarette!* The woman officer, Marsha Dinsdale, caught his look and rolled her eyes.

"Don't you know it's illegal to smoke in bars?"

Thin shoulders lifted in a shrug. "What? They got detectives arresting people for breaking bylaws now?

You should seriously consider your job options." Her voice was threaded with anger, but at least she was speaking.

"No, but there's a few things I could arrest you for."

Back to the hot-eyed silence. Bamber sighed, sensing Meade's restlessness beside him. The man was still furious that this Kerry Loman had duped him with one of the oldest tricks in the book. Her eyes slid sideways to look at him, and a small, knowing grin played around her scarlet-painted lips. Meade all but growled.

"Look, Kerry, I'm not really interested in you. Hardly worth the paperwork in chasing you up and arresting you. But if I must, I will. It's your choice. We have you on video tape helping Joel Alvarez out of the hospital. That's helping a convicted murderer escape custody."

Stony silence. Bamber could see by the flicker of her eyes that she was listening despite the disinterested pose.

"So, now we come to the get-out-of-jail free question: Who hired you? I want a name, Kerry, or you can kiss your grubby little freedom goodbye for two or three years, just on what we have on you now."

Aside from a tense tightening of her fingers around her beer, the girl held onto her silence.

Bamber sighed then motioned to the constable that they were going to escort Little Miss Innocent down to the station. "Maybe a night in the provincial hotel will help your memory," he told Kerry in answer to her scowl.

Chapter Eleven

Fern took a deep, calming breath as she entered the hospital. This was a place she always felt safe, in control, competent—a direct opposite to the way most people felt when entering through the power-operated double doors into the brightly lit world of medicine.

No matter how brightly lit, how cheerfully decorated, no matter what aura of calm and efficiency the surroundings projected, most people entering a hospital felt ill at ease, covered with a cloak of anxiety about themselves or a loved one. Hospitals to most people were associated with pain, illness, death, or anxiety and dread—*What will the tests show? Will it be positive? Negative? Will it hurt? Can they stop the pain? Will my loved one be all right?* And bargaining with a God they might never have given thought to for years about what they would offer if only, only, He would make the test results come out right, the news good.

But for Fern—and, she suspected, many of the hospital staff—it was her element, a place where she could do good, could ease pain, could challenge mortality, be in control. A place where she donned a white coat and an authority in the eyes of others that was possibly, sometimes definitely, misplaced. People looked to doctors as if they were some sort of demi-god, someone who could press and prod, look at an xray and pronounce a simple cure, waving their hands over a prescription pad to take the pain away.

And sometimes it was like that. For Fern, who worked with the trauma unit and specialized in emergency trauma work, the divide between cure and oblivion was blurred by the in-between limbo that faced many, like the construction worker who'd fallen from scaffolding. His family had been ecstatic to learn that he would come out of the drug-induced coma and his chances of survival were great. Then two days later, when she'd had to tell them that injury to the spinal column meant the man would probably never walk again, they'd clung to each other and wept.

Now she hurried to the pharmacy station, her mind on Joel Alvarez and his seeping wounds. She needed to prevent infection, needed to close the wounds to prevent further damage, and treat him with antibiotics. She grimaced at the idea that she was picking up supplies to keep Rose's killer alive while she'd fantasized seeing him die as painful a death as he'd bestowed on her sister.

But his words, *When the real killer is still walking around enjoying life,* had robbed her of what little peace of mind his conviction had offered. Because in the back of her mind she still found it difficult to equate the evil act of murder with a man who'd risked his own life to rescue others from burning buildings and fiery car wrecks. She'd listened in amazement as his defense attorney, Glory Jordan, spoke in court passionately at the sentencing about her client's previous good standing in society. Everyone in that courtroom could see that Glory believed her client could not be guilty of so heinous a crime. If she hadn't seen Joel with her own eyes, Rose's blood on his hands, she would have found it impossible to believe, too.

She'd assumed that the trial and the life sentence in prison would have brought closure for her, but it hadn't. Now the idea that Joel Alvarez might be innocent, however slim that possibility, gave her no choice but to try and find out the truth. Even if it meant a pact with the devil.

And when she knew for sure that the law had convicted the right man, she would make sure he never walked in the sunshine again.

"My, but you are serious looking." A deep, rich voice so close to her ear that Fern jumped. She'd been so engrossed in her thoughts as she waited for the pharmacy clerk to fill her requisition that she hadn't seen Dr. Morgan James enter the waiting area, and she startled at the sound of the other woman's voice.

"I'm sorry, I didn't mean to make you jump! You were miles away!" Dr. James, a tall, rangy woman with a mass of auburn hair caught up in a French pleat that usually became an unruly mass of curls by the end of her workday, looked serious as she examined Fern's face.

"Oh, you know how it is. Everything sometimes closes in on you." It had taken Fern some time to get used to the fact that her friend and former college buddy Morgan had been the same doctor who performed the autopsy on her sister and had given evidence of the awful wounds Rose had endured. As she had given her evidence in detail in the court, Morgan's glance had occasionally strayed to Fern as if she wanted to apologize for the graphic phrases she had to use to describe what had been done.

Later she had approached Fern and apologized for the further indignities she had had to visit on Rose's body in order to gather evidence. They'd cried in each other's arms and then gone out to a bar and gotten drunk, one of the few times Fern could remember ever being drunk in her life. To her surprise, it had felt good to let the alcohol and the noise of the rowdy bar numb her feelings.

Until the morning after, when she and Morgan both went through the day looking green about the gills as the hangovers took their toll. They hadn't repeated the experience.

"I haven't had a chance to really talk to you since the sentencing. How are you coping?"

"Well, it's kind of up and down."

"You didn't find Alvarez being put away for twenty-five years was a closure, eh? I didn't think you would."

"No, I don't think there'll ever be closure. The only real justice would be if Rose could be returned to us as if none of this had ever happened. Isn't that what justice is supposed to do? Put things right?"

"Some things can never be put right," Morgan said somberly. "But at least we can punish the guilty."

Fern bit her lip. "I find it hard to equate the man everyone knew as Joel Alvarez, the hero, the man I dated myself a few times, with the monster who killed my sister." She blurted the words out. Somehow it was a relief to admit what she was thinking.

Morgan took a deep breath and blew it out, the air making her curly bangs float up from her forehead. "The evidence would seem pretty conclusive."

"You mean the DNA evidence?"

Morgan nodded. "Well, that and the evidence of your own eyes. It's hard to deny scientific evidence, although it's really not as easy or conclusive as the television programs would have us believe. There are constant new revelations about the human genome that take us closer and closer to accuracy."

"Are you saying that the DNA might not have been from Joel Alvarez'?"

Morgan gave her a sharp look. "Don't get me wrong. DNA is pretty accurate. Unless Alvarez had an identical twin, mind you. And there was nothing in his background that would suggest that he had. Remember, the defense tried to float the idea that maybe someone related to Alvarez was responsible for Rose's death, and the prosecution nipped that one in the bud with evidence that he had no relatives and was an only child."

"I don't recall that. But then I had missed a few hours of the trial when there was that multiple car pile-up on the 401, and the gas tanker overturned. It was all-hands-on deck in the ER, and I stayed on." Fern shuddered at the memory of mangled bodies and wrecked vehicles.

"All that aside, honey, you saw the man with your own eyes. The bartender gave evidence that Alvarez was with your sister, even identified him and named him. Alvarez had no alibi for the time Rose was killed. I'd say it's just a sad case of a previously decent man going off the rails for some reason. Although, the police looked into his background pretty intensively and didn't find anything, even though this is the sort of crime a killer usually builds up to."

Fern was silent for a few moments. The pharmacy

assistant came back with a brown bag containing the items Fern had requisitioned.

"Did I ever tell you that I was always grateful that you were the one to…to autopsy Rose? I know you loved her and would have treated her with dignity. That meant a lot."

"Oh, Fern! You've no idea how it broke my heart to have to do that!"

The two women hugged.

"Morgan, thank you. You've taken a load off my mind."

Fern's next stop was her department head's office, where she explained that she needed to take some time off. Dr. Don Barnaby looked at her with compassionate eyes across his neat desk. "I'm glad you've decided to do that," he told her. "You've been running on empty since before the trial, and we've all been worried about you. Get some rest and recharge those batteries, and I hope you feel better when you get back. If you need longer than a week, well, you're owed time. Just let us know so we can cover for you."

She thanked him, relieved for his understanding and that he hadn't asked her any awkward questions. Minutes later, after stopping in to inform the department secretary and the receptionist that she was spending a few days in a friend's place in cottage country and to give them her cell phone as a contact number, she walked out of the hospital doors into the chilly afternoon. Fern wondered what people, especially Detective Bamber, would say if he heard she was going to spend days at a cottage belonging to Alvarez' defense lawyer. And that she wouldn't be alone.

There was no time to waste on considering what

she was planning. A glance at the clouds told her she needed to get on her way. Snow was threatening, and the rural roads could get treacherous.

She just had one more stop to make before returning home to pick up Joel Alvarez.

****

Richard Phelan swore and hit his fist against the scarred veneer of the cheap kitchen table that served as his. desk. One more attempt at reaching The *Facilitator* on Instant Messaging had received no reply. The man wasn't answering emails, wasn't responding to Instant Messages, didn't seem to be on Twitter. Where the hell was he?

A dark shadow of foreboding touched him. His earlier anxieties about *The Facilitator's* loyalties weighed heavily, followed quickly by a stab of anger. He stood, smashing his fist this time against the greasy tiles of the kitchen wall again and again until the roaring pain in his knuckles brought him to his senses.

The pain may have erased the anger, but it didn't erase the question. *Where was Joel Alvarez? And where was Slater?*

Could it be that even now the man was baring his soul to a captivated and encouraging Ontario Provincial Police or Royal Canadian Mounted Police detective? Was he pouring out the story of how he'd been contacted and asked to report on a murder trial and to arrange for the convicted man to be attacked and almost killed? Then paid to have the same man sprung from hospital on the bidding of a virtual employer he knew only as Mr. Brown?

Richard checked his computer inbox again. Still no message. *What the fucking hell's going on?* Was the man simply still out and about following Joel Alvarez? But he knew he was supposed to check in with Richard, to give progress reports so that his employer could plot the next step in his punishment of the man who'd ruined his life.

A grim smile, a smile that wasn't quite sane, lit up Richard's face. He knew all about Joel Alvarez, but Joel knew nothing about him. Of that, he was convinced. Otherwise, if the man had known, he would have connected the dots that led to his present predicament. No, Alvarez was dangling on the end of a puppet's strings that Richard held and tugged hither and thither.

And one day soon he would cut that string, and Joel would come tumbling down. Forever. And then he, Richard, would be living the high life on some tropical paradise with his lottery winnings. Maybe he'd send Alvarez a postcard to pin up in his miserable hole of a forever jail cell.

If he decided to let the bastard live, that is.

****

"So, Kerry, I'm glad you've finally decided to be smart and tell us what you know." Bamber turned around the hard plastic chair and straddled it. Kerry wasn't looking anywhere near as perky now as she had when they'd brought her into the interview room two hours earlier.

In fact, she looked downright wilted, her makeup faded and streaked, eye shadow and mascara looking like bruises around her eyes. Taken out of her barroom environment and away from the people she could impress by her aggressive silence and defiance of the police, she had quickly lost her starch. Especially when the two officers took the time to explain to her just how long a jail sentence could be imposed for the charges they could bring against her unless she helped them.

Officer Meade had let her see his anger at being duped by her in her Candy Striper hospital volunteer disguise and made it clear that he would have no trouble identifying her from the witness stand at her trial. Bamber had then shooed the angry corrections officer from the interview room, and his seat opposite Kerry had been taken by Lee Groves.

"Who do you think the courts are going to believe—a long-serving Corrections Canada officer, or a juvenile delinquent who's just moved along into an adult rap sheet?" Bamber had snarled at her. The girl shrank back into her chair but struggled to hold on to her silence.

Then they produced still shots from the hospital surveillance tapes, grainy though they were, and it was clear that she was the one steering Joel Alvarez towards the exit and escape. Kerry's bottom lip began to quiver, and tears filled her eyes, running in tracks down her pale cheeks. The impending waterworks cut no ice with the two officers who were rapidly becoming impatient to move on with their investigation. They knew she held some vital information, and they wanted it now, if not sooner.

With a sniff, the young woman capitulated and began to tell them everything she knew. Which was disappointingly little, Bamber thought wearily. Still, they knew someone had paid her handsomely to get Alvarez out of jail, a man who claimed to be a private investigator and went by the name of Slater.

"I don't know his first name, so don't ask. But

there is one other thing…"

"What's that?" Bamber snapped. He didn't have time to play games.

"Well, he had a business card and, well, I laughed. He called himself The Facilitator. You know, kind of like someone who makes things happen?"

"Yeah, we know what facilitator means. Did he say who he was working for?"

"No, he was petty cagey about that, but it must have been someone with deep pockets 'cos Slater was handing it out like candy."

So some anonymous someone had a motive for spending so much cash on causing maximum damage to a man who had no family and few, if any, friends left. Or was the unknown benefactor actually trying to help Alvarez escape justice? Bamber voiced this thought to his superior who suggested that it was a possibility, but a pretty dangerous one. He pointed out that the 'rescue' was pretty rough, and Alvarez could have died.

"Not exactly a humane way of treating someone you wanted to save," he commented. Years of experience told Bamber that you gather all the evidence, and sometimes things that don't seem to have much meaning suddenly mesh with new information and picture forms that solves the case.

"Do you have this business card?" he questioned Kerry Loman.

"It's in my purse, somewhere, I think…"

Groves handed her a cheap, grubby-looking pink purse, and she started rummaging. The police had already been through the items there but hadn't seen a card.

"Ah! Here it is." Kerry pulled a battered looking

tube of cardboard. The business card had been rolled up and stuck through a hole in the purse's lining.

"Will we find traces of cocaine in this nice little tube?" he asked.

Kerry's eyes went wide. "No, I never did that!"

Out of the corner of his eye he noticed Grove fidgeting. The two detectives stepped outside of the interview room, and Bamber asked impatiently what was bothering his sergeant.

"That man you know, the one beaten up in the back alley…"

"Yes, the case that we got this morning. So?"

"So his name is Slater, and he had a business card in his pocket that said The Facilitator!"

Bamber swore under his breath, but his heartbeat sped up. Could this be the solution, the key piece of evidence they'd been missing? "Get a car. Let's finish with Little Miss Innocent and cut her loose with a warning not to go far from Primrose Hill. Then we're going to the hospital to talk to this man." Bamber smiled. *Could it really be this easy?*

Kerry was looking more confident when the two officers returned, but something about their faces made her swallow back an anxious exclamation.

"So you expect us to believe that this guy approached you, handed you a wad of cash and a to-do list for springing a total stranger from hospital? And you just said, *gee, thanks so much, Mister, I'll get on it right away*?" Bamber let the disbelief thread through his words.

Kerry screwed up her pretty face in a scowl but held her silence.

"You didn't ask any questions, like, why am I

doing this? Who wants this done? Who the fuck is this guy they want out?"

"Look, I needed the money. I've got a kid, needs new winter stuff and all. Kids grow fast. I knew who Joel Alvarez was when I saw his name. I look at the TV news, you know," she declared as if claiming she read Tolstoy in the original Russian. "You can't talk to me like I've shit for brains. I'm not a dummy, jus' cos I don't have much schoolin'. You should have a bit more respect."

Bamber ignored the disgusted snort of the detective next to him, focusing his attention on Kerry as if she were the only woman in the world. And a smart one, too.

Am I a good actor, or what? "Kerry, you're doing fine, and no one intended to insult you. You've shown you're smart enough to co-operate with us. Now, I want to know everything that happened again—descriptions of anyone who approached you, any names, contact information, whatever you can remember."

Another few minutes of prodding and poking and alternate tears and angry silences, but finally they knew they had got as much as they could from the young woman. Bamber told the desk sergeant to turn her loose without charges.

"What? Turn her loose after everything she did?" Meade's face was suffused with angry red that the satisfaction of revenge was being snatched away. The corrections officer had been waiting at Bamber's desk all this time, wanting to see his young nemesis dragged away, preferably whipped and in chains.

"She co-operated with us," Bamber said mildly, noting with irritation that the man had made a chain of

147

all the paper clips from the holder on his desk. "And besides, we know where she is if we need her for something more."

"These kids can disappear into the woodwork," Meade spluttered.

Bamber shrugged, turning his attention to more urgent matters. If they needed to reel Kerry back in, they'd do it.

But now they were going to sweet talk some doctors into letting them question a severely beaten man who just might have the answers they were seeking.

****

Fern waited until she was well north of Kingston, flitting on side roads where frost-rimmed trees and grasses sparkled like Christmas lights in her headlights on the edges of the fields and woodlands. When she was sure she was far enough to have a good head start on anyone who might pursue her, she pulled onto the side of the road in the welcoming shadow of a giant, leafless maple tree and made the call. After a couple of rings, it went to Detective Bamber's voicemail, and she sighed with relief. At least she didn't have to speak directly to the sharp witted man.

"Detective Bamber? I've been thinking about what you said. You know, about going away for a while. I was pretty nervous alone at home, so I decided to take your advice and go and stay at a friend's cottage. I'm going up to near Cloyne. It's a little place in cottage country well north of Kingston. It's a bit remote, but this whole thing with Joel Alvarez escaping has really got me spooked. You can reach me by cell phone if you need to, but I believe the reception isn't the greatest. I hope there's good news about Alvarez soon."

Fern spoke calmly, her voice betraying none of the tension she felt. It wasn't a lie. She really was heading northeast to the Land O' Lakes area. Glory Jordan had offered her the use of her country property near Cloyne, where she would meet with them later. It was the sin of omission in what she was saying that made her nerves stretch taut for fear Bamber's keen mind might read the underlying tension in her voice and guess at its cause.

Fern relaxed her tight grip on the cell phone. Right now, she felt caught in the crossfire, between the evidence of her own eyes and the strange nagging doubts in her heart.

That's why she wanted to get Joel out of Primrose Hill, out of the orbit of a police search, to a place where she could have him to herself. He'd told her he was going to find out who had killed her sister and Fern had decided to help him. *Even though she was sure all the evidence was going to lead directly to Joel himself.*

And this time it wasn't a nearly harmless Taser gun she carried. Reaching into the deep pocket of her fleece jacket, her fingers caressed the cold metal of a small pistol.

One way or another, she would see that her sister had justice.

Chapter Twelve

Joel woke up with a start, groggy and disoriented, as the car braked to a stop in almost total darkness. Where the hell was he? He couldn't even remember falling asleep, and the thick blackness that pressed against the car windows gave no clue as to where he was. He hurt all over and knew he was running a fever. Did his feverish mind imagine the sexy, feminine perfume, a mix of citrus and something feminine and womanly floral that he couldn't name, that drifted to him from somewhere close by?

Not the sort of smell you find in a prison cell. I must be dreaming.

Then his thoughts cleared, and he was catapulted into reality.

He was in a car driven out to the middle of nowhere with a woman who hated his guts and wanted him dead. He was weak as a kitten and totally at her mercy, and this woman had made it plain she'd cut out his beating heart, given half a chance. Except she doubted he had one.

He recognized Fern Adams' scent then, remembered breathing it in deeply on their third date, the date he'd actually worked up the courage to kiss her goodnight.

And his body remembered the warm, soft shape of her body against his, the sound of her laughter, her breath tickling his ear…

Joel shook himself out of such thoughts. *It's been too long since I enjoyed feminine company. My mind's playing tricks and putting things that don't belong in my head. 'Course, right now it's not my head that's responding. Damn it all, I must be really feverish!*

And then he figured he must also be insane. He was trusting Fern Adams with his life—and she was the one who'd stolen it from him in the first place. What was he doing out here in the middle of nowhere with a woman who hated him so much she'd actually threatened him with the biggest kitchen knife he'd ever seen? That's after head-butting him and knocking him unconscious?

Of course, he had to admit that he had frightened her by grabbing her, holding her, desperate to make her listen to him. *Don't go there, pal. You're enjoying the memory of holding her too much. You need to keep your guard up. And if she catches one smidgeon of these thoughts on your face, she'll probably gut you like a fine lake bass, and with less compunction then she'd deal with the fish!*

Wonderfully cool air washed over his face, reviving him, as Fern opened the driver's door and leaned out into the night. Through the opening, Joel saw a dark canopy of trees against a slightly lighter, starlit sky. Somewhere he could hear a steady trickle of water. They certainly weren't in Primrose Hill anymore, and his stomach flip-flopped as he once again questioned his decision to go along with Fern to this remote cottage in the woods.

She said she'd help him find the real killer of her sister, but he knew from the ice in her eyes that she was still giving him top billing for that role.

Fern got out of the car and opened the rear passenger door but made no move to help Joel out. In his weakened condition, he had to fight the dizziness that enveloped him as he stood. Pride made him resist grabbing hold of the door for support, but he was gasping in pain as his wounded chest and back protested the movement. *Damn her, she'd caused him so much pain already. He'd die before he'd let her enjoy seeing him suffer.*

He looked around at the cozy looking cottage, the trees enfolding it on three sides and the softly lapping, moon-silvered water on the fourth. No other lights visible as far as he could see. There was nowhere to run, cries for help would go unheard in this remote location. And bodies could disappear without trace.

He drew in a sharp breath as the car's courtesy light illuminated the emotions warring on Fern's face, and it occurred to him that this would be the perfect place for a murder.

His.

****

He should have known that any idiot calling himself The Facilitator would have dogshit for brains. Richard's guts had turned to jelly when he read the paragraph in the paper about the man left for dead in the slum alleyway. He'd known right off that it was his faithful servant, The Facilitator. What other middle-aged guy would have been stupid enough to wander alone into that side of town? Unless he was there for a purpose, like following someone. And screwing it up wholesale.

And this was a screw up *par excellence*. A beating

this severe would involve the police, and they'd ask the same questions Richard was asking: W*hy were you in that area of town, Mr. Slater? What was your business there at that time of night?*

Perfectly sensible questions with no perfectly sensible answers. He was pretty sure that The Facilitator wouldn't be fast enough to think up any good reasons. And now, stressed out, in pain, and scared in a hospital bed, he'd be certain to spill the beans about what he'd been up to and who'd put him up to it. And paid him handsomely for the work. In the hands of a forensics computer expert, his email account and texts could be accessed and would supply all the police needed to know.

Richard's bowels threatened to give way. It had been some time since he'd last had an attack, but it seemed The Facilitator's stupidity was enough to set off his irritable bowel syndrome again. Sweeping the newspaper off the kitchen table, along with a pot of marmalade, teacup, and several dirty dishes, Richard got up and fled to his bathroom.

It wasn't all bad, either. The smallest room was where he did his best thinking. And he had lots to think about—like how to make sure that The Facilitator kept quiet and received adequate punishment for his stupidity.

****

Glory could see Fern watching through the cottage window as she pulled carefully into the parking spot behind the car Fern and Joel had driven to the rural lakeside cottage. It was so very quiet here, something she'd always valued. She hoped what was happening now wasn't going to destroy this ambience forever.

The door to the cabin was pulled open before she had even slammed shut her car door. Fern Adams was outlined there in the pale light from the cabin's generator-powered low wattage lights. She opened the door farther and stepped back to let Glory in, but the lawyer couldn't read the other woman's stiff and unsmiling expression.

At least Joel looked happy to see her. He tried to stand as soon as she entered the room, his smile wide in a face so pale and strained looking. Too weak to actually make it to his feet, he collapsed back into the chair with a groan. He was obviously in pain and exhausted.

Turning on Fern, Glory demanded, "What have you been doing? The man's white as a sheet and looks about dead on his feet! It's enough to break a person's heart. Surely as a doctor you could help him!"

"No, Glory. Fern's been good enough to me, considering she set me up for a life sentence for a crime I didn't commit." The bitterness in Joel's voice was unmissable and Fern scowled at him; her face pale and her lips drawn tight.

"They tell me eighty percent of the guys in jail are innocent, just like you," she sneered. Turning to Glory she added, "Mr. Macho Man has been refusing to take pain killers, although he's had antibiotics and the wounds are looking better than they did when he arrived in my kitchen."

Glory could see the anger on Fern's face, and hear it in her voice, as if the woman was demanding: *What more did they expect of me, these two people, one who probably killed my sister and the other who defended him in court?*

154

"I really don't think it's fair to accuse me of medical negligence."

Glory sighed and dropped her bag on the floor "I'm sorry, Fern, I didn't mean…I guess it's been a long, stressful day for all of us. Especially you."

"It's not exactly been a walk in the park for me, either" Joel interrupted, but there was a smile hovering around his lips. The smile disappeared as a thought struck him. "Glory, what the hell are you doing here? Even though you're my attorney, you're also still an officer of the court and bound to inform the police." Joel paused, a defeated expression on his face. "You haven't already told them where I am, have you?"

Glory didn't think a man's face could go any paler than Joel's had been when she arrived, but a look of sheer despair had engulfed him at the idea of his freedom coming to an end.

"I could get into a lot of trouble for not telling Detective Bamber where you are. But I'd be in a lot more trouble with my own conscience if I didn't help you now and see what we can do to prove your innocence."

Fern snorted and looked unrepentant at the sharp look Glory pinned her with.

"I gather you're still not quite convinced?" she asked the other woman.

"After I saw this man—and it was him, unless he has a double—leaving my sister's apartment, covered in her blood? No, I have to believe the evidence of my own eyes."

"So why are you here? Why didn't you call the police as soon as you got an opportunity? Instead, you came to me claiming you were going to help Joel prove his innocence."

"No. I wanted to prove his guilt beyond any doubt."

"So you do have doubts?" Joel asked quietly.

Fern laughed, an ugly sound that echoed around the massive beams in the cabin's cathedral ceiling. A sound that didn't belong within these log walls, with the bright knitted afghan blankets, the family photos, the cottage-y décor, and the stack of well-thumbed novels and board games on the shelves. "Don't start thinking I'm on your side, Joel Alvarez. I'm not. But you planted that seed of doubt when you asked me how I could live with myself if the man who'd killed Rose was still walking around free."

Joel struggled to his feet and Glory saw him wince as she recognized the pain the movements cost him. He stood in front of Fern; their eyes locked with the intensity of longtime adversaries. "I don't understand you at all, Fern. I really don't."

"Then let me spell it out for you," Fern hissed back at him, refusing to allow him to see how disconcerting his proximity was. She could almost feel the heat of his gaze on her skin, feel the force of his sharp intelligence pushing at her mind, trying to convince—or intimidate? Which was it? *No, no, I can't let him confuse me like that!*

"I don't believe in your innocence, Joel. But while ever there may be a tiny, tiny iota of doubt, or while there may be anyone—" She aimed a glance at Glory. "—who may be taken in and believe you may be innocent, while there's the slightest chance that some clever lawyer could come up with a means of getting you off the hook, I want to make sure all possibilities are covered. When I've erased all possible doubt, I'm going to make sure you're punished."

Glory squirmed in the heavy silence. Seeing these two staring at each other, locked in mental combat, she found herself holding her breath wondering what would happen next. Would the emotions roiling in the room explode? She'd never before realized how close hate and love could be, but the intensity of emotions that hammered between Fern and Joel made her wonder what was driving them. *Could it be that the feelings growing between the two before Rose's death still lingered? And just how did Fern Adams intend to carry out her threat to see that Joel was punished?*

In her line of work, Glory had seen too often the bloody remains of acts motivated by revenge. She shivered even though the cabin was warm with the aromatic scent of pine logs in the woodstove.

****

Bamber pushed back from his desk, wishing once more he had a cigarette, and cursing Alvarez, Slater, and all those involved in this mess for bringing him to the edge of lighting up again after so long…but he finally felt they might start making some headway. Recapturing Joel Alvarez had gone to the top of his case list, not just because the man was a convicted killer, but because the top brass feared a public panic if the man who'd committed the most horrific murder rural Primrose Hill had witnessed in many years, maybe ever, wasn't soon back behind bars.

There were other cases demanding his attention. Just as he returned to his desk with Kerry's statement, Groves hurried in. "Hey, boss, just got word from the hospital on the mugging victim they called in this morning. The one that Loman woman mentioned. Dan Slater. Also known as The Facilitator. He's conscious and able to talk to the police. In fact, the nurse that called said he's insisting on talking to the police."

"Nice to hear that someone wants to talk to us," Bamber retorted, grabbing a bottle of aspirin from his desk drawer and tossing back two pills with the remains of his cold coffee. "Okay, you go and take his statement."

"Actually, sir, he's asking to speak to you. Or rather, the officer in charge of the Alvarez case. Says he won't speak to anyone else." Groves looked excited. "Do you think that maybe he knows something?"

"More likely that Alvarez is the one that beat him up, and he's just seen the photo in the evening paper." Bamber glanced at his watch. After nine. It looked like a long day had just gotten a whole lot longer. He grabbed his woolen overcoat, threw his car keys to Groves, and picked up the Slater file to reread in the car on the way to the hospital.

****

It was so easy. Richard Phelan was amazed at how easy it was to kill a man, right under the noses of the people whose job it was to save that man's life. He almost burst out laughing, although that would have been inappropriate and would have brought attention to him.

"And you definitely don't want anyone to call on Dr. Phelan for help. It might be injurious to their health!" He grinned at himself in the stark light of the men's washroom as he pulled off the white coat he'd "borrowed" from a hook in the doctors' locker room. The stethoscope that he'd also picked up as a prop he slipped into his leather jacket pocket as a memento of this fun day.

"What?" He raised an eyebrow to his own image in the mirror. "People always take little mementoes of great days. Although for most people, it's the tat that's sold in souvenir shops. Mine's better!"

He held his hands under the hot water, scrubbing at them as if he really were a doctor about to perform surgery. But his job was already done. Instead of saving his patient, he'd dispatched The Facilitator to meet his Maker.

And the look on the man's face when he realized what was about to happen had been priceless!

****

"Seeing as you're the one who doubts everything I say, why don't you tell me why you're lying about seeing me?" Joel's face was set in hard lines as he arranged his lean body on the old-fashioned leather settee that suited the cottage. "After all, I'm at your mercy. What have you to lose?"

"I'm not lying!" Fern snapped. "Why should I believe you'd answer me, anyway?"

"You have my word that everything I tell you will be the truth." He wriggled and winced as his battered body complained. His battered mind also screamed with complaint, demanding sleep and oblivion from the horror his life had become. Strangely enough, despite everything that had happened, despite the fact that she had been the major card in the prosecution's case against him, Joel found a desperate need to convince Fern that he wasn't the monster he'd been branded.

He watched her searching his face, hunting for the truth behind his words. Her look remained stormy and unconvinced. "Like your word would count for anything. But maybe there's some reason. Like maybe something in you snapped, and you think you're telling the truth. At least, the truth as you know it." The subtext to her words was, *which didn't rule out the possibility that the man was crazy as an outhouse rat...*

"What brought you to Primrose Hill? You're a TO firefighter, and Primrose Hill's not exactly a popular vacation spot, yet you told the court that you were taking some much-needed vacation time."

"Yeah, Primrose Hill leaves a lot to be desired for someone who wants to take a bit of time out and relax." Joel gave a crooked smile at the irony of how his "vacation time" had turned out.

"So why were you really here?"

"He's already told you, the police, the courts, and me! He was doing a bit of travelling after his parents died." Glory defended him.

"Hold on, Glory. There was more to it than that, and I never thought—okay, here's the long version of my story." And he told them how his father had been killed in an accident shortly after retiring, and then his mother had given up and died. "She died of a broken heart, although on the death certificate it said congestive heart disease," Joel said, knowing his eyes had filled with tears and wiping them away impatiently with his sweater sleeve.

"When I went through Mom's things, clearing out the house so that it could be sold because I knew I couldn't live there any longer, I found a lockbox of papers. They looked like old letters from years ago, and they were actually yellowed with age. I was going to just dump them out without reading because if Mom had kept them a secret for so many years, then she deserved to have her privacy left intact.

"Then I saw one of the letters was addressed to My Dear Rachel—that was Mom's name. It was only idle curiosity that made me read it, or at least, it was when…at least when I first started. The letterhead said Dr. Arthur Stone, Family Health Practitioner, Copper Junction. He addressed Mom and Dad as if they were old friends, telling them that someone named SueAnne was pregnant, and everything was going well.

"I was really lonely. And maybe grief had made me a bit crazy. After they were gone, I realized that I knew so little about my family's past. Mom and Dad never had close friends. It was like all they needed was each other. And they told me their parents, my grandparents, had all passed. Neither of my parents had ever mentioned other relatives, and this letter made me curious about my mom's life before I was born. I thought maybe she'd been brought up in Copper Junction. I had to look it up on a map. Suddenly, it meant everything to me to know who her friends had been, what she had been like growing up. Maybe even relatives I had never known about.

"There were several letters from the doctor, all talking about this SueAnne. For some reason I thought she must be his wife, and in one letter he promised to let them know as soon as the baby was born. He sounded excited and told them he'd look forward to seeing them when the baby arrived.

"I read the final letter so many times I almost know it by heart. It said, basically, '*congratulations, we have a healthy baby boy. Come and see us as soon as you can*'."

Joel looked down at his hands, which were clasped together so tightly his nails would leave white half-moons in his skin. How well he remembered the childlike emotions he'd felt, a mixture of anger that his parents had left him with this mystery and a budding hope that maybe, somewhere, he had family.

"I started imagining there were all kinds of dark secrets, maybe estranged family members. Maybe I wasn't alone, after all. I felt driven to find the man who'd written these letters, who called my mom Dear Rachel…" Joel's voice trailed off, and he shrugged apologetically. "Probably makes me sound a bit pathetic."

"Not at all, Joel. People pay thousands of dollars on ancestry sites, trying to research their ancestors. Why should you be any different?" Glory said, giving Fern a hard look.

"But why did they never mention anything about their past lives? I used to ask questions when I was a kid because all my friends had grans and grandpops, aunts and uncles, cousins. Looking back, the answers were never satisfactory. It never made sense that we had no one." Joel lowered his gaze to study his hands, clasped across his stomach. Even in the dim light of the cabin, Fern saw his eyes shone with unshed tears. Somehow, the idea of a lonely young boy searching for family made her sad.

"I kept thinking about the whole thing, couldn't get it out of my mind. It sounds a bit pathetic, but I was so lonely after they died, and the thought hit me that maybe I did have relatives, people who maybe didn't even know that my parents had passed before a rift between them could be healed." He shook his head. "It never crossed my mind that they might not want to know me. I just wanted to know more about my parents and to know that I had blood relatives somewhere. Mom and Dad were usually so open with me, and maybe it sounds a bit unhinged, but this was a mystery I had to solve. Funny, but when you're grieving, all sorts of little things become so important.

"I had vacation time coming to me from the fire crew, so I figured I'd go and investigate a bit, see if I could find the doctor who'd written to my parents."

"That brought you to Primrose Hill?" Glory asked.

Joel sighed. "No, or rather yes, I guess so. I was just passing through on my way to this place called Copper Junction. My old car had alternator trouble in Primrose Hill, and the mechanic at the garage on Elm Street said he'd have to order the part and, it being a foreign make, it could be a week or so before it arrived. Primrose Hill looked like a nice place, so I thought I'd hang around a bit, have some free time from work, explore, have some R&R.

"Just goes to show how wrong you can be."

"Yeah, murdering a defenseless woman must be really hard work," Fern snapped, and Joel's pale face turned a sickly gray.

"I just needed a break after that horrendous year. I was heading off to Copper Junction, looking for family. I never intended to stop in Primrose Hill, and I can tell you this, if I'd known what was going to happen, I'd never have come within a hundred million miles of the place." *He didn't add that, before everything hit the fan, he'd thought the car trouble was Fate's way of making sure he met Fern.*

"So, you might have some living family up North.

Big deal. Do you have some sort of complex about rejection and Rose turning you down led to some massive paranoid explosion?"

Joel flushed at the mocking tone in Fern's voice, and his screwed-up fist slammed down on the wooden arm of his seat with enough force to make him wince as the jarring in his arm caused lightning bolts of pain in his wounded ribs. "What the hell are we doing here? You're so set on not believing me that I'm surprised you don't just call that detective you know and have me dragged back to jail."

"Sounds like a damned good idea to me." Fern stretched, trying to look casual, but Joel's obvious pain and weakness had shaken her. Fern and Glory exchanged glances, and Fern stood from the low-slung armchair she'd been perched in. "Let's freshen the coffee pot. Maybe you'd help me, Glory."

Glory followed Fern into the narrow galley kitchen, pushing the door closed behind them. She glanced around at the rustic cabinets and folksy charm of the paintings on the walls. "You know, all my memories of this place are happy times."

"Well, once we're done, maybe you can have the place smudged with sweet grass or maybe a church blessing, or whatever." Fern tossed out the coffee that had gone cold, rinsed the pot, and refilled the container with fresh grounds. "Is he on the verge of confessing that he killed my sister? Is that what he means by he'd never have come to Primrose Hill if he'd known what was going to happen?" Her face was flushed and her eyes hectic in the stark halogen lights of the kitchen.

Glory shook her head savagely. "He's not up to this. Even talking is wearing him out!" she hissed.

"You've got to stop this third degree, this interrogation!"

Fern, pouring water into the coffee maker, nodded. It was obvious that even talking about these issues was exhausting Joel in his weakened state. "I know that. But he's on the brink of confessing. I know he is! We can't stop now. We've got to press on."

"Why? So that you can act as Judge, Jury, and Executioner?" Glory demanded. "I can see from the guilty look on your face that I was right to drive out here to check on you. You're looking for more than a jail sentence to avenge your sister, aren't you? You intend to take the law in to your own hands."

Fern sucked in a deep breath, knowing her face was burning. *How on earth could Glory have guessed what was in her mind?*

"Oh, guessing what you were thinking was pretty easy. You'd be amazed the number of survivors of crime that I've worked with who've had the same revenge fantasies. Only you," She grabbed Fern by the shoulders and forced her to look at her. "—only you, *Doctor* Fern Adams, you intended that it would be more than a fantasy!"

Fern glared back at her, keeping a determined silence which spoke volumes.

"I'm calling myself all kinds of fool right now, for trusting you! I've handed you the perfect murder location on a plate! But hear this, *Doctor* Fern Adams. This cottage has been in my family since my granddad was a kid, and nothing bad has ever happened here. Let's keep it that way. If you do one thing, just one thing, to endanger Joel Alvarez, then I'll hunt you down and you'll stand in court yourself!"

Fern looked down at her feet, guilt and anger mixing to confuse her emotions.

"I guess you ladies are talking about the gun that's been dragging Fern's pocket out of shape since we left Primrose Hill?" Both women swiveled around to face Joel, who'd entered silently and now leaned casually against the door jamb. He grinned at their startled looks, but when their frightened eyes fell to his hands, he cursed.

"Don't worry. I haven't touched Fern's new toy. Just that someone who's so law-abiding is so damned transparent. Couldn't you at least have hidden it in your purse? Or were you afraid I'd jump you on one of the back roads?" The smile turned to a scowl as disgust and pain hardened his voice.

Fern chewed on her bottom lip, her chest tight with shame and fear as she thought of the weapon in the side pocket of the sweater now hanging on a hook by the cottage door, the gun so easily accessible just steps away from where Joel had been sitting.

He had the perfect opportunity to grab my gun and use it to have both Glory and me helpless at his disposal—literally his disposal! And what a perfect place this would have been. Hardly anyone comes to the cottages in the winter. There'd be no one for miles around to hear our screams...or find the bodies.

Fern gulped; one hand pressed to her chest to try to contain her racing heart. Joel turned his back on them, stalking away into the cabin's living room and out through the front door onto the small porch.

****

He'd been right! Of course, he'd have been surprised if he'd been wrong. He now understood that he was far smarter than most people, even that stuck-up bitch of a lawyer who had sniffed around Joel like a cat in heat during the trial.

Still, it seemed the bitch might still be sniffing around Alvarez even at the risk of her own career. For a brief moment, he toyed with the idea of sending an anonymous tip to the police, informing them of Joel's whereabouts and the fact that his lawyer, an officer of the court, had failed in her duty to notify them immediately. *Was, in fact, sheltering and giving succor to—or sucker to.* Richard grinned nastily at his own crude wit.

But he had a much better plan. One that would give him much more gratification than simply turning that bastard and his whores over to the police.

He watched as Joel stomped from the room, slamming the kitchen door behind him. Fern Adams pulled the drapes closed over the kitchen window, shutting Richard out of the light and heat and comfort that was within. *That doesn't matter. I've been shut out all my life,* Richard thought, but his fingernails drew small, red half-moons in his palms as he clenched his fists.

Slipping out of his boots, ignoring the chill from the icy pellets that clung to his socks, he crept on silenced stocking feet up to the side window of the cottage and peered carefully inside at the living room.

The pretty blonde lawyer was there, her back to the window as she spoke to Joel. She'd called him in from his perch outside on the porch where he'd been standing, trying to cool off. Richard's stomach clenched as he saw Joel start to smile. *Probably looking forward to fucking the bitch. Well, they don't have much longer because I plan to have more fun with Joel Alvarez and his little friends. Oh, she thinks she's so smart, does that one, and yet not smart enough to cover her tracks.* The gleeful thoughts helped to stave off the bitter breeze that blew across the lake, hitting him full force even in the shelter of the cabin. After all, few things that are worthwhile can be obtained without a little suffering. He pulled the collar of his woolen jacket and plaid shirt up around his neck, wishing he'd thought to pick up some gloves and a scarf.

It had been a pretty easy job to look up the land registry and discover that the blonde lawyer owned a remote family cottage up here in the middle of nowhere. He hadn't even had to follow her, just get directions from a teenager behind the counter of the small store on the edge of Cloyne where he'd stopped for gas. He'd also picked up a ham sandwich and a couple of cans of beer to keep him company as he made his own way here in a leisurely way.

A leisurely way which had given him time to get the lay of the land and to formulate a new plan.

One which hardened in his mind as he saw that there was a third person in the room. *What the hell was Rose Adams' sister doing here with that bastard Alvarez and his bitch lawyer?* It hadn't taken much ingenuity to follow Fern Adams to the lawyer's office, although it had been a bit of a surprise to speculate that the two women were friends. But he had the smarts to recognize that the two sluts were planning something. He'd remembered the look he'd caught on the doctor's face in court when she'd looked at Alvarez, the brief look of, what? Sorrow? Caring? Whatever. He found the fact that she'd been dating the jerk before her sister's murder to be a very interesting tidbit indeed. It opened the doors to many fascinating paths.

Hidden alongside the cottage, Richard Phelan smiled as he'd watched Joel Alvarez limp across the small plain cedar deck and enter the cottage again, slamming the door closed behind him.

Trouble in paradise, eh? He wondered.

But then Richard's irritable bowels contracted, and he thought he was going to lose his control right then and there. *Pity the poor forensic tech who had to analyze that DNA evidence!* He pressed his palms against the rough wood of the logs and used his mind to control the pain. Watching Fern Adams as she spoke to her sister's killer had provoked an unexpected arousal that dismissed his anxiety about his loose guts with a more pressing problem—a huge hard-on that needed some relief.

And he knew just where he could get that. *There's a lot to be said for planning as you go,* he thought as he turned and walked quietly back through the anonymous inky darkness of the woods to his car. Even the sharp stones and twigs that jabbed at his stockinged feet didn't dissipate the anticipation that sang in his blood.

Chapter Thirteen

It was obvious that the man on the hospital security tape was Joel Alvarez. The bastard hadn't even tried to hide his face--in one frame, he'd looked up at the camera perched above the exit doors on the corridor that Slater's room was on, given the camera a brazen thumbs up, and smiled.

The kind of smile that made even hardened men like Detective John Bamber shiver.

"Son of a bitch! That's Alvarez, no doubt about it!" he cursed soundly.

Lee Groves echoed his boss's vitriol, pointing to the time stamped on the bottom of the film. Alvarez had murdered Slater just twenty minutes before they had arrived to see him. *Now they would never know what it was the badly beaten man had wanted to tell them about Alvarez—the motherfucking bastard had made well sure of that!*

"The hospital was on lock down within 15 minutes," Jed Atkins, the grim faced security chief, told them. "But that would have been plenty of time for the asshole to dump the doctor's white coat and walk out of here as if he didn't have a care in the world."

"This man didn't have a care in the world—Slater being dead was one less thing for him to worry about. As far as Alvarez was concerned, killing his employee was just a matter of housecleaning!" Bamber couldn't keep the fury out of his voice.

Atkins handed them a list of everyone who had been into Slater's room. The man had had no personal visitors and had, to all intents and purposes, been isolated for his own protection. Who knew if the person who'd administered such a terrible beating might want to return to finish the job? Everyone who'd gone into that room was a medical professional, law enforcement officer, or cleaning staff. Except for a stone-cold killer who'd borrowed a medic's white coat to carry out his evil deed.

Bamber nodded. "Did he have any keys among his personal possessions?" Bamber demanded. "I think it's time to take a look at Mr. Slater's office and his home. Maybe there'll be something there that will shed some light on the connection between Joel Alvarez and Slater."

****

Joel stomped back inside the cottage after Glory called him back, slamming the door and refusing to meet the eyes of the two women who sat at opposite sides of the room studiously ignoring him and each other. No one spoke as he strode through into the kitchen, pulled open the door of the refrigerator, and pulled out a beer.

"Dammit! These are non-alcoholic!" he swore as he marched back into the room.

And just like that the mood in the room changed. Glory snorted with laughter and, before she knew what was happening, Fern joined in. Joel glared at the two women but couldn't hold back himself. With the kind of tension they'd all been under, still were under, the laughter was like a splash of cold water on a hot and humid day. It cleared the supercharged atmosphere and lowered the anger quotient, although mistrust still hovered within swooping distance.

"Okay, the first thing we need to do is get hold of any documents your parents left, their own birth certificates, that sort of thing. Anything that might help us trace any other family members. And we'll get the name and address of the doctor, the one you think might be related, look him up on the medical register." Glory spoke directly to Joel, ignoring Fern. "We'll have to go up to Toronto and...Oh, damn!"

Glory grabbed her briefcase and pulled out a thick leather-bound diary, frowning as she riffled through the pages. "Shit. I've got a court appearance tomorrow, and there's no way I can get out of it!"

"This can't wait. All the documents are in a box in my parents' bedroom in the TO house. I never thought I'd need them as evidence of any kind...I need to get a car." Even as he spoke, Alvarez realized he had no money, no credit cards, no driver's license. And even if he did have the documentation, he knew the chances of getting a rental vehicle in this area were slim to none, not without the police being informed before he'd even fastened his seatbelt. By now his face would be on every newspaper and television news bulletin throughout the area. That was, of course, if he could even physically manage the drive. He was weaker than a kitten. *With my luck I'll probably pass out on the 401 and run straight into a concrete bridge abutment.*

A quick glance at the faces of the two women sitting opposite him confirmed his thoughts, and he dropped back into his chair with a defeated sigh.

"You can't get a car—but I have one." Fern spoke

a few moments later, her voice startling the other two.

"You'd be willing to loan me your car to go to Toronto? What if I disappear in the city and head down for South America or somewhere?" He couldn't keep the incredulity out of his voice.

"Oh, I wasn't planning to let you go alone. I'm coming with you." He saw from the set of Fern's face that she meant it. A tiny part of his being was pleased that she'd give even this much ground, and he quickly told himself that having a doctor travelling with him in his condition could only be a good thing. *Provided she remembered her Hippocratic Oath.*

"Remember, we're looking for information that might clear me of your sister's death. I'd have thought you'd be reluctant to have anything to do with that."

"I've come this far, haven't I?" Fern tried to look him in the eye, saw herself reflected in their soft brown, and looked away. "And if we don't find it, *when we don't find it*, then I'll know that you're lying. And as you said, I want to make sure that the man who killed Rose is not still walking around free."

The cold steel that laced her voice sent a shiver up Joel's spine.

****

In the cottage just a few hundred yards from the one that belonged to Glory Jordan, twenty-two-year-old Lucy Lee Maxwell stepped out of the shower and toweled her slender body dry before turning her attention to her long, dark hair. The blow drier teased it into thick waves that fell onto her shoulders and framed a pretty face with the exotic features and almond-shaped eyes she'd inherited from her Vietnamese mother.

She smiled at her reflection in the mirror, thinking of her mother and how proud she'd been that her only daughter had gotten into Queen's University. Now Lucy was studying for the entrance exams into the school of medicine, and her mother and father were proud enough to burst!

It had been Mom's idea that she come and spend a weekend alone at the cottage to study. She'd said that the peaceful atmosphere and no distractions would help Lucy relax and focus her mind. And she had an early Christmas family reunion to look forward to. Her immediate and extended families would descend on the lakeside cottage in a day or two for a party before the cottage was finally closed up for the winter.

She pulled on a terrycloth bathrobe, basking in the heat from the woodstove that made the cabin warm and cozy despite the falling temperatures outside. It was so private here. The cottage was on a small promontory, surrounded on three sides by the lake, public on only one side. In summer there was some boat and canoe traffic, but generally this spot was quiet. The last time she'd been to the cottage was during the August heatwave, with a group pf friends.. They'd gone skinny dipping, laughing and chasing each other on the sandy shoreline, diving into the clear waters and splashing about like playful lake otters.

That weekend had been the very first time she and Terry had made love. And she had known, right then, that she was in love with him. She sighed. *How she wished Terry was here with her now, making love to her in front of the golden orange glow of the woodstove.*

She had invited him to the family get together, but

he'd said he'd find it a bit overwhelming to meet all her family and relatives at once. They'd agreed he'd come to meet with her mom and dad for dinner once the exams were over. She found his shyness endearing, and he was so sexy with his gentle, serious nature.

The knock at the door startled her. She hadn't heard a car, but her thoughts were on Terry. A jolt of excitement shot through her as she wondered if she had somehow conjured him up. Could he have decided to drive up on the spur of the moment for a few stolen hours with her?

Flicking the heavy weight of her slightly damp hair over her shoulders, heart beating loudly in anticipation, she let her robe fall unbelted around her body as she went to answer the door. The smile on her face would have spoken volumes of welcome to Terry, but someone else stood there on the doorstep.

A stranger.

A handsome man with a twisted grin and hard, cold eyes. Then she saw the flash of the porch light on the fine steel of the knife in his hand.

His smile was enough to freeze her soul.

****

"I think we may have a break!" Lee rushed into Bamber's office waving a telephone note. "I just took a call from a sergeant in Copper Junction. That's somewhere up North—who says he's sure he recognizes the man in the fax we sent around."

Bamber felt his heart rate pick up. This might be the first real lead they'd had in this goddamned case, especially since the lead of The Facilitator, Mr. Slater, private eye, had fallen through with the man's death. "Don't keep me in suspense. Spill!"

175

"The sergeant in Copper Junction says this is a guy who used to live in his area. Guy's a real nutter, according to the officer. But he says the guy's name is Phelan, not Alvarez." Lee stopped to check his notes while Bamber tapped his fingers on the desk.

"Okay, he says the guy pictured in the wanted material is the split image of a Richard Phelan. He's faxing us a copy of this Richard Phelan's records. That's the guy he says is our Joel Alvarez. He also said this guy was a bad actor from being a kid, and a few days after he disappeared, his mother was found in her burned-out shack. Sergeant Roberts said it was considered a suspicious death."

Bamber could feel the stirring of excitement as he looked over some sheets of new information faxed by the officer in Copper Junction. It carried over to his team as they considered the new information and became energized..

"Let's get checking out some of his known associates to see if there's anyone who might be likely to take him in around this area. Sergeant Cam Roberts has sent us a list of Phelan's cronies, and it's a very short list. He said we'd probably find a number of them were serving time in jail. Richards and Peterson, go and talk to anyone you can find in Toronto, from the fire chief and his colleagues to any family, neighbors, whatever, who may have something to say about the man." John Bamber brought his colleagues up to date on their latest investigation results.

"I still don't get how he could be a thug from up North and a hero firefighter in TO," Detective Liz Bennett commented. "It just doesn't seem right, somehow."

"Do you have anything to base that on?"

"No, sir, except that—well, you said the officer in Copper Junction thought Phelan was guilty of several rapes, plus the murder of his own mother and the burning of her cabin, his childhood home. But there was nothing they could prove. Sounds like a bit of a psycho to me, and guys like that, well, they don't usually take a sabbatical from that kind of behavior to work as firemen in the big city, unless they're in jail, caught, or dead. At some point it seems our guy changed completely, became a first responder brave enough to risk his own life to rescue people from blazing buildings..."

"That psych degree itching in your mind, Liz?" Detective Bill Stevens teased her and ducked to avoid the paper clip she aimed in his direction.

Bamber held up his hand to quell the snickers. "Either the Copper Junction lead is a wild goose chase, or Alvarez had some kind of epiphany after strangling his mother, maybe tried to quell the need to kill, made a good life in Toronto, and then something set him off again."

"Or maybe Alvarez is being set up," Bennett insisted.

"What, you got some kind of hard-on for this guy? Don't let the good looks fool you, honey."

"Knock it off, Stevens," Bamber snapped.

"Yes, sir." Stevens said humbly, but the grin he flashed around the room belied his hangdog agreement.

"I just can't see how he could be like two different people. Split personality, maybe? Did Sergeant Roberts say when he became aware that his guy had moved to Toronto full time?"

The room fell silent. Someone muttered "Damnation!" under his breath.

Bamber hoped his face wasn't as red as he thought it might be, showing his embarrassment at missing that tiny detail. "Liz, you call Sergeant Roberts and see if you can fix a firmer timeline. Check in with the TO fire dept. for when Alvarez was hired. Let's just follow through with what Liz is suggesting, that maybe Alvarez is innocent of Rose Adams' murder, and he stepped on toes somewhere hard enough to make someone want to frame him. Where would that take us?" Bamber invited his colleagues to play the "What if?" game. Maybe they'd get inspired.

"He'd probably have only one thought in mind—to get as far away as possible. Maybe even head down into the States and disappear," Groves offered.

"I don't think so," Bamber replied.

"No, I don't, either. But I'm not sure just what he'd do. A lot depends on whether he still has the help of whoever organized the hospital escape," Lorimar contributed.

"Alvarez did claim innocence all the way through. He didn't even try for a lesser sentence with a guilty plea, or try for an insanity angle," Bennett said.

"And if he really wants everyone to believe he's innocent, or if he actually is innocent, then what would he be most likely to do?" Lorimar, the chief of detectives sat in Bamber's chair, Groves sat in the hard visitors' chair, and Bamber stood with his shoulder against the doorframe. He looked like a man who was poised for any action that came along and was frustrated that none was in sight.

"What are you thinking? Surely not that the man is

innocent! You've seen the evidence!" Stevens exclaimed.

"I think we have to look at every angle. What was it that Sherlock Holmes was supposed to have said about eliminating everything, and what's left is the truth, no matter how impossible?" Groves said.

"Maybe you've a point," Bamber admitted. *Maybe Groves wasn't the over-enthusiastic puppy he seemed to be.*

"Sherlock Holmes was a fictional detective," Lorimar's sharp reminder was interrupted by the bleating of a cell phone. Looking embarrassed, Groves got up, slipping open his phone, and walked from the room.

"According to the file here—" Bamber crossed the room to lean over his desk and ruffle through the pages of the file that was pitifully thin despite the work that had gone into it. "Alvarez insisted that Fern Adams had set him up, that she'd lied on the stand. And he wanted to see her and shake the truth out of her."

"My God! That's where he's gone! He's gone to find his victim's sister and…" Lorimar sat bolt upright, worry furrowing his already wrinkled brow.

"Okay, now. Fern Adams called me a while ago, said she was heading up north to a friend's cabin. Cloyne, I think. It's pretty unlikely that Alvarez would know where she was." Then his face went pale as a sickening thought hit him. "What if Alvarez has already found her? What if he was with her, forcing her to drive to some god forsaken remote area?"

Lorimar stood and paced the room. "I don't think he'd have had her call the police and say where she was going, would he?"

"I don't know. The man may be extremely smart, especially if he has set up all this escape plot and everything that has gone with it. In fact, all she said was that she was going to a cabin in the—what did she say? The Middle of Nowhere? A place called Cloyne in cottage country, would probably be pretty quiet at this time of year. And Alvarez could somehow have managed to tail her."

"You're all forgetting one thing. If he's innocent, that means Fern Adams lied to the police and in court. What would her motive be for that? Is there anything to connect the victim's sister to Alvarez?" Bennett asked, sitting forward in her chair

"You mean like a woman scorned, that sort of thing? She had a fling with him and then the sister pushed in and took him over?" Lorimar joined in.

"She wouldn't be the first woman to want revenge on a straying lover or another woman who screwed her man," Bamber admitted. But somehow it didn't sit right with him. "Fern Adams seemed truly broken up about her sister. Hard to imagine her setting Rose up for such an awful death."

"Could be guilt, not heartbreak." Lorimar got up and walked towards the door. "Liz, your brief is talk to Sergeant Roberts, see what you can consolidate about Alvarez' movements in Toronto, see if there's any way to fit him in as this Phelan character. Stevens, take a uniform and go see if you can sweet talk the hospital admin or some of Adams' coworkers into giving you her vacation location. Someone out there must know where she's gone. Make sure you ask them if Fern could have been infatuated with Alvarez and royally pissed when her sister got her claws into him. Tactfully, of course."

"Yeah, like he'll probably have to look the word 'tactfully' up in the dictionary," Bennett said, rolling her eyes.

"Better check with Alvarez' associates in Toronto, too. I believe Rose Adams sang for her supper in a couple of bars in TO," Bamber told him.

At that moment Groves returned with a handful of official-looking papers. "The go-ahead for a search of Slater's apartment and car if we can find it. I've put the license number out over the radio," he told Bamber.

Bamber tapped his fingers on the desk. He wanted to go out and join the action, but instinct told him to wait for Liz Bennett's information and the files from the Copper Junction officer. The best use of his time was here in the office. He sighed. He'd kill for a cigarette right now.

"Lee, you go. Take a couple of guys and search Slater's apartment. See what you can find there that might tie the poor bastard to Alvarez. Look for emails, especially. Maybe he has a laptop in the apartment. There must be a reason Alvarez risked going to the hospital to kill him."

The detectives got busy with their assignments. At last something to do beyond tossing fruitless ideas around.

****

Richard Phelan had had a very busy day but the interlude the previous day at the cottages had invigorated him and he'd approached this day with gusto. First he'd dispatched his not-so-very-faithful employee, the Facilitator, to meet his Maker. *The look on that man's face when he saw who his new 'doctor' was – and knew what the treatment would be!* He'd enjoyed masquerading as a doctor, too. Indeed, maybe he'd be good at that – he could be the kind of doctor who helped the very sick to cross over. *No, on second thoughts, maybe not his style.*

Then he'd had to hare over to Slater's apartment, taking the stairs to the twentieth floor in order not to bump into any nosy residents who might later remember him if the police came sniffing around. It had taken him several precious seconds to force open the flimsy lock – *oh, my, Facilitator, surely you could have done better than that!* He picked up Slater's laptop and a couple of notebooks, plus a stack of other paperwork, stuffed them into a very official looking briefcase, and left the building with the only evidence he knew of that could have linked him to the now deceased private investigator.

Altogether a good day's work, he smiled to himself as he left the building. As he exited he saw an Ontario Provincial Police car arrive at the parking spot in front of the building.

"Ah! Cops are always one step behind!' he grinned as he hurried away, looking for all the world like a professional on his way to an appointment – and unnoticed by the police officers.

Chapter Fourteen

The simple brick semi-detached house near Toronto's Yonge & Eglinton area didn't look like the kind of place that would spawn a crazed killer. It looked just like the other houses on the street—neatly trimmed front lawn, a small peach tree in its center, now leafless and frost rimed against the coming winter. The short driveway had been cleared of snow. Was it a helpful neighbor, or did Joel have a contract with someone to keep the house looking lived in?

Fern parked in the driveway and looked around at the neighborhood Joel Alvarez had grown up in. All the other houses on the street boasted colored lights, some with more elaborate decorations such as sleds piled high with gaily wrapped "gifts" or the ubiquitous blow-up plastic Santas and Frosties. She imagined his house, like all the others, would have been trimmed with lights and Christmas decorations when his parents were still alive. The lack of any sign of festive cheer made the house stand out from its neighbors, giving it a sad, dejected look like a new widow at a Christmas dance.

It was quiet now as the night rushed towards dawn, but she imagined on late summer evenings the street would be alive with kids, riding bikes, playing street hockey, chasing each other around on imaginary adventures. Would Joel have been one of those happy, cared-for kids? Fern imagined that parents would sit on the porch, gossiping and watching over the youngsters.

What had happened, in this Norman Rockwell environment, to make a small boy grow up into a vicious murderer?

They'd stopped at a roadside café for takeout coffee, but other than that had driven from Cloyne through the night to arrive at Joel's Toronto home in the small hours of the morning. Fern took a deep draught of her now cold beverage, hoping the caffeine jolt would keep her alert enough for the next step in their journey. She had insisted on driving, and now she was exhausted. Her training as a doctor had given her the stamina to cope with long periods of time without sleep, but even so she longed to lie down.

"I'll go inside, grab what we need, and be back in five minutes. The neighbors will be up and about soon, and we shouldn't hang around here." Joel slipped out of his seatbelt and pushed open his door, wincing as his wounded body protested. Fern did the same, telling him there was no way she was leaving him alone, not even for a second. *The man could have an arsenal of guns tucked away in that house, or he could just disappear through a rear door and leave her sitting there like a fool.*

"Suit yourself," he muttered back, closing the car door as quietly as possible and walking slowly up to the steps leading to the front porch. Stooped over with one hand pressed against his wounded side, he bent down and tilted a small flowerpot to remove a key from a box hidden there.

She'd been wondering how they'd get access to the house. *A housekey under a plant pot?* Not exactly security conscious. Fern grimaced. Despite his lean, muscular strength, Joel Alvarez moved like an octogenarian. Her prisoner was obviously so weak he couldn't run if he wanted to. The dedicated doctor in her winced, and she flushed with shame, a feeling that quickly dissolved as she thought of her sister's terrible death.

****

The memory of that girl's soft skin, her silky hair, her trembling body against his, her mewling fear…It had kept Richard warm all the way back to Toronto and the next day at his shitty job at the car detailing plant. She was so beautiful that he'd momentarily regretted that she had to die. But, as he'd explained to her while she lay naked on the floor, bound and gagged with duct tape, it was necessary in order for him to finish his plan. He would finish this game he was playing and then retire to somewhere warm to enjoy the life of the wealthy while Joel suffered the misery of life behind bars with no hope of ever seeing the outside world again.

And, with his money and contacts, he'd see that Joel lived a long life full of pain and humiliation so that every day he woke to the fear of what might be done to him next, of rape and brutality and hunger, just as he, Richard, had done all his early life.

Richard was delighted at the sight of the lovely young woman who answered the door, her house coat hanging open to display her youthful beauty. He knew with crazed certainty that she had been waiting for him and welcomed him into her home with eagerness. That belief made him hard and ready, and he had thoroughly enjoyed the charms of little Lucy before finally putting her out of her misery. And he had few regrets. She'd begged him to kill her in the end, just as urgently as she had begged him to let her live in the beginning.

Women! They're so mercurial—one minute wanting to let you have them if it'll please you enough to let them go on breathing, an hour later wanting you to kill them so you can't enjoy them anymore! No wonder they cause a man so much misery.

Memories of his mother flashed through his mind, and his rising hard-on shriveled. He could still hear her easy laughter and feel her vicious right hand, the wire coat hangers that caused such pain against his delicate flesh, the way she'd been able to turn her back when her boyfriends had enjoyed themselves with her small son.

Anger flared up in his mind when he remembered how he'd gone crying to her, blood still congealing on his ass, telling her what Uncle Joe had done to him that first time. She'd been furious and given him a whipping for making things up and trying to spoil her good time with her new boyfriend.

Later, when he had again tried to complain after another man had used him viciously, instead of the cuddles he had hoped for she had turned on him, slapping him so hard across the face that his jaw had ached for days. Then she told him that the man had paid well for his fun and that he, Richard, should be pleased that he could finally bring some good into her life after all the misery he'd caused her and all the sacrifices she had made for him. And the next time one of the men asked for him, he'd better damn well open his mouth or pull down his pants and give them what they wanted.

And all this time Joel Alvarez had lived a cushy life, pampered in a family who had cossetted, fed, and cared for him, while Richard had been tortured, neglected, and abused.

The anger turned to rage and lodged behind his eyes, a slow, simmering burn that required little to flare it into consuming, destructive life.

****

Detective John Bamber and his sergeant, Lee Groves, stood looking down at the body of what had once been a beautiful young woman. Traces of that beauty still lived around her eyes, the set of her mouth, the slender length of her naked body. But it was marred by the bruises, by the cuts that ravished tender flesh, the cracked ribs and the obvious marks and bites consistent with sexual assault.

"I'd say she's been dead about six hours. And probably wished she was for an hour or more before that. This bastard really enjoyed himself. What kind of psycho tortures a young girl like this, a little thing with such a good life, a useful life ahead of her, for hours, and gets his kicks like this?"

The police surgeon, a rotund and generally genial man called Stokes, was red-faced with anger and disgust. "I've seen a lot in my time, but few as bad as this. And, in case you hadn't thought this already, she looks a lot like Rose Adams, your other murder victim. I'll know more when I've done a full exam, and I'll give you a better report, but I think it's probably fair to say that this one hasn't left much behind."

"There looks to be semen, though, and her fingernails are broken. Poor kid fought like a devil. Maybe we'll get his DNA and nail this one quickly," Bamber felt the anger burning through him as he looked at this woman, barely more than a child, who had met such a terrible death.

"I hope so, because looking at this kid, I'd say the guy enjoys himself too much to stop now," Stokes warned.

Groves and Bamber watched as the body of Lucy Lee Maxwell was gently placed inside a body bag and then loaded onto a gurney to be wheeled out of the cottage. The sad burden was accompanied by the paramedics who had the gray, taut looks on their faces of men who knew they had arrived too late to do anything useful.

As the body was being loaded into the waiting ambulance, a car drove up and a woman flung herself out before it had even come to a full stop.

"My baby! No, no, that can't be my little girl!" Lucy's mother grabbed at the body bag on the gurney, pleading with the paramedics to let her see, so that she could tell them this wasn't her daughter.

Dr. Stokes gently disentangled her frantic grip on the body bag and turned her into her husband's arms. Shock and grief were evident on the man's face as he put his arms around his wife's shoulders and tried to comfort her. Hearing the cries, Bamber and Groves hurried outside.

"Is there any possibility that she isn't Lucy?" Mr. Maxwell asked, his eyes pleading even though the hopeless tone in his voice gave him away. This was a man shocked beyond pretense; in his heart he knew that pathetic burden on the gurney was his child.

Mrs. Maxwell turned her ravaged face toward the detectives. "Why won't they let me look? I can tell them that it's not Lucy; it's some other poor mother's daughter, but not my Lucy."

Bamber, a veteran of too many scenes like this, still felt something twist in his stomach at their grief. An angry knot lodged behind his breastbone as he gently told her it would be better to wait until they could see the deceased at the mortuary.

Her eyes widened at the unsaid words, the silent horror that prompted him to advise she should see her child in more civilized surroundings when some of the worst work of a madman had been cleaned away. Not naked and bruised and bloodily defiled.

Still the parents looked at him from grief-darkened eyes. Waiting for a miracle to happen.

Bamber cleared his throat. Better to take that hope away now and let them begin to deal with the pain. "We have a driver's license here with a photograph on it, Mr. Maxwell. Is this your daughter?"

He nodded to Groves, who came forward holding the license in its evidence bag. The man's face went even grayer, but he took in the small plastic rectangle. Tears sprang into his eyes as he studied it, and he nodded. Feeling the positive movement of her husband's head against hers, Lucy's mother began to cry fresh sobs that tore at the hearts of the people present.

"She was going to be a doctor, you know. She wanted to help people…"

"Sir? Here's a list of the owners of the neighboring cottages you asked for," a uniformed officer spoke respectfully.

Bamber took the papers and cursed as Glory Jordan's name leapt out at him. Holy Christ, had the lawyer lied to him? Is the reason they couldn't find Alvarez because his lawyer had stashed the man away in her cottage—the property right next door to the Maxwell cottage?

Had her misplaced faith in her client's innocence brought this evil to the Maxwell family? Another thought followed fast on the heels of the first. In helping a convicted killer, had Glory Jordan put herself in danger? Was she at this very moment lying battered and cold in her own cottage while the madman she had befriended roamed these woods?

****

The cottage listed as belonging to Glory Jordan stood calm and peaceful, trees sheltering it and the waves lapping gently at against a sandy beach at its feet. It wasn't at all unlike the Maxwell family cottage, a place so serene it was impossible to imagine evil could exist there. Or that a cold-blooded killer could be lurking inside.

He sent two uniformed officers to cover the rear exit of the cottage, then turned to Groves.

The dreadful thought that Glory herself might have become a victim caused Bamber to speed up their search of the cottage. " In the circumstances, we have just cause to enter the place. Get onto Glory Jordan's office, talk to her secretary and find out where she is and tell her we want to interview her. Don't say a word about this murder. We're not waiting for a warrant for this cottage—and don't mention that to the secretary, either."

Groves stabbed at the quick dial numbers, spoke briefly and succinctly to whoever answered at the police station, and then turned back to his boss. Snapping the phone shut, he said, "It's all in the works. Er, Boss, er John. They're working on the warrant, and

Bennet is contacting Jordan's office as soon as the secretary arrives. It'll take a while, though. Have you thought she may be inside and…and hurt?"

"That's where you come in, son. You and those size twelve copper's boots of yours. Get the door open. But ring the bell first, just in case."

"What? Like they do in American cop shows?" Groves looked a bit doubtful, but at Bamber's nod, he took a kick at the solid wood door. It didn't budge. Groves flushed red to the ears but aimed a second kick just below the lock and, with a splintering cry, the door swung open.

The cottage answered their invasion with silence.

Bamber stepped inside, weapon in hand, afraid of what he might find. How the hell could a smart woman like Glory Jordan put herself in this kind of danger? It quickly became apparent that the cottage, with its old-fashioned furniture, artistic splashes of bright color, and whimsical touches in cushions and covers, was completely empty of life.

As he walked through checking the rooms, Bamber swallowed down a sigh of relief that Glory wasn't here, that his sense of foreboding after seeing Lucy Lee Maxwell's body had been without foundation. Groves called his name, and he hurried to find out what had caught the younger detective's attention.

His fear for Glory's safety morphed into fear for Fern Adams when Groves showed him the small brown empty plastic bottle of morphine pills, with Fern's name as the prescribing doctor.

He'd been disappointed that his hopes of finding Joel Alvarez holed up here had come to nothing. The idea that Fern Adams was with the man, either voluntarily or against her will, left him with a hard knot of anxiety in his chest.

Someone, somewhere, had to have some answers.

His gut told him a pretty, blonde defense counselor should be his first stop in finding them.

Chapter Fifteen

Fern followed Joel into the neat, cozy middle-class home he'd grown up in. Through a narrow hallway lined with family photos she passed a flight of stairs with a white painted banister rail, and entered a large, bright family kitchen. Joel was already standing at the sink filling an electric kettle.

"Thought we could maybe have coffee while we sorted through the papers," he told her, giving her a sideways glance.

Was he expecting me to yell at him? Or was he afraid I'd find this the perfect moment to use the gun, execution style? The inner knowledge that she had once considered doing just that first shamed her, then the hard rage that had dogged her since her sister's murder bloomed in her heart. *Why shouldn't Joel die for what he'd done? Didn't the Bible say a life for a life, an eye for an eye?*

"So you had the hydro kept on?" she asked. "A pretty expensive idea. Were you expecting to be back here anytime soon?" She knew her words had a sting in their tail, but Joel just looked at her with that disingenuous smile of his.

"No, it's cheaper to keep the power on for the heat than to have to replace all the house's water and sewage systems, to say nothing of interior damage, when the winter storms hit. I have a little money that my parents left me, and some investments I can use, unless it looks like I'm going away for a long, long time. Then I'd have to sell. But I'm not ready to let go of my home yet."

A picture of her parents' century old farmhouse flashed into Fern's mind's eye, the home she loved, and she suddenly understood why Joel was so reluctant to give up on the home his parents had left for him.

"I think Mom and Dad had visions of grandchildren playing here in the yard, and street hockey with the other neighborhood kids..." Joel's voice trailed off and an expression of unbearable sadness flickered across his face before he turned away to busy himself with making coffee.

Fern shrugged, trying to shake off the shock of compassion she had experienced. To feed her hatred she watched him through slitted eyes as he put on the kettle and took down mugs from the cupboard over the stove. Lots of small, everyday actions that her sister would never be able to carry out, thanks to him. Ordinary everyday actions, as if he were innocent, as if he deserved to enjoy a quiet cup of coffee in this calm, neat kitchen while her sister moldered in her grave.

Joel Alvarez acted like an innocent man.

Was he a man without conscience, or could he truly be innocent?

The contradictions, the doubts, were tearing her apart.

The man she'd briefly dated had been kind, considerate, and intelligent. And dangerously attractive. A guilty shame lurked in her heart that forced her to admit she'd been so very strongly attracted to him. She'd read somewhere that psychopaths were charming, too. Sometimes, when she glanced at him when he was unaware, the character in his face took her back to that kind, intelligent man she'd thought he was. And for a moment, she felt again that flare of attraction.

And that brought the anger to the boiling point.

She came out of that painful reverie at the sound of his voice. "It was just supposed to be a road trip, you know. Just a way to get away from all the grief here, the loneliness, maybe find that I might still have some family left." Joel placed two mugs of black coffee on the small, round table, along with a cow-shaped sugar bowl and spoons. He turned to the cupboard again, rummaging until he emerged with a package of those dark cookies with the white icing sandwiched between them. He grinned triumphantly. "Still fresh after all these months."

"I'm surprised the house is still, well, in such good condition. No damage or vandalism while you've been away. The neighbors must have known where you were and why…?"

His look mocked her. He knew she couldn't say it. "While I've been locked up in jail? Incarcerated? Actually, I own the house outright, courtesy of my parents, and the neighbors we have, well, they're a good sort and not likely to take hell out of the house, despite my conviction. My parents were very well respected, and they'll watch the place until I get out – or sell…"

"Twenty-five years is a long time for a house to wait."

"Long time for a man to wait. But I'm going to be exonerated. You're going to help me."

Fern shrugged. "Whatever gets you through the

day, I guess."

"If I didn't believe that I'd take that gun you have hidden in your purse and blow my own brains out."

Fern shuddered. She didn't doubt that he meant those words.

He crossed to the small kitchen table and sat, resuming his story as if they were just two people visiting. "So much had happened, and I needed a time out. The house fire that they mentioned in court, that happened a week after Mom's funeral."

"The newspapers called you a hero fireman," Fern said. Her voice dripped with sarcasm. "How can you be a hero and a murderer, all in one body? Are you some sort of psycho?"

Joel's shoulders hunched as if she'd struck him. "You're right. It wasn't courage that sent me into that house. It was that I really didn't care if I lived or died. I thought maybe the flames would make the decision for me—and then I heard the woman crying. Sobbing so hopelessly, and the fear in her voice shook me. I managed to get through the smoke and find her. She was huddled in the baby's nursery, a place she'd created for her unborn child. I don't know what instinct took her there, but I knew in that moment I couldn't let her and her baby die."

He pulled in a deep breath, spooned sugar into his cup, and then stood and made for the door. "I'll get those letters."

He returned moments later with a biscuit tin decorated with whimsical woodland creatures. "Here are the letters if you want to read them. Perhaps you can make more of them than I did." Joel handed her the box. "We probably shouldn't hang around here much longer. This is the kind of community where people notice anything unusual going on."

"We wouldn't want the police to arrive before I prove beyond any doubts that you are a murderer," Fern said coldly. *It was getting harder to keep her hatred of him going. She needed to strengthen herself against him.*

As she took the box from him, their fingers touched, and a shiver of shock, of *knowing,* ran through her. The same effect Joel had on her when they dated, that tingle of attraction. *Before she knew what a monster he really was.*

Joel didn't seem to notice her reaction, or if he did, perhaps he thought it was revulsion, not desire. "Ah, so you have doubts?" He managed a shaky grin which only served to highlight how pale he was. It didn't need a professional medic to see that the man was reaching the end of his strength as the stress and his wounds took their toll.

"None at all." Fern steeled herself against feeling any pity. She eyed Joel as he reached for a handful of cookies. "Don't you ever eat anything that doesn't come out of a cardboard box and is ninety-five percent sugar?"

"These are the best cookies ever made. After prison food, I'd probably eat the cardboard box as well and enjoy it," he replied, popping a cookie whole into his mouth. Fern caught herself watching as his tongue swiped at crumbs on his lips. His upper lip was fuller, generous, and his lower lip a thin, hard, masculine line.

She snorted. "Pack a change of clothes and your toothbrush. That hobo look you've got going doesn't make a good impression. Then we'll get out of here.

We'll stop at a coffee shop somewhere out of town, and I'll read the letters, for whatever they're worth."

Joel smiled at her, wishing with all his heart that he could turn the clock back to the time he had first met Fern Adams. He remembered every minute of their time together, from the first date—dinner at a small Mexican restaurant—to the last time they had seen each other. That last evening they'd stayed at her home, watching movies until it was time for her to pack her things for the medical conference in Boston. When she walked him to the door, he had taken her in his arms and kissed her. A kiss she had returned with a heat that he had felt right down to his toes.

"Why are you smiling?" The look she gave him told him he had nothing to smile about.

"I was remembering the last time we were together. That last kiss…" He noted the faint blush that bloomed on Fern's cheeks. *So she remembered.* He flinched as her hand lashed across his cheek.

She'd kissed him back and left for her conference in Boston. And on her return she'd gone to call on her sister, and claimed she'd seen him running away with her sister's blood on his hands.

"The last time we met was on the stairs to my sister's apartment. You nearly knocked me down the steps, but I still had time to see that Rose's blood was all over you."

His jaw set grimly. "Honey, I'm innocent, and you're going to help me prove it."

Fern was smart. Dummies didn't qualify as doctors, and he knew she was hoping that helping him would only give him enough rope to hang himself. Whatever he had believed at the trial, that she was deliberately lying, he was now sure that Fern Adams really believed she had seen him running away from her sister's apartment on the day of the murder. *But how could that be?*

And even if he was able to convince her of his innocence, the specter of Fern's sister would always stand between them. His hands fisted in frustration as he climbed the stairs.

****

Richard Phelan paced the small space between his battered brown charity shop sofa and the makeshift desk that held his computer. Tension held his body rigid; he could barely swim against the tide of manic energy and excitement that filled his body.

That, and fury. He knew he had Joel on the run, knew from that morning's newspaper headlines that his archenemy was being blamed for little Lucy Lee's murder. *Chalk yet another victory to Mr. Brown, the Avenging Angel!*

But something was eating at him, a sense that something was about to go very wrong in his best-laid plans. He was convinced that the something—or someone—was Fern Adams. He'd seen her and that lawyer woman with Joel at the cottage. What the hell was the woman doing, consorting with her dear dead sister's murderer?

Had she lost her mind? It certainly hadn't looked like she and that blonde lawyer bitch, Glory Jordan, were being held at the cottage against their will.

Were both the stupid whores fawning over Joel, just as Richard's not-so-very-dearly-departed mother had done?

He'd been by the Adams' farmhouse yesterday, but

all the lights were out, the mailbox crammed with a couple of days' worth of fliers and free newspapers. A light dusting of snow on the driveway showed that only a wandering deer had passed that way. No humans had entered or left the house; no car tracks marred the silent snow.

Later, he'd sauntered into Glory Jordan's' office, enjoying the thrill of his own bravado.

Shit! He cursed himself for that little mistake. The receptionist had been nervy, suspicious, but she'd politely told him her boss was out of the office for a few days taking some much-needed R&R at her cottage. Then she'd clammed up when he'd asked her the whereabouts of that cottage. He was pretty sure she'd called the police the moment he'd closed the office door behind him.

Still and all, she wouldn't have been able to recognize him as anyone other than Joel Alvarez. Which probably accounted for that look of fear he'd enjoyed seeing on her face. She had probably called the police to tell them their wanted escapee had just visited Glory's office.

Richard grinned to himself at the flurry of confusion he expected the police would be in, thinking that their escaped convict had been seen in a respected lawyer's office right under the nose of the police instead of on the run from Primrose Hill! He popped open a beer can and settled down in front of his computer to read the latest news about Joel Alvarez' troubles and all about the terrible murder of poor Lucy Lee Maxwell at the hands of the vicious killer, Alvarez.

****

Bamber tidied up the papers on his desk, stuffed a

couple of file folders into his expensive leather briefcase—a gift from his ex-wife some years ago, when divorce was something that happened to other people—and closed his computer. He'd been on the go nonstop for the past few days, and they were getting nowhere. He'd told Lee Groves to go home, get some rest, and he intended to do the same.

"If anything comes up, I'll be at home. Call me, no matter what," he instructed the young officer on the reception desk. "Especially if we hear from the lab about the DNA samples I sent as a rush."

"Yes, sir," came the reply. Bamber had almost made his escape through the big glass doors when he heard his name called.

"Detective Bamber, sir! There's a woman on the phone asking to speak to you." Bamber reluctantly returned to the desk and reached for the telephone. The uniformed officer covered the receiver with his hand. "She says it's urgent, sir. Sounds a bit scared if you ask me."

Bamber wasn't asking him, but he agreed the moment he heard Vera Worthing's voice. The woman did sound scared. For a brief moment, he had thought the caller was Fern Adams or Glory Jordan, and his stomach lurched.

"I'm so sorry to bother you, detective, but something weird happened," she told him, identifying herself as Glory Jordan's secretary.

"It's no bother, Ms. Worthing. What can I do for you?"

"Well, you won't believe what happened earlier today. Took me a bit to really believe it myself. That man who escaped from prison—Glory's client?

Alvarez? He walked in here, large as life, wanting to know where he could find Glory. Scared me, it did, when I recognized him."

****

Fern didn't try to stop him returning upstairs. Short of climbing out through a second-story window, how could Joel escape from her? She'd made sure to take her car keys with her and, even if Joel had managed to snag his own car keys, if his vehicle was in the garage there was no way he could get out with Fern's car parked right behind it. Not to mention that he was as weak as a kitten. So weak she knew she could easy fight him off if he tried to attack her.

Travelling around in a cab or public transport, he'd be easily recognized, and the police hotlines would be burning up with tips from responsible citizens. Joel would be back behind bars faster than you could say "jailbreak".

Fern grasped her coffee in both hands, grateful for the warmth that passed to her cold fingers. The house was cold, the heat on at a minimum to save money, she guessed. Just enough to keep pipes from freezing. What would become of Joel's childhood home if he were to be in jail for life? Or any of the things here, his parents' furniture, his own boyhood mementoes? Would Joel be somehow able to keep the basic payments met in hopes of saving a home to come to, if someday he was free of prison bars?

Still holding the cup, she wandered into the hallway. Upstairs she heard Joel's footsteps, the flush of the toilet, water running in an upstairs sink. Then his slow steps along the upper hallway, she guessed to one of the bedrooms.

Slowly she began to walk down the hall, looking at the many photographs that stood out in mismatched frames on the forest-green painted wall. They formed a pictorial family history of Joel's life: his parents' wedding photo, his baby pics. What a cute kid he had been! Most of the photographs were of Joel with either his mom or his dad; later there were school photos, photos of Joel with friends. One of him with a group of other teens, proud with musical instruments, caught her eye.

So he'd been into rock music. Maybe it was a hackneyed thought, but had he been involved in drugs? Had there been an addiction that, even though past, had left him with flashbacks and paranoia? She'd heard that happened sometimes. Maybe long term drug abuse explained how the hero had become a murderer.

The final photograph caught her eye. Joel stood with his parents, both of them beaming with pride. He wore his firefighters' dress uniform, and his face glowed with achievement and anticipation of the future.

He was damned handsome.

Now where had that thought come from? Fern slammed the coffee cup down on a small table which held a telephone and a now-dead plant. Rubbing her hands up and down her arms, she fought a wave of nausea.

Could she really still be attracted at some level, some purely sexual level, to the man who had murdered her sister?

What sort of woman did that make her?

She bit her lip as a small voice in the back of her head asked what sort of doctor was she that she could plot to execute a seriously wounded man?

****

"It was ever so strange, Detective. He walked right through those doors as if he didn't have a care in the world and asked for Glory. Got quite snotty when I said I couldn't tell him where she was, he did." The thin, gray-haired woman rolled a pencil between her thumb and forefinger as she talked. A nervous tic, Bamber decided, seeing the woman's hands shake slightly. He'd gone to interview Glory's secretary, Ms. Worthing, in her small apartment not far from her employer's office.

"You're sure this was the man who came in here?" Groves offered her a photograph of Alvarez taken from his arrest folder.

Mrs. Worthing's lips thinned as she stared at the black and white likeness. "Yes, that's…I think…"

"You're having second thoughts? You were so sure when you called…"

The secretary swallowed. "I know this sounds a bit odd, but I never actually met Joel Alvarez. I know Glory thought he was innocent, but to be honest, when I typed up her files and notes from court and interviews she'd done, I thought the evidence was too strong. Felt a bit sorry for her, I did.

"Yet there's something…I don't know. Just that the man who was in here was far cockier than he looks in this picture. Downright aggressive, in fact. Arrogant. Glory said Joel was always low key and charming. But the man who was here….do you think he could be, what do they call it on Criminal Minds? Decompensating?"

"Mrs. Worthing, I need to be sure that the man who was here was Joel Alvarez," Bamber said, beginning to suspect that this very strait-laced looking woman was a bit hysterical.

With a sharp look as if she read his mind, she told him, "I'm not given to imagining things, Detective Bamber. I'm sure it was this man who was here. Just he seems a bit different. Maybe it's because he was just arrested in this photo and not feeling quite so arrogant. The man who was here looked just like this." She tapped the photograph. "Except his expression was different."

Bamber nodded. "Could just have been due to the situation, then," he agreed.

"Could you tell me where Ms. Jordan has been today? Has she taken a few days off?" *Was she out and about in cottage country with Fern Adams and a double murderer?* He wondered.

"Oh, no, Detective. Glory works very hard – she was at her desk early this morning because she was due in court for the early morning session. She was in court all day and had a meeting with her client afterwards. I imagine she's probably just got home and gone to bed, exhausted, poor dear. I only told that awful man she was taking a vacation. It seemed worth the lie." Mrs. Worthing's cheeks flushed at admitting that she'd told an untruth. "I thought if he believed she was out of town, he wouldn't come here again looking for her.

"Well, please ask her to contact me first thing tomorrow. And Ms. Worthing, you might consider taking a day off yourself, or at least keeping your office door locked, just in case Alvarez decides to visit again." Bamber saw the older woman go pale and could have kicked himself for frightening her so baldly. "I don't expect there's any chance he would be still around. He's been spotted way away from this area, possibly going to Toronto."

Mrs. Worthy sighed with relief. "Whatever. I hope you find him. I've been worried about Glory since she took this case on. It's like she can't see the man for what he really is. Like maybe he's got that split personality disorder, you know, a bit like Jekyll and Hyde."

Bamber sent a silent curse to the producers, directors, and writers of all television and movies based on CSI programs. In his view, they'd made every lay person think they were a forensic expert while offering a whole mess of inaccurate expectations of the real police work. Which made him wonder how long their overworked lab would take to get the DNA results he was sure would help untangle the puzzle of how Alvarez could be in two places at once.

Because the latest word from Sergeant Cam Roberts in Copper Junction was that the man he referred to has Phelan, a rapist, suspected murderer, and all-round bad guy, had been absent from Copper Junction for some time before Rose Adams had died. If Roberts had got his dates right and also his insistence that Phelan closely resembled Alvarez, then Rose's murder had been carefully planned, timed, and carried out by a cunning psychopath.

Or Phelan and Alvarez were two separate people. And, according to the DNA left behind at the scene of Rose Adams' murder, the sample could only belong to Joel Alvarez. No two DNA results were the same. But what about the murder of Lucy Lee Maxwell? Could the DNA results be the same, making Alvarez her killer, too?

Bamber turned towards the door, but the secretary

stopped him, her voice quivering a little. "I told him that Glory had gone to her cottage up north. It was a lie, but I didn't want him to find her. She was actually safe in court that day. Could…you don't think…could he track her down?"

Stifling a sigh, he called for a couple of uniformed officers to canvass Glory's office building and the immediate area to see if anyone remembered seeing Alvarez enter or leave. There was no security camera, and he made a mental note to advise Glory Jordan to have one installed. As a criminal lawyer, she was very vulnerable. He pulled his thoughts away from his attraction to the lawyer as Groves brought their car around to the front entrance.

"I guess split personality would explain a lot of things about Alvarez," Groves said thoughtfully as he climbed into the vehicle. "He's a firefighter hero in one identity, a brutal murderer in another."

"Or maybe he's trying to set up for a plea of insanity," Bamber said. "Perhaps this whole business from Copper Junction, this man Phelan, is a dead end." He wished he knew where Alvarez and Fern Adams were.

Why would two smart, sane women put themselves and other innocents in jeopardy to help a murderer like Alvarez? He knew Glory believed in her client's innocence, but what was Fern Adams doing with her sister's murderer? Why would they risk the same fate as Lucy Maxwell?

A cold lump seemed to settle in his stomach as he considered the possibility that Fern might be prepared to forget her law-abiding upbringing and Hippocratic Oath to dispense justice herself.

Chapter Sixteen

"John, I believe in the law. I wouldn't be doing this work if I didn't. But sometimes the law makes mistakes, and Joel Alvarez' conviction is one of them." Glory Jordan raised a

pink-nailed hand to stem his furious response. "I know that the evidence seems incontrovertible, but it's wrong. Everyone deserves a chance to prove their innocence, and the only way that Joel could possibly have that chance was to be free long enough to find the evidence that exonerates him.

"I have no idea who finagled his escape from prison, whether it's someone who feels he is innocent and deserves a chance—"

"Such as yourself?" Bamber's tone was hard. They were in Glory's office early the next morning.

Glory smiled without humor. "Oh, no. I wouldn't go so far as to plan a jailbreak for the guy, no matter how much I believed in him. What worries me is that it could be someone who believes he's guilty and should pay a price greater than jail time."

"Glory, someone is sheltering Alvarez. He couldn't have disappeared so readily, not in his condition, if he didn't have help."

Glory chewed her bottom lip, wondering just how much she should tell the detective without landing them all in a deep pile of trouble. Finally, she sighed. It was her duty as an officer of the court to reveal what she knew.

"I have a confession to make."

"Yeah? What did you do? Rob the office coffee jar? Jay walk?' Honestly, despite his earlier comments, Bamber couldn't imagine Glory Jordan abusing her position as a lawyer, an officer of the court. But looking at her serious expression, those white teeth worrying her bottom lip, a dark feeling began to tickle his gut.

"I know it's a lawyer's duty to defend her client, to keep him safe. Sometimes, though, there is a clash between what's right in terms of humanity, and what's right in terms of the law.

"I have information as to the whereabouts of Joel Alvarez. I should have given you that information in a timelier manner, but I was concerned about the welfare of my client."

Bamber drew in a deep breath. "You know that aiding and abetting a convicted felon to escape the law is an offence that can carry its own jail time? Where is Joel? He needs to be returned to custody immediately. Are you aware there has been another murder, the brutal killing of a young woman in the same manner as Rose Adams?"

Glory's face drained of blood so quickly he thought she was going to faint. But the lawyer pulled herself together. "That would be the murder of Lucy Lee Maxwell? I heard about it; it took place near my own cottage. When did it occur?"

Reluctantly, Bamber gave her the information that he had about the time and place of the young student's death and was surprised to see the color flood back into Glory's cheeks as she breathed out a sigh of relief.

"Then Joel couldn't be responsible for that death. Even though he was at my cottage, he was with myself and Fern Adams the entire time. He didn't leave our sight, and he couldn't have killed that poor young woman, unless you think we had something to do with aiding and abetting him…"

Bamber raised both hands to his face, trying to make sense of the incredible tale Glory was telling. "Alvarez was at your cottage with yourself and Fern Adams? Does this get any worse, or have you finished your meddling? Is Fern Adams actually involved voluntarily in the escape of the man who we believe murdered her sister? The man she herself gave damning testimony against in court?"

Glaring at the woman across her desk, Bamber picked up her telephone and ordered Groves and another detective to meet him with a police car immediately.

"Where are they now?" He demanded. He watched her intently, and Glory knew that whatever she said in the next few minutes would affect the way the detective carried out the rest of his duty to recapture Joel Alvarez. She sent a little prayer to St. Jude, Patron Saint of Hopeless Cases, for help in framing her words. She explained about her visit from Fern Adams and her reluctant agreement to allow Fern to use her cottage. Still, she felt uneasy about the whole deal and knew it could land her in a whole heap of trouble if Bamber wanted to be nasty about it.

"Fern said she needed to get away to think about things. I asked her point blank if Joel had been in touch with her, and she said yes, he'd come to her home and said some things that made her wonder about his guilt.

She felt he was no threat to her as he was still extremely weak and in pain from the wounds and surgery. I advised her to call the police, and she said she was considering all her options." She caught sight of Bamber's stormy expression and decided it was the better to be completely truthful and admit she'd voluntarily travelled to cottage country and seen Joel with Fern. "I was very concerned when my assistant called me last night and said Joel had been to the office and upset her. You see, as far as I am aware, Fern and Alvarez were travelling to Toronto to pick up some documents, and then going on from there…there was something wrong if he was in Primrose Hill visiting my office last night.

"From what Fern had said about his condition, I can't imagine he could have driven himself to Primrose Hill. And I know without a doubt that Fern wouldn't have loaned him her car…and he wasn't strong enough to put up a fight.

"Because I wasn't sure Joel was safe with her, in his condition, I called her to check on them. I'd hoped that Joel could have come up with some leads, and I was afraid that if he went back to prison whoever is behind this would make sure that he was murdered this time. Apparently he had never left the cottage after I left, until they left together to travel to Toronto in Fern's car overnight. Whoever came to my office, it couldn't have been Joel."

"So Fern Adams is willingly involved in this?" Bamber couldn't keep the incredulity out of his voice. *Were both these women crazies?* "Why on God's green earth would the woman want to aid the man who murdered her sister? At the trial it was perfectly obvious that she was sure he was the one, and she was equally determined to send him to jail."

Glory saw the rage and disbelief in Bamber's eyes and looked away. She chewed her upper lip, trying to figure out how much she should tell him. The law, and legal ethics, demanded that she declare all her knowledge. But loyalty to her client said no.

Uppermost in her mind was her suspicion, confirmed by Fern, that the other woman was intent not just on seeing justice done but on carrying it out herself if need be. A vigilante justice. Should she tell Bamber that she had actually seen Fern in possession of that ugly snub-nosed little gun, and of her dark suspicions that Fern intended to use it to carry out vigilante justice? She shuddered. *Had she made a terrible mistake? One that would cost Joel Alvarez his life? Or was Fern the one in danger now?*

"Ms. Jordan?" Bamber's voice, harsh and demanding, called her back to reality.

Glory looked around her neat, unpretentious office. It was always bright, with a southwest facing window where her plants flourished. The polished wood desk, a gift from her parents, provided a reminder always of who she was and where she came from. On one wall the sturdy bookshelves held her collection of law books and related publications, a symbol of work she had loved with a passion since she was a teenager. *I could lose all this, everything.*

The memory of Fern Adams' faraway expression when Joel confronted her about the gun had haunted her since she'd left the two of them alone at the cabin. *Was Fern honest in her declaration to at least try to help him find evidence of his innocence or guilt? Or had she,*

Glory, unwittingly delivered Joel to his executioner?

Her jaw trembled briefly as she began to speak. "I believe that Joel Alvarez has been set up. I thought Fern Adams was a part of that, but now I'm not so sure. To be honest, I'm not sure what her agenda is. She claims she arrived home and Joel was waiting for her, that he forced his way into her home and grabbed her when she tried to escape. He overpowered her, but she hit him, and he fell down unconscious. She says his wound and blood loss had made him weak."

"So why didn't she call the police or run screaming from the house and enlist the help of a passing motorist?"

"An alternative agenda, I guess. Because...because she claims Joel challenged her. He raised doubts in her mind, and I can't help but wonder if those doubts were already there to be so easily resurrected. He said that he was innocent, and if she carried out vigilante justice, or handed him back to the police, then her sister's real killer would go Scot free."

Bamber sighed and swiveled his chair around so that he could gaze out of Glory's office window. None of this made sense, and yet he had a gut feeling that even though it was crazy, it was so crazy, it was the truth. "Are you trying to tell me that Fern Adams went voluntarily up to an isolated cottage to hide out with her sister's murderer?"

Glory frowned. It did sound crazy, put like that. "You must understand that Joel was very weak, and Fern didn't—doesn't feel as though he's a threat to her. I agreed that they could use my cottage because I needed time to try to find the missing piece in the case against Joel."

"And what might that be?"

"The name of the person who really killed Rose Adams."

"You're forgetting another missing piece. What motive would someone else have had? It looks as though Alvarez was out drinking with Rose Adams most of the day she was killed, because the barman and a couple of other people at the Wild Turkey Inn have identified Joel as being with her that night.

"Afterward, either they got into drugs or more booze, and somehow an argument. Maybe Alvarez wanted sex and Rose didn't want to give out, and Alvarez lost it.

"And before you say anything else, Glory, you should know that an OPP officer from Copper Junction, where Joel used to live, has identified Alvarez from a photograph as a bad actor from his own town. A man suspected not only of a couple of rapes or attempted rapes, but also of the murder of his own mother."

Glory began to protest, to demand to see the evidence that had not been produced at any trial. But his next words left her shocked and shaking.

"It also looks as though your dedication to helping a convicted killer may have cost a young woman, a woman planning on becoming a doctor, her life. The daughter of the family who own the cottage next to yours, Lucy Lee Maxwell, who was raped and murdered last night died in exactly the way Rose Adams died." He admitted to himself a grim satisfaction at Glory Jordan's sudden intake of breath. "Your claim that you and Fern Adams were Alvarez' alibi is suspect because of your relationships with him."

"This is the guy you and Fern are trying to shelter, but in fact you may have let a monster loose in the community."

Chapter Seventeenth

"Hey boss, where's Phelan?" Mitch Kramer poked his head into the cramped office of the car valet and detailing firm, Donnelly Motors. His boss, Keith Donnelly, was working on a calculator, sorting through the week's invoices that cluttered his desk.

"I dunno. The lazy bastard's late again. He's started to treat the place more like a sinecure than a job. In fact, he gives me the creeps, with that weird stare of his. What you want him for, anyway?"

"You're right, the guy is a bit off the wall. He's kind of odd. He thinks he's better than the rest of us. And I said to him one day, why d'you think you're better than the rest of us? And he just looked at me as if I was a dog turd or something, you know, something to be scraped off his shoe. And he said, *'Because I am better than you lot.'* The other guys went into fits of laughing and it's been a catch phrase for a while now. Phelan walks into the place, and someone will say, *'Because I am better than you lot,'* and everyone curls up laughing."

"Rather you than me. I don't find the fucker funny. To be honest, I'll be glad when he's out of here."

"If he's this late, maybe he's not coming in at all. So should I start on the Culver car now? You know old man Culver said he wanted it ready for their road trip this weekend."

Donnelly rolled his eyes. "Dammit to hell, that Culver account is a biggie for us. I'll fire that bastard's ass when he finally shows up. You go ahead, Mitch. Get Andy or one of the other boys to help you if need be. Can't keep the old man waiting."

A knock at the door and another employee poked his head in, his face streaked with engine grease and wearing a puzzled expression.

"Hey there, Boss, have you seen Phelan?"

"No, I've just given Mitch here instructions to do the Culver car. You can help him."

"Well, Boss, something kinda weird. Have you seen the picture in the paper of the guy just escaped from jail? The one who murdered that chick in Primrose Hill about a year ago?"

"No, don't have time to read the paper till I can go to the can. What's up?"

"The guy, Alvarez, who raped that woman and slit her throat, well, he looks the spit image of Phelan. We were wondering if the crazy asshole has an even crazier brother. But the guys are fit to be tied with plans to tease the idiot when he gets in."

Donnelly stared at him. "You won't be teasing that asshole any longer. I'm firing his ass the minute he shows up." Donnelly heaved his scrawny frame up from the battered leather chair. "Anyway, gimme that paper. Sally Anne…"

A pretty, petite woman poked her head in from the next office. "You bellowed, Boss?" she asked, rolling her eyes at Mitch, who grinned back.

"I'm off to the little boys' room. See to the telephone, will ya? And try not to chat up the paying customers."

217

"Umph. Why do you think the paying customers keep coming back? It sure isn't for a chance to chat with you, you old sourpuss." She disappeared back into her office, slamming the door behind her.

"Damned if I can get decent office help," Donnelly muttered, following Mitch out to the workshop where a couple of his employees stood staring at the screen of a small television that was on the wall above the staff coffee machine.

"Do I pay you lot to watch the idiot box?" he snarled at them as he passed heading for the washroom.

"Well, I'll be damned. Hey, Boss, come here and look at this!" Pete Angelo shouted to make himself heard over the noise in the car detailing shop. He couldn't take his eyes off the television news that was playing.

"Angelo, get your fat ass back to work. What do you think you're doing? Omigod..." Donnelly stopped in his tracks while he took in the grainy video that was filled the screen of the local news channel.

"Fuck me with a feather, Boss. Ain't that Ricky Phelan up there dressed like some friggin' doctor?"

Donnelly shook his head from side to side. "If it's not Phelan, then he's cloned himself. Shut up, won't you, and let me hear what that cop is saying."

"Police are seeking the help of the public in locating the whereabouts of this man, believed to be escaped prisoner Joel Alvarez. He is possibly still in the Primrose Hill/Kingston area, although it is possible he is also in the northern Land'o'Lakes cottage area. He is considered to be dangerous and should not be approached. Anyone with any information should contact police at the TIPS number that appears on your

218

screen now."

"What the hell? If that is Phelan, and this happened yesterday so I guess it could be. The lazy bugger— been off work sick, so he says, for almost the last week...."

"Seems he was just off murdering some poor guy in the hospital. Who'd have thought that wimp would have it in him? And maybe he's offed two women, as well."

"Stop yammering, Pete. I'm calling the police." Donnelly pulled his cell phone out from the pocket of his grimy coveralls.

****

Bamber was late getting to the station after his frustrating interview with Glory Jordan. He'd grabbed a coffee from the break room and was tempted to ignore the ringing of his internal office phone, longing for a few moments to assimilate all he'd learned from Alvarez's lawyer. But the idea that the caller could herald a break in the Alvarez or Slater cases changed his mind.

"Detective Bamber?" The desk sergeant said, his voice bright with excitement. "Sir, sorry to call you when you've just got in, but the fingerprints fax from Copper Junction that you were waiting for has just come in, and there's a report from the techie guys about the laptop that was recovered from the search of Slater's home. Terry the Geek said he thought you should see it right away. And that lawyer, Glory Jordan, called and asked that you call her back ASAP. Oh, and a guy from a detailing plant in TO says he recognises the man in the video pic as one of his employees. He asked if someone would call around and talk to him and his crew."

Bamber glanced at the clock. There was a little tingle in the back of his brain that told him this could be the break they'd been hoping for. After what seemed like a long dearth without progress, all of a sudden, the case might be bursting wide open…he'd been dog tired, but suddenly the adrenaline was flowing and he rushed to drag on his coat.

Time for one quick call while Lee Groves brought the car around. *Let's see what Glory Jordan has to say for herself.* As he dialed, his pulses revved up at the memory of the softness that underscored the lawyer's professional exterior, the light perfume she wore. *The softness and scent that a man could easily forget himself in….*

Then she was answering, her voice catchy as if she'd run for the phone.

"You wanted me to call you?" It came out unintentionally brusque. *It's not her fault you were indulging in an erotic fantasy about the woman just as she picked up the phone,* he admonished himself.

"Detective Bamber? John?" Her use of his name revved up the feelings, and he rushed to tamp them down again.

"No, it's Santa Claus. Who the hell did you think it was?"

His sarcasm was met by a warm chuckle. "Well, you know, Detective Santa, I do get calls from other people. But this time I may have a gift for you."

Bamber swiped a hand over his eyes. If only she knew what he'd been thinking.

"Go ahead, surprise me."

That chuckle again, as if she'd heard a double-entendre in his words and was thinking of acting on it.

Pull yourself together, mate. This is business.

"I just confirmed the time of death for Lucy Lee Maxwell with the Coroner."

Well, that brought him down to earth. "Just a minute…" He had brought the file with him, but it took a few moments to locate it in his briefcase and open to the right page.

"Looks to be between ten p.m. and one a.m., last night or this morning."

"Yes, and that confirms that Joel Alvarez couldn't have killed that poor girl.."

"And you know this how?"

"Because Fern Adams and I were with him yesterday evening and into the early morning hours. Both of us can swear he was with us throughout that evening and the night. I didn't leave until about 3 a.m., to get back to Kingston for a 10 o'clock court hearing in another matter. Joel Alvarez did not kill that poor girl."

"And you were with him the whole time?" Something that could have been called jealousy tweaked at Bamber's ego. "And you decided not to reveal that little detail when I interviewed you this morning?"

He was pleased at the embarrassed hesitancy in Glory's voice as she continued:

"He was only out of our sight for five minutes, when he stepped outside the cabin for a cigarette and he stayed on the deck, and for a couple of pee breaks in the cottage bathroom. Like I said, Joel Alvarez could not have killed that poor girl."

"How do I know you're not making up an alibi for

him because of your feelings—"

"My feelings?" Irritation threaded her tone.

"Your feelings as to him being innocent?"

That light chuckle again. "If you're thinking what it sounds like you're thinking, you're wrong. Joel Alvarez was with me and Fern Adams until well into the wee small hours, discussing how to go about proving his innocence. Or his guilt, in Fern's case.

"Let's face it, detective, I'm sure you're not going to suggest that Fern would make up an alibi; she'd be far more likely to put the noose around Joel's neck herself."

Then she was gone, and Bamber was holding a silent phone and wondering again if he wasn't against an almost unsolvable case.

Chapter Eighteenth

Fern sipped early morning coffee in an almost deserted roadside cafe and studied the letters Joel had given her. She had to admit, there was certainly something fishy about the whole thing, particularly the anonymous note suggesting Joel should go to Copper Junction.. If it truly was a note and not something he'd added himself...

Why would a doctor write a personal letter on his office notepaper? Why was there apparently no further correspondence once the child was born? If it was truly about a happy event in the family, why was there no further news, photographs, replies to letters that Joel's mom would have written to express delight at news of the new baby? Surely the woman called SueAnne would have wanted to send her relative some pictures, maybe even arrange to visit, if they were celebrating a happy family event?

And why did Joel know nothing of these relatives? If, in fact, they were relatives. Suddenly a disturbing thought tickled the back of her mind. She didn't say anything to him, but she'd heard of doctors directly arranging adoptions. Only a couple of weeks earlier, she'd read a report online about a doctor who'd been doing just that, and apparently making a fat living charging fees to desperate pregnant women who felt unable to raise a child and couples who were desperate for a child. If Joel was adopted illegally, then that would explain his parents' wish to keep the whole thing a secret. *Couldn't people be prosecuted for adopting without going through proper channels? Had the Alvarez's bought a baby on the illegal black market?* She made a quick phone call to Glory Jordan for legal advice.

"Glory, this is Fern Adams. I'm still with Joel, and we're heading off to a town called Copper Junction. Listen, this might sound weird, but I need to know if it's illegal to adopt without going through some kind of regulated agency? Like, can doctors arrange adoptions?"

"You're wanting to adopt a child?" There was a smile in Glory's voice as she answered.

"Don't be ridiculous!" Fern was in no mood for joking. "Just answer the question."

"My, but someone got out of bed on the wrong side. You think Joel may have been adopted? I'm not a family law solicitor, so I can't really answer that, and I don't know what the laws would have been governing private adoptions nearly thirty years ago. I know there are rules about how adoptions should take place. There's no real answer to that. I'd say it's more a case by case issue as it stands right now, depending on how aware they were that the adoption was illegal. Some people prefer not to know the facts, just to assume that an agency or a doctor is legit, and the fees are to cover medical care, etcetera. I think people facilitating such adoptions could be prosecuted. I'll find out." Glory's voice held less eagerness than Fern expected. Her next words explained why. "I'm glad you called, Fern. I've just been talking to Detective Bamber. He's hot to trot in blaming Joel for the murder that took place at the cottage next to mine, at the same time we were there with Joel."

Fern sucked in a sharp, fearful breath. "When? How the hell could Joel have—"

"That's it, you see. He couldn't have done this one. The modus operandi is exactly like Rose. But Joel Alvarez was with us the whole time. I checked with the coroner. No way could he have done this, given the time of death. I'm sure you'll appreciate the irony of this – that you and I are witnesses that Joel could not have murdered this latest victim."

Fern chewed her bottom lip. The news threw her for a moment, and then she said, "So it's a copycat, right? Some sick bastard has been following the news reports and decided to have some fun the same way."

She heard Glory give a deep, exasperated sigh. "Oh, Fern…"

"Anyway, I'm calling because I'm a little wary of what I've read in these letters." Fern continued. " And I'm not really sure what it means, but there are letters from a doctor about an upcoming birth, then the birth of a child. I'm getting the strangest feeling that something doesn't add up. Joel is convinced that these letters are about family that he never knew he had. I haven't mentioned this to him, but I'm thinking maybe the doctor was facilitating adoptions."

The silence at the other end went on so long that she thought they'd lost the connection. Finally Glory replied, "That explains your questions about the law back then. You're saying that you think Joel was adopted? That he might have blood relatives in Copper Junction? I doubt they'd be happy to have an unclaimed relative show up on their doorstep. Especially the adoptive mother, who probably wouldn't want anyone to know about her little 'mistake'." She couldn't hide the tingle of excitement in her voice. Fern was quick to squash it.

"I don't see it will take us too much further. Even if he has relatives, it doesn't change the fact that he has been identified by myself, and by the barman...and that his DNA matches that of the killer. Give it up, Glory. Joel is guilty."

Neither woman spoke of the tiny worm of suspicion that was beginning to wriggle in their minds. Fern refused to admit to herself that maybe there was a way that the killer could have been in two places at once. And that thought made her heart beat faster when she caught the longing expression on Joel's face as she returned to their table at the coffee shop.

She took a few moments to explain her theory about the possibility of adoption. Joel's face lit with hope, and she wished she'd kept the idea to herself. *No sense raising false hope.*

"Glory will be in court most of the day, but she's going to find out about illegal adoptions," she told Joel when he returned from the café counter with a second round of coffees for their journey. "I've asked her about the legality of an adoption being arranged by a doctor."

"Why would it matter now how it was done? If I was adopted, it was as a newborn, and that's thirty years ago." His face fell as he realized the problems. "And I don't see how it can help. I don't know much about DNA, but I do know that even samples from related family members have differences." Fern gave him a hard look. He'd been excited when she'd agreed to investigate this with him, but as they traveled, he'd become more and more morose.

"It matters because it will affect the way this Doctor—" She consulted the letters. "—Dr. Stone, reacts to your request for information. If it wasn't legal, then he'll deny everything. We can use our knowledge of what's in the letters your mother received, along with our knowledge that it was illegal, as leverage to force him to talk."

Joel managed a quick smile. "You should have been a detective or a lawyer."

"I don't think so," she replied. "I'm a damn good doctor, and I get to mix with a much better class of people."

When they left the welcoming warmth of the coffee shop and returned to the highway, Joel sank back into heavy silence.

Fern knew she should be relieved not to have him attempt to chat to her and win her over. But the longer she was with him the harder she found it to believe that he was a cold-blooded murderer.

No doubt her sister had been charmed by Joel Alvarez, too. And look where that got her. Yet if Joel was innocent... Fern's face heated at the reaction to that thought.

****

Detective John Bamber leaned back in his chair and stretched his cramped shoulder muscles. He'd happily given Groves the job of going through all the TIPS that came in after the hospital security tape video of Alvarez was shown on the TV news at lunchtime and again in the early evening. There would no doubt be lots of sightings of Alvarez, and many would be false starts.

If they were lucky, some observant member of the public would phone in with a lead that would put them hot on the trail of the escaped killer. Word had come down from on high that they had to make catching Alvarez ultra-top priority. Neither Corrections Canada, the hospital, nor the Ontario Provincial Police wanted to appear like total incompetents in full public view. Heads would roll if asses weren't efficiently covered.

Right now, he was working on the new case of the man who'd been found beaten and left for dead in a back alley, only to be murdered in hospital in plain sight by someone who looked just like Alvarez. It seemed a huge coincidence that a stranger would beat up this guy with obvious fatal intent, and then a completely new killer—Alvarez—would risk entering the hospital to finish the job.

Ergo, the two cases were linked, and Alvarez was guilty of at least three murders. Four, if the Copper Junction OPP sergeant's gut feeling was correct that Phelan/Alvarez had murdered his mother as well.

Bamber's thoughts kept straying to Fern Adams. He knew Glory Jordan was safely in court arguing a case before Judge Peter Hardy—not a task he envied her, having time spent himself testifying before that notoriously difficult judge—but Fern was still on the missing list. He'd put out an all-points bulletin in hopes that she'd be spotted. *Dear God, the insanity of women! Why would she take off with the man who'd murdered her sister?*

Bamber could think of only two reasons. One was that she didn't believe Alvarez was guilty. Given that Fern had given the evidence that clinched the evidence against Alverez, it seemed pretty unlikely that she'd now be running around the countryside trying to prove him innocent. Another option was that she was travelling under threat of violence from Alvarez. But it seemed unlikely that, injured as he was, the man could hold a strong, resourceful woman prisoner.

The option that made his blood freeze was that she intended to become judge, jury, and executioner herself. No doubt Fern had bad intent, and he was afraid her life would be ruined in her quest for what she may have seen as justice for her sister. The woman was a dedicated doctor. Could she see her way to murder?

He hoped Glory Jordan could shed some light on where Fern and Alvarez were planning to go. Then he found himself looking forward to seeing the sexy, smart blonde lawyer in a way that went way beyond his questions pertaining to the Alvarez case. Despite his fury at her for keeping back information about Alvarez' whereabouts, he still felt a frisson of pleasure at the thought of her.

As for Fern, her car license plate and description had gone out to police across the province. And had been circulated to other provincial forces as well as the Royal Canadian Mounted Police and also to police in the U.S. in the event Joel tried to cross the border. At this point they were hesitating to put her photo and missing persons information out on the news media but, if she wasn't spotted safe and sound within the next 48 hours, they would have to go that route. *Wouldn't the Press have a field day with that—no doubt putting two and two together and getting their sums right in this case.* It was definitely no coincidence that Fern Adams had gone missing at the same time her sister's murderer had escaped from custody.

He winced as he imagined the headlines about incompetency in all ranks in not protecting the dead woman's sister from the man who'd sworn revenge against her.

Bamber swigged down the last of a now cold cup of coffee and opened the file containing printouts of the emails the techs had found on Slater's laptop computer when they'd searched his apartment.

He didn't know that two new pieces of information were about to change everything.

****

Copper Junction turned out to be a two traffic light town whose prosperity had once been built on mining for copper which had blossomed, made a few folk rich, and just as quickly deserted the town again. With the mining gone, the railway quickly departed, and residents without a car were now dependent on a twice weekly Greyhound Bus service that stopped here on its way elsewhere.

In fact, Joel thought, looking out at the closed storefronts and graffiti on main street buildings, it looked as though just about anything coming here was on its way elsewhere, rather than staying. *Would he find his truth here, or had all leads to it left on the last bus?*

Fern was wondering the same thing as she navigated to a parking spot at the sidewalk in front of a Stedman's department store that seemed to be doing a fair business, judging from the customers going in and out. She hadn't voiced her thoughts to Joel and Glory, but for the life of her she couldn't see what connection there could be between a possible long-lost relative of Joel's and her sister's murder. Or if Joel had been adopted, how would that help? She sighed. She'd promised that she would explore all angles of Joel's alleged innocence. She had to be sure that he truly was the guilty party, although logic insisted he was the man she had seen leaving her sister's apartment that awful night.

But her heart—perhaps it was a mistake to spend so much time alone with him. Psychopaths were notorious for their charm. Many people in contact with them found it hard to believe that they were cold-blooded monsters until they witnessed for themselves the horrible deeds that spilled from the beast's mind.

And Fern, despite all the evidence against him, despite all the evidence of her own eyes, was finding it increasingly difficult to believe that the quiet, decent man she thought she was dating could be guilty of brutal murder. Still, she was determined not to be taken in. Her mind went to the hard gray gun nestled in her shoulder bag, within easy reach. *Justice takes many forms.*

But then there was Lucy Lee Maxwell's terrible murder. Could that really be a copycat killer? Despite all her attempts to rationalize how Joel could have killed the young woman, she was forced to admit that it would have been impossible. After all, he'd scarcely left their sight – even when he stood outside, smoking and sulking, he'd been in plain view of both herself and Glory. She told herself that this didn't mean Joel hadn't murdered her sister. After all, she'd seen him with her own eyes…

What was really causing her some disturbance was she couldn't deny that something strange was happening to her feelings. The more time she spent with

Joel, no matter how hard she tried, the more difficult she found it to believe he was capable of the awful brutality done to her sister. The dichotomy of what she knew to be fact and what her emotions were telling her was starting to drive her crazy.

Oh, stop it! she told herself, yanking the keys from the ignition.

"Come on, let's get on with this. I want to get out of here," she snapped, unlocking her seatbelt, and flicking off the car lights.

****

Richard Phelan was still coming down from the high the murder of Lucy Lee Maxwell had left him feeling, boosted by the experience of killing the Facilitator under the noses of an entire hospital staff.. *Oh, it had been a treat! The expression on Slater's face! And that little bitch had tried to fight him, and then she'd pleaded for her life. But in the end, just like them all, she'd lost all her fight and been like a sacrificial lamb that suddenly accepts its fate. That's when the fun leaves and the depression sets in.*

Now he was dog tired. It was important to show up for work, even though he'd missed a couple of days, he should still keep to a routine. But maybe he'd take another couple of sick days, read the newspapers and online commentaries, glory in the slow destruction of Joel Alvarez. His brother.

The brother who'd been chosen for a good life, a life Richard had paid for in his own suffering. He'd endured cruelty and abuse so that Joel could be warm, happy, fed, and loved.

And now it was time for Joel to pay the piper.

Chapter Nineteen

A sharp *rat-a-tat* sounded on the solid pine door of a backwoods cabin in a remote Northern Ontario community. Visitors this late at night never brought good news.

The old man who lived there grunted with the effort as he roused himself from the battered old recliner. In front of him an ancient television set played on with the sound turned off, some 'real life' drama featuring well dressed, glamorous folk who'd never had to give a second's thought to where their next meal was coming from or how they'd manage to find the cash to mend the hole in the roof.

Elegant ladies in designer clothing, dripping jewelry. Just the way *she* had wanted her life to be. Tall, handsome men, too wealthy to need to be strong, demonstrated in make believe what the likes of him could never have even in their finest fantasies.

That hammering at his door continued as Chief Joseph took a last drink from his herbal tea and carefully gathered together the cup, bowl, and cutlery he'd used for his simple supper of moose chili and fresh wild greens. He burped genteelly into his hand as he walked the few steps into his kitchen area.

"Blast it, who invented this chili pepper anyway!" he murmured to himself, pressing a hand to his chest where heartburn was beginning to rage.

The banging at his door continued. The visitor was not to be ignored. The large-faced clock over the cookstove claimed it was close to ten o'clock. A sudden chill of precognition caught him, rippling down his spine with the slow deliberateness of pine resin from a wounded tree.

The old man put the dishes down on the wooden counter and made his careful way through the sparsely furnished cabin to the door, peering out of the window before drawing back the bolt after recognizing his visitor.

"What brings you here tonight, Sergeant Roberts?"

"I thought maybe you'd have not heard—I know you don't bother much with the newspapers or the television news," the heavyset police sergeant said as he accepted Joseph's nodded invitation to enter his home.

"Waste of money, the newspapers, and the TV news is just more of the same served up like pablum." The older First Nation man stated, gesturing to the only other chair in the room as he reached over to turn off the silent television set.

"A call at this time of night is never good news. Bad news is hard to tell, so why don't you just come right out and let me know what I'm going to wish you hadn't?"

Sergeant Cam Roberts sat politely in the seat he'd been offered, glancing around the cabin. He knew Joseph lived alone, had never married, and yet the place was spotlessly clean and tidy. There was an orderliness that spoke of self-respect and a sense of dignity that was lacking so much these days. If he hadn't come on such a delicate mission, the police officer would have been happy to accept the beverage Joseph offered him and sit a while to chew over old times with the man he'd known since they were both young.

But he didn't expect this to be an easy interview. He held onto his official mask as he cleared his throat. "Chief Joseph, I can't help but think that SueAnne Phelan would have been a whole lot better off if she'd married you."

The old man's expression was unreadable. "And why do you think that, Cam?"

"Because you'd have given her the stability she needed to keep her on track."

" SueAnne had great dreams, dreams I couldn't fulfill for her."

"And look where those dreams got her. An early grave. You could have saved her from that."

"I long ago realized that there wasn't anyone real who could save her. Her head was filled with fantasies. And her daddy would never have let her marry an Indian. He was a hard man whose mind could never be changed." Joseph stared for a while at the now blank television screen, as if he could picture the past—or the future as it might have been—there.

Sergeant Roberts pulled out a folded piece of paper from his pocket and handed it over to the older man.

Joseph drew in a sharp breath. There was no mistaking the man in the grainy photocopy of the newspaper article photograph, but the terrible headline, *Killer On the Loose!* cut his heart to the quick.

"Is it true?" he asked as soon as he could speak without the tremble in his voice giving him away.

Roberts nodded. "Let's not beat about the bush, Chief. I know he's your son. Everyone in town knows he's your son. It was one of the major scandals in Copper Junction all those years ago. And even if I hadn't heard the rumors, one look at him would tell the tale of his parentage, wouldn't it?"

Chief Joseph nodded. "But the newspaper says this man is Joel Alvarez. So why have you brought this trouble to my door?"

"It seems he took on another name after he made the move to the city. If the man in the picture isn't your son, then he's an amazing look alike. I thought for one thing that you ought to know. And for another…well, I'm afraid that boy may make his way here, thinking that you'd help him."

"Or maybe to get revenge because I didn't help him so long ago." Chief Joseph held up his hand to stop the officer's protest. "Oh, I heard all the stories, all the things that she got up to with her man friends and how she neglected that child. I should have done something. But I didn't."

"We should all have done something and didn't."

"But I am his father. I had a responsibility to see that he got the care he needed to grow up right. They whisper that he murdered his momma. And if this is true, if he murdered this woman, then I have a responsibility for that, too.

"I see that he even changed his name. But it didn't change who he was."

There wasn't much else to say. Roberts dismissed the easy platitudes that sprang to his lips. He'd known that Joseph would take the evidence of his son's evil behavior badly, yet he'd had to warn the man because it could well be that the boy would return and seek help, or revenge, on his father.

No one broke the silence of the cabin, and a few minutes later Roberts got up and, with a gentle pat on Chief Joseph's back, quietly let himself out of the cabin.

The other man sat, staring at the past while the logs in the woodstove flickered to ash and the chill of winter began to lick at his bones.

****

"What makes you think that the man we're looking for, the man we know as Joel Alvarez, is this man, Richard Phelan?" Bamber's head was going to explode. So many mismatched details were flying in. *First, Alvarez was a hero fireman. Then he was a convicted psycho killer. Now he's a man named Phelan working for minimum wage on a car detailing and body shop. And not to forget that he'd apparently won big on Lotto Ontario. And at some point, while spiffing up cars and rescuing victims from blazing buildings, he managed to multi-task and murder Rose Adams, the private eye Slater, and Lucy Lee Maxwell?*

What the fuck is going on?

He was interviewing Keith Donnelly; the owner of the car detailing shop whose claim to fame was that he employed a man named Richard Phelan.

"Well, this guy here—" Donnelly tapped the photo Groves had supplied with an oil and paint-stained fingernail. "That guy is Ricky Phelan. A dead ringer."

"Yeah, you reckon our Ricky has been living a double life? Like geeky car detailer boy by day, crazy psycho murderer at night?" Pete Angelo asked, peering at the photo over Donnelly's shoulder. "'Cos I can tell you this—the minute I saw that video on the TV, I knew this was Phelan. Nothing would convince me otherwise."

"Yeah, and we always knew he was a weirdo," one of the other employees commented. "He never fit in here, that's for sure."

Bamber continued to probe, eliciting dates and times, comparing them to the dates and times that the crimes Alvarez was accused of had been committed. He considered employee records and testimony from co-workers and Donnelly, the boss, and it soon became evident that Joel Alvarez had managed to perform a miracle.

The man had been in two or even three places at once.

****

"Two places at once?" Lorimar asked, his eyebrows climbing toward his receding hairline. Bamber, Groves and Lorimar were in Lorimar's office, chewing over the information that had been gathered.

Information that made absolutely no sense at all.

"I can see that the man could possibly have held down a second job in Toronto as car detailer between shifts as a hero fireman, although why he'd go by a different name, I can't imagine. Tax dodge, perhaps?" Lorimar's incredulous expression matched that of the other men in the room. "But that he simultaneously spent time in prison awaiting trial after murdering Rose Adams? And here in Primrose Hill, a five-hour drive from the city? Shit, detectives, I think you've got crossed wires here somewhere."

"So far as we've been able to ascertain, Alvarez has no living relatives. Same seems to go for Phelan, according to Sergeant Cam Roberts. And the fascinating news is that Phelan is a big-time lottery winner who's wanted for questioning about the murder of his mother."

Lorimar held up his hands in a defensive gesture. "Stop. I can't take all this in at once. Where did that information come from?"

"A local cop from some backwater named Copper Junction." Bamber outlined the information he'd received from the files Sergeant Roberts of Copper Junction had faxed to him.

"SueAnne Phelan, that's this guy's mother, was found dead in the charred ruins of her backwoods cabin. She'd apparently been strangled then had her throat cut before the place was torched."

"The same MO as Rose Adams and the Maxwell girl." The three detectives were silent for a few minutes, digesting this.

"So, we've been working on the assumption that Phelan and Alvarez were one and the same." The detective handed out copies of a police arrest photograph of Phelan provided by the officer in Copper Junction. "You can see why the sergeant thought the wanted pic of our man Alvarez was the same person as this Phelan." Everyone nodded. "But as for the rest…" Lorimar scrubbed at his face as if his hands could erase the puzzlement that had settled there.

"Seems this Phelan was the carefully groomed type," Bamber said with a smile. "Luckily for us, he left a hairbrush and toothbrush in his locker. Donnelly from the car detailing biz where a guy named Phelan, who is the split image of Alvarez, worked, was all too happy to point out that the locker was company property and therefore anything left there was company property or considered abandoned, and he could let us take it without a warrant."

Groves rolled his eyes. "Good thing he wasn't well-liked among his colleagues. They thought him an arrogant bastard. Maybe this is one time we should be happy for all those CSI programs all the civilians watch." Bamber quelled him with a glance.

"It seems that for each event we know about in Alvarez' life, Phelan was somewhere else. With witnesses like his co-workers. But there's no record of his whereabouts after he headed for TO, where I might add, he had picked up a very substantial lottery winners' cheque, from Copper Junction until he surfaces working at the car detailing place. His employer states that Phelan was in work on the day of Rose Adams' murder but had been sent out to pick up some supplies just before lunch. Seems he was gone the rest of the day on a task that shouldn't have taken more than a couple of hours, and he didn't show up to work the next day. They said Phelan took a couple of unauthorised days off around about the time of Lucy Lee Maxwell's murder. We have testimony from his lawyer, Glory Jordan, that both she and Fern Adams were with Alvarez during the time frame of the Maxwell murder. And Phelan hasn't shown up to his job yet."

"But Alvarez always claimed innocence of the Adams murder. Glory Jordan always said he was innocent, but she's his lawyer. Her receptionist identified Alvarez from the photograph we had but said the man who came into her office was 'different, somehow, arrogant.' A description that fits Phelan but not Alvarez. And if we accept what his lawyer said, then Alvarez was somewhere on the road to Toronto from cottage country when his double was giving the receptionist the creeps, to use her words, in the lawyer's office."

"So, what do you think? Borderline Personality Syndrome?" Groves asked.

Lorimar snorted. "It would make a nice, simple solution, maybe even a get-out-of-prison-free card. But even if he had two different personalities in the one body, that one body couldn't be in two places at once," the police chief said.

At that moment Alex the Geek, the forensics expert, knocked on the door and entered the office. "Oh, have I got news for you! Ready to have your theories blown away?" he said with a grin.

"If it takes the case any farther, then you can blow up as many theories as you like." Bamber told him.

"Well, I examined the DNA sample from the Maxwell murder and checked it against the sample from the Rose Adams murder. They looked identical."

Bamber sighed. "Do I hear a 'but' there? You're just about to muddy the waters further, aren't you?"

"Prepare to be blown away, my friends. The DNA from the toothbrush – icky thing, not kept clean – also matched Alvarez. But here's the kicker: First, you see, those fingerprints you got from the guy up in Copper Junction, well, they're not quite the same as Alvarez' prints. Close, and maybe the differences could be explained away. Now, twins, as you know, can be either fraternal or identical. Identical twins do not have identical fingerprints.

"It's long held that identical twins have identical DNA, but my friend at the university is working on some means of identifying differences. You don't want me to go into the details, do you?"

"Just give us the basics," Lorimar said, rubbing his temples where a headache was starting to bloom.

"Patience, patience. Now, if our boy Alvarez is a fraternal twin, which is to say, Momma had two separate eggs fertilized, then the DNA samples are different. Fraternal twins are formed from two different eggs and different sperm, which is why fraternal twins may have two different fathers."

"The basics, Alex, just the basics."

Alex looked puzzled. "That is the basics…"

"To you, maybe, but not the rest of us. Go on."

"What we have here is a Sherlock Holmes type puzzle. We have a man who can be in two places at once, but there is only one DNA. But if Alvarez comes from a single egg that split, which means he's an identical twin, then the DNA of he and his brother should be identical."

"I think my head is going to explode. You're saying that, if Alvarez and Phelan could be twins, identical twins, then there's no way of telling their DNA apart?" Bamber rubbed his temples as the headache there grew.

"Ah, up until recently, no, you couldn't tell them apart. They are literally identical. But as I say, I have a friend at the uni who's studying this actual subject, and she says her work shows there should be a slight but traceable identifiable difference in the identical twin DNA."

"And is there?" Bamber couldn't keep the impatience out of his voice. "Bearing in mind we don't have any evidence that these two are related, yet alone twins. The resemblance could be just accidental. Or somehow or another, they are the same man."

"Not so fast. This test takes time. I talked my friend at the uni, she's a professor and expert in the field. Now, given that there are differences in the fingerprints, I felt uneasy about declaring they all came from the same person. Soooo, what I'd like is permission to take the DNA samples we have, one definitely from Alvarez and one from the apparent lookalike, over to her. She's agreed to take a look. And we should tentatively have some results probably late tomorrow or the day after if I can convince her to put a rush on."

Lorimar nodded his approval, and the tech dropped a file folder on Bamber's desk, sketched a wave, and left the room.

"Is it just possible that the phrase you used earlier, John, identical twin, may be the answer to that puzzle, although it doesn't absolve Alvarez. Maybe they are twins working together? Let me know when the DNA results come through, too. That should answer a lot of our questions. And see if you can get a search warrant on Phelan's apartment, or wherever he goes to ground."

"Well, if the Geek is right and they are identical twins, could it be one is setting the other up? Although we don't know which one." Lee Groves scratched his head. "You know, it's possible that Alvarez claiming his innocence was telling the truth."

Bamber scowled. "I don't know whether to hope this solves our case, or what. If you're right and Alvarez has been set up, then there has been an appalling miscarriage of justice."

****

It had all been going so well until that asshole, *the*

Facilitator—Phelan snorted at the name—had screwed everything up. *Well, I've made sure he won't be talking, but what if he had written things down, maybe was smart enough to keep his notes somewhere safe, like in a bank deposit box and not his office?* He remembered how he'd been concerned that the investigator had kept incriminating evidence of their conversations in case he was ever called to answer for his actions to the police.

Then there was that other problem. Where in hell was Joel Alvarez and that stupid bitch, Fern Adams? He'd returned to the cabin where the pair had been shacked up as soon as it was safe and the police investigating that sweet thing's murder had left, only to find them gone, the cottage filled with innocent emptiness.

He'd tried to contact Glory Jordan, but that snotty cow of a receptionist had insisted she didn't know where the lawyer was, and later, when he'd walked into her office, he'd enjoyed something in the woman's tone when she recognised his face. Fear.

Not that he minded if she was afraid of him. Fear was a certain aphrodisiac; Richard had learned that at an early age. But she'd continued to tell him that she had no idea where Glory was or when she'd be back, and the more he'd listened to that slight waver in her tone, the more he'd begun to think there was something more to it than simple fear of him.

What if somehow the police had twigged to who he was? What if Glory's office was tapped, burly and brutal officers listening in, waiting for their chance to trap him and...

Richard slammed his hand against the desk, his palm slippery with sweat. A cold sweat that lingered despite the red-hot fury that surged through him.

Nothing, and no one, was going to get in the way of his plans.

He was the Avenging Angel to Joel Alvarez's Guilty Soul, and he intended to see the man molder in jail for the rest of his life—or dead. It didn't really matter which.

His brother had enjoyed the good life while Richard carried hell on his shoulders. Turn about was fair play.

****

In the Copper Junction cemetery, Chief Joseph knelt awkwardly on the frozen ground, hating the arthritis in his legs that had robbed him of a young man's agility. Tears formed in his eyes and ran unfettered down his cheeks as he leaned forward to touch the small granite headstone with his ungloved hand. "SueAnne, what have we created between us? Why wouldn't you let me care for you and love you and the boy?" He caressed the name carved into the cold stone. "No, it's wrong that I should blame you. I should have been stronger, insisted on keeping you on the straight and narrow, insisted on being a father to our boy. Whatever terrible sins our son has committed must be on my shoulders, too."

He knelt there, singing a dull keening song of sorrow from his native culture until a passerby recognized him and came to persuade him to leave the graveyard before the increasingly bitter winds carried him off to his own grave.

Chapter Twenty

The drive to Copper Junction was long and made difficult by the slick, icy covering on parts of the road once they left Highway 401. Fern was exhausted; even so, she refused to let Joel drive. Not just that she didn't trust him, but she was aware of how weak he still was and was pretty sure he wouldn't be able to handle a skid in the not unlikely event they might hit one.

The weatherman was predicting snowfall later that evening. Fern was resigned to the idea that if the weather turned before they completed their investigations they would have to book into a motel for the night. They'd need to do it before the evening rush of people wanting to stay put and avoid travelling in the bad weather. The idea of a motel room, a hot shower, and a chance to catch up on sleep was overwhelming. She doubted she'd slept for more than a few hours since she'd got the news that Joel had escaped from prison.

But the idea of an overnight stay brought with it a whole host of problems. There was no way she'd let Joel have a room of his own, oh, no, she was pretty sure he'd be gone before she woke up, taking her car and money, too, probably. And to her horror, the thought of sharing a double room with him in such close proximity sent heat rising to her cheeks and reminded her that, not so long ago, she'd been attracted in all ways to this man.

Not so long ago, until he'd murdered her sister.

But what if he was innocent? The thought constantly gnawed at her mind. *If for some reason he'd been visiting her sister and found her murdered body, why had he run away? As a trained first responder, why hadn't he called for help? Why had he let Fern herself make the grisly discovery of her sister's bloody body?*

There seemed to be no way past the fact that she had seen him with her own eyes, her sister's blood streaked on his face, his hands, his blue patterned woolen sweater…

Round and round she went, until she caught herself with eyelids drooping as she sped along the road at 40 kph over the speed limit. If she didn't pull herself together, she'd kill them both and maybe some other innocent drivers as she spun out of control.

But she really needed a break.

And that meant sharing a room with Joel Alvarez. The idea set a funny little quiver going on inside her, a reaction she remembered from the first time he'd kissed her, in the shade of some lovely old oak trees in the park in Primrose Hill, with a statue of one of the town's founders looking on. *She sighed. She hated him. She had to hate him.*

Joel had felt the tension in the car's speed ratcheting up and was relieved when he felt the vehicle slow down somewhat. If he was exhausted, then Fern must be totally worn out. She needed to rest, but he got the angry vibe from her, could sense that she was struggling with everything. *Was she feeling guilty that she'd fingered him as a killer when she had to know he was innocent?* Because he knew for certain that she was lying when she said she'd seen him running away from her sister's apartment, splattered with blood.

He knew that for sure because he'd been nowhere near that place, didn't even know where her sister lived. Had someone paid off the barista at the Wild Turkey Bar & Grill, as well? Because Joel was willing to swear on his mother's grave that he'd not been having drinks with Rose Adams that afternoon.

He'd been hiking the rugged hills around Primrose Hill, daydreaming about maybe making a life for himself in this small town. He thought of leaving behind the hectic city which had been his home since he was a child. A life perhaps with someone like Fern Adams...

A daydream that just made him feel like a fool now—like the fool she'd obviously played him for.

How could he have been so wrong about this woman?

What he couldn't figure out was why. Why did someone who didn't know him want him convicted of a terrible crime and put in jail for life? And why would Dr. Fern Adams be willing to help that person?

"Fern, I...I can't get over the idea that I've been framed." He heard her derisive snort but pressed on. If nothing else, his questions would help keep her awake until they passed somewhere they could stop.

"What I still can't get, is why? I never met you before I came to Primrose Hill, and I never met your sister, except when you introduced us. I know nobody there. Never even been that far east of Toronto before."

He heard Fern take in a ragged breath, her knuckles whitening as she gripped the steering wheel. But before she could speak, they spotted a motel sign off the highway and she sped across two lanes without signaling, to the horn blaring annoyance of cars behind them and oncoming, to follow the sign.

"Cut that a bit fine, didn't you?" he snapped. He was rewarded with a glare as Fern slammed the brakes on and parked the car in front of the motel office. Named the Copper Break, the place looked the part of a classic slightly rundown motel, something out of a horror movie, all but several steps above a rent-by-the-hour dive. There was a light on in the office window, proof against the dull clouds darkening the midafternoon. On the rear wall a television set showed the news headlines.

"Okay, we have two choices. If you come into the office with me, there's a good chance you'll be recognized. Seems the clerk has the TV tuned to the 24/7 news headlines. He or she is sure to call the cops, and you'll be arrested.

"If I leave you in the car, and when I come back you've taken off, then I'll call the cops, and you'll be arrested. Either way, you'll be back in the Primrose Hill pen before you know what hit you. So, what's it to be?"

Joel glanced sideways at Fern. Her face was set in a dark frown that convinced him she meant what she said.

"I have no intention of taking off on you," he said quietly. "After all, I need you to vouch for me when we prove that I'm innocent. I'll be right here when you get back."

Fern glanced at him, one eyebrow raised to show her disbelief. Then she nodded, gathered up her leather bag, and grabbed her jacket from the back seat. "I meant what I said. Be here when I get back."

Then she was gone, pushing against a cold wind

that blew along the car park and flirted with her hair, playing with the ends of the silk scarf she wore over her heavy Aron sweater.

Joel sat still a few moments longer after Fern had stalked away. He understood her ill temper. But was it because she really believed he was a murderer or because her inexplicable attempt to frame him might be unraveling? Was she sure he was a killer and thought looking farther afield was a waste of her time and his? In fact, she probably hated him just for planting that tiny seed of doubt in her mind about his guilt. Either way, he was surprised that she hadn't already called the police and given him up. He looked at her through the window of the motel office, seeing her straight back, the deep set of her face, her fine mouth turned downward in a scowl, the deep frown line between her eyes at odds with the rich and generous fullness of her lips. That the weather was closing in on them in Copper Junction, a one-stoplight town that, judging from her expression, wasn't doing anything to improve Fern's mood.

Crap, I wish I'd met this woman under other circumstances. He shook the thought from his mind. It was crazy to think she could ever have feelings for him. *Even if I'm ever able to prove that I didn't kill her sister, she's going to think of that terrible time every time she sees me. She's not going to remember the connection we had growing after just a couple of dates, the instant attraction...*

...and I'm going to remember how easily she was convinced I was a killer. Not much of a solid basis for a relationship. He sighed, swamped by a sense of loss of things that could have been.

Fern returned to the car and climbed into the driver's seat without a word. She slammed her door shut and put the car in gear. Ignoring Joel's questioning glance, she reversed and then turned to pull out of the parking lot and onto the road. The motel was located on the edge of town, and Fern turned right to take them towards the main street and Copper Junction central. It was a short journey.

"Not much of a place," she muttered as she parked the car in a spot on a street pockmarked by empty stores and others with signs screaming "Closing Down! Everything Must Go!"

"That should make it easier to find the doctor who signed the letters addressed to my mother."

Fern gave a derisive snort. "I know the letter was real. I read it myself. What I don't know is what it was about. This SueAnne could have been an old college chum of your mom's, a relative of this doctor who wrote to her to share the happy news that she was pregnant. Maybe she even wanted your mom to go and stand up for the baby."

"If they were such good friends, then I'm sure my mom would have mentioned it. And she'd have had photos. Mom was always snapping shots of us."

"Sometimes the best of friends grow apart. And I noticed, well, you say she was always snapping photos, but all I saw in your house, and in your mom's box of letters and photos, were pix of the family. Did your parents not socialize?"

Joel paused; his forehead creased in a frown. It was true when he thought about it. "No, we were a very self-contained family. And my parents were very close. It was like they enjoyed each other's company, and they didn't need a social life outside of that. Although they came to all my school and university events."

Fern pulled into a parking spot at the curb near a large department store. "We probably don't have much time before they roll up the sidewalks and everything closes for the day. Wait here, and I'll go ask about the doctor's office." Out on the sidewalk, Fern hesitated, then stopped a woman who was just passing by. The woman, a middle-aged matron clutching several shopping bags, stopped with the ease of smalltown folk to talk to a stranger. Hearing Fern's request, looking at the notebook where they'd scribbled down Dr. Stone's address, the woman frowned.

Joel saw the frown, then the woman said something to Fern that produced a matching frown on her face, too. Then the woman suddenly smiled. Joel pushed his way out of the car in time to hear the woman say, "…but his office is still open. Perhaps the receptionist there will be able to point you to someone who can help you."

Fern thanked the woman, who smiled and said, "You're welcome" in a way that sounded genuinely meant. Then she once more hoisted up her shopping bags and moved towards an elderly Fifth Avenue car sitting at the sidewalk several cars behind where Fern and Joel had parked.

"What was all that about?" Joel asked.

"Well, is seems that Dr. Stone was well known in town, but that woman seems to think he retired about three years ago." Seeing Joel's face fall with disappointment, Fern added, "But she gave me directions to his office, which is still open with a new medical partnership, and said the receptionist there might be able to tell us something. I guess they may still have his old records."

It took only a few minutes' walk to find the low-slung board and batten building that housed the medical clinic. The waiting room was filled with people looking in various states of illness. A man with a cast on his leg grunted a warning as they brushed past him, and several very pregnant women eyed the newcomers with varying degrees of interest.

The receptionist slid back a window and smiled a welcome. She was young enough not to have become dour with the ground down town.

"Can I help you? I'm afraid if you're looking for a doctor, we have only one partner taking new patients at the moment. Or you can see the nurse practitioner if there's an emergency, provided you don't mind waiting in line?"

"Actually, we're trying to find some information about Dr. Arthur Stone."

The young woman's smile evaporated. "Oh, dear, I am sorry. The doctor died a year or two ago. He was very old, you know. Did you know him personally?"

Fern didn't miss a beat. *She should have been an actress*, Joel thought admiringly. "Dr. Stone treated a relative of mine before she moved away quite some time ago. She's now in a nursing home—Alzheimer's, they say." Fern paused as the young receptionist made sympathetic noises. "Anyway, it seems there were some surgical issues some years ago that her current doctor needs to know about in her treatment. Unfortunately, her records didn't follow her when she moved, and of course, she can't remember what was done. I was so hoping Dr. Stone might remember or be able to check his records."

"That's dreadful! It must be such a strain for you. Alzheimer's is a terrible thing to happen to anyone. But I'm sorry. I wasn't working here when Dr. Stone retired, but I know he took all his records with him, except those for current patients."

"Perhaps his next of kin would have them or know where they went?"

The young woman's face went grave. "I don't think he had any relatives living. His only niece was SueAnne, and she's...passed away, too. But I doubt you'd have found any of his papers, anyway. Dr. Stone's house was burned down, and everything went up in smoke."

"Oh, dear. That's a shame. I would say it was a good thing the poor man wasn't at home when that happened but..."

"No, he was in the funeral parlor." The receptionist finished the sentence, looked suitably serious before adding, "It was very strange. His niece's house was burned down, too." Then pasting on a happy, competent face, she announced, "Mrs. Western, the doctor can see you now."

Fern and Joel were just exiting the building when the receptionist rushed after them. "I am so glad I caught you," she gasped, her face red from rushing. "One of the doctors remembered that Dr. Stone's nurse, a lady by the name of Hartnell, is still alive and might be able to help you. Here's her address."

The young woman held out a piece of paper, and Joel thanked her.

Outside on the sidewalk, he commented: "At last, a possible contact who may have known my mother!"

Fern gave him a hard look. "Don't get your hopes up, Joel. You may be chasing after shadows, and this woman may know nothing. Her memories could be faint after all this time, anyway."

****

"Fern, tell Joel to look up the name Phelan, SueAnne. I have a man here who claims to be Joel's birth father, says the child's mother, who wouldn't marry him, was named Phelan." Glory's voice reflected her excitement even over the hundreds of miles of cell phone signal.

"How do you know all this?" Fern couldn't keep the excitement out of her voice. At last, perhaps here might be the answer to the riddle that was holding them back, and perhaps, too, the missing link that would prove or disprove Joel's assertation that he was innocent. *Funny,she was starting to think that a tiny part of her heart was wishing he really was innocent.*

Then she shook herself, because it was so hard to let go of her belief that he was guilty.

"This gentleman is from Copper Junction." Glory was saying, "He says he saw all the information on the news, as well as heard from his local police chief that a man going by the name of Joel Alvarez appears to be the same as Richard Phelan, his son. Phelan apparently won the lottery and disappeared from the town of Copper Junction some time ago."

"But unless he's a terrific liar, and that may well be, I could swear Joel had never set foot in Copper Junction until this trip."

"Honestly, Fern, I don't know what to think. I've been behind Joel one hundred percent only I had nothing concrete to go on until I just heard this weird story from Chief Joseph and saw the photograph of his son. If it's Joel, Fern, then it's a Joel we don't know. This photo shows a different side of him. My secretary was shaken when someone who appeared to be Joel appeared in her office and, well, she said this man didn't seem like the photos she had seen of Joel. Perhaps I've been mistaken all along. Perhaps he's got multiple personality problems. Or maybe, just maybe, Joel does have a twin. An identical twin. I'm going to research twin DNA. And then there's the murder of that young student in the cottage next to mine. It's impossible for Joel to be responsible for that – he was never out of our sight, and I don't believe he could be in two places at once. Could there really be a copycat killer? There's been so little information put out about the actual murder of your sister...

"In the meantime, I'll hassle that Detective Bamber a bit to find out what the police are up to. Fern, for your own good, please take care with him. If he is this Phelan character, then being back in Copper Junction could set off all sorts of repressed memories. Keep safe and be on guard for anything strange..."

Fern gave a shaky laugh. "It seems there's been something strange going on for years. How would I tell the difference now?" And the phone was put down, leaving Glory listening to the dial tone.

Chapter Twenty-One

The motel they'd chosen on the edge of Copper Junction looked even more rundown as they returned in the foggy twilight. Fern drove into the almost deserted car park, her eyes so gritty with tiredness that she could barely hold her head up. Beside her Joel was sunk in some kind of deep fugue that had enveloped him since the news that Dr. Stone was dead. The one person who might have been able to verify his hopes about the letters he'd found. He couldn't help but wonder how much an elderly nurse might remember from nearly thirty years ago – or how much she might want to admit.

He'd reacted with the same kind of shock on the news of Lucy Lee Maxwell's murder and had drawn back into himself. Fern glanced over at him, not sure whether the news was a surprise or if somehow he'd already known. He reminded her of some of the shell-shocked victims of accidents and disasters that she'd treated as a doctor during her career in emergency medicine.

If he were a soldier, it would be easy to diagnose Joel as seeming like a man with post-traumatic stress. He certainly looked haunted.

When she stopped the car several spots down from the dimly lighted office, Fern turned to her passenger and asked if he wanted something to eat. He looked at her blankly, and with a sigh, she told him to wait where he was while she picked up the key to their room. "It's not exactly the Ritz, but after all, we have to sleep somewhere. We certainly can't sleep in the car."

But she'd lost Joel again. He was staring unseeing at some scene that was beyond her sight. She got out into the icy chill of the evening, her feet scrunching on the frozen gravel that carried a thin coating of snow as she walked to the neon sign that flashed *Office: Vacancies*. Part of the sign was blown. It flashed forlornly as if it was losing hope. Just like everything else in Copper Junction seemed to be.

The balding man behind the counter scarcely took his eyes off the television when she checked in. "Do your rooms have coffee makings in them?"

"Yep, we have an electric kettle and some of them packets of instant coffee and powdered milk. There's snacks from the vending machine outside; we don't do room service," he replied with what Fern took to be an attempt at irony. She shrugged and picked up the keys he placed on the counter. The man turned back to his television as if had Fern ceased to exist.

Quickly she returned to the car and opened the passenger door. To her relief, Joel stirred himself enough to get out of the vehicle and then to take the overnight bags they had brought. He went into the stuffy, small room while she went to the machine several doors down along with some change to buy snacks of potato chips and cookies. She added a couple of candy bars, aware that neither of them had eaten since late morning when they'd stopped at the coffee shop outside Toronto as they'd begun this odyssey.

Her stomach sour with tension, she'd passed the

point of hunger without knowing it but could feel the lethargy that low blood sugar brings. As she opened the room door she glanced at Joel's pale face, his immobile features. Perhaps coffee and some sugary confection would bring some life back into him.

Although it was likely it would require much more than that, but sugar was good for shock.

Joel looked around as if he were noting their surroundings for the first time. "You just got one room? Are you afraid I'll disappear while you sleep, or are you hoping that I will so that you can use that gun you bought?" He took a bite of a candy bar, chewed, and then asked: "Tell me about this second murder I'm supposed to have committed. When, and where, was I supposed to be when it happened?"

Fern chewed her bottom lip for a moment. If she told Joel about the murder of Lucy Lee Maxwell, he'd immediately put two and two together and point out that he couldn't have murdered the young student. And he'd know that Fern and his lawyer, Glory Jordan, would be witnesses to that fact.

And if he knew these things, would he use it to push her to believe in his innocence?

And, come to think of it, surely she had to believe he wasn't guilty of that murder. After all, weren't she and Glory with him all during that time? But that didn't exonerate him from Rose's death...

She told him this much and pointed out that the second murder could be a copycat killer. The look of hurt on his face when she obstinately refused to believe in his innocence actually made her heart hurt.

But she couldn't let go of the memory of Joel rushing away from her sister's apartment, Rose's blood on his clothes and hands…

"So even knowing I couldn't have killed the second poor woman, you still won't give me a break?"

His tone was bitter, and Fern's cheeks flamed. "Can you blame me for not trusting you? I still don't know who the hell you are."

He gave a grim smile. "Neither do I, Fern. Neither do I."

****

"Sir…er, boss, er…" Bamber looked up from the papers he was studying on his desk, not hiding his irritation as Lee Groves rushed into the room. "Sir, I've just been going over the material on Brown's laptop computer…you know, the guy who was murdered by Alvarez in the hospital?"

Bamber nodded impatiently. *Of course he remembered who Brown was. Alverez' third murder victim.* There was a second, Lucy Lee Maxwell, possibly a copycat, and Fern Adams was missing….

"Well, he's been very discreet, but from what I can tell, the man works as a kind of private investigator. Unlicensed but carrying out various jobs for people. That's what he meant by Facilitator. His main customer seems to be a guy named Brown and, from what I saw, it seems like this Brown was paying this Facilitator to get someone who was housebound out of hospital and then to watch him."

"So? Who was he hiring? A nursing service?"

"Not a nursing service. I looked at his list of contacts. One of them is Kerry Loman…you know, the Candy Striper imitator who got Alvarez out of jail, we got his business card from her. My guess would be that this Mr. Brown is actually Phelan, but I can't see how

Alvarez/Phelan could have made these arrangements. For one thing, I asked, and he didn't have access to computer email or texts during the time he was in the pen. I also checked bank records. Alvarez hadn't made any withdrawals or sent money to anyone other than the agency looking after his house in Toronto. We got a look at Slater's bank accounts, and there are large sums of money coming in at erratic intervals. Nothing to match Alvarez' account, but they roughly match the dates of the prison attack on Alvarez, and another large amount into Slater's account around the time of Alvarez' escape from the hospital. Then there's a large debit, which matches the information from Kerry Lomond.

"Could it have been Alvarez using an assumed name who hired this man?"

"I don't know, sir. It doesn't sound like that, given the information about his computer access in the jail or his bank transactions. Maybe Alvarez is cleverer than we give him credit for. However, even if he had managed to access a computer without the authorities knowing, outgoing and ingoing emails, and search histories, would be checked out routinely by prison officials. At least, that's what the deputy warden told me. Ditto for any online financial activity.

"The computer crimes lab is going through Slater's laptop and his bank accounts, trying to trace the email and IM address. They've given it priority, so we should have something soon."

Bamber raised his eyebrows. "Well done!" The young office blushed with pleasure. *Well, well, seems like Groves isn't as dumb as he looks. Maybe I can make a cop out of him yet.* Bamber grinned as he stared at Groves, his mind working furiously. Was this Mr. Brown Joel himself? But how could he possibly have access to computer or email services from inside the prison without it being noted and checked by prison officials? The poor bastard hadn't even had any visitors he could have roped in to help. Or was it someone, Phelan maybe, assuming Alvarez and Phelan were two different people, who hated Alvarez so much he was willing to go to great lengths, great cost and risk, to get the man out of jail? And what did he intend to do now? Execute Alvarez?

And what would happen to Fern Adams, who was probably with Joel?

Then another thought struck him again, causing a shiver to run down his spine. *What if Fern Adams herself was planning to execute her sister's killer?*

"Lee, would you do a search and find out if Fern Adams has a gun license?"

Groves' eyebrows rose to his hairline. "You think that maybe…Oh my God, that would explain her behavior! She wants to do what the courts didn't—give her sister what in her eyes would be justice!"

****

Getting a room with two beds, instead of separate rooms, had been a big mistake. Fern lay in her own narrow bed, totally conscious of Joel just a few inches away from her, within touching distance. And he was restless, tossing and turning just as she was.

Her heart ached with accusation that she was so aware of the man who all the evidence suggested had murdered her sister. And yet there was still, beneath the hatred she stoked in her mind for him, a sense of attraction, physical, mental. *And what if Joel was an innocent man, somehow caught up in some kind of weird plot*...but she couldn't get past the reality of seeing him with her own eyes, running from her sister's apartment...

Fern said a prayer that morning would come quickly, and they'd be able to get on with the task at hand. Which, she persuaded herself, was to prove Joel's guilt and free her from this burning doubt that had slunk into her consciousness as she spent more time with him.

What about the second murder? Was it possible that enough details had been put out for a crazy monster to commit a copycat crime?

She turned over and tried to plump up the flat and saggy pillow. There was no way that Joel was out of her sight for long enough to have done what was done to that poor child.

If he was innocent, then some awful miscarriage of justice had been done. And she, Fern Adams, had been a major part of that injustice. *Would he ever forgive her?*

Just a few feet away from her, Joel rolled over and groaned as he pressed against the wounds on his side and back. He struggled to find a more comfortable spot on the thin, worn mattress, but in his heart he knew he couldn't sleep. Not with Fern so close he could smell the faint ghost of her perfume and the underlying notes of that fragrance that was just Fern herself, close enough to touch, to hold...no! He needed to nurse the anger he felt towards the woman who'd accused him, on whose word he had been investigated and convicted.

Sure, other people had lied, like the barista at the pub who claimed he and Rose had been there laughing and drinking together all that afternoon. Dear God, what moved people to do such things, to lie and cut away the life of another person?

Because sure, he hadn't been sentenced to death—there is no death penalty in Canada. But he may as well have been executed, rather than live with this pain and hurt and anger, the injustice of it all. To say nothing of twenty-five years moldering in prison...

And the betrayal of the woman next to him stung a much as the longing for her.

Morning couldn't come quick enough as far as Joel was concerned. They'd got the name of a nurse who had worked with Dr. Stone, and tomorrow they would visit her. Somewhere, out in this rundown little town, lay the answer to all his questions, and he wanted to get out and find them. Whether Fern believed him or not.

****

Bamber slammed the phone down. His colleague, the country cop in Copper Junction, had come up with news that threw the whole case into a new light...and created even more confusion. He punched in a familiar number on his cell, experiencing again the shiver of pleasure and exasperation at her voice.

"Ms. Jordan, I want the truth. Are Fern Adams and Joel Alvarez in Copper Junction? And please remember, it's a citizen's duty not to lie to the police. And that goes double for an officer of the court."

"If I tell you where they are and what they're doing, will you give me one piece of information?"

"I'm not in the business of bargaining, Ms. Jordan." The silence that followed was thick. He capitulated, with the brief thought that Glory Jordan was a hard woman to refuse. "All right, one question, if I can answer it without jeopardizing my case."

Her heard her sigh. "Yes, Fern and Joel are in Copper Junction. Joel seems to think he might have relatives there, and they will somehow prove his innocence. You do know that Fern and I were with Joel when poor Lucy Lee Maxwell was murdered.? There's no way he could have committed that crime."

"I wish I could believe you. Seems both of you have a dog in this fight."

"I just want what Joel wants, to prove his innocence."

"And is that what Fern wants? That Joel Alvarez be proven innocent of her sister's murder?" Bamber couldn't keep the question out of his tone.

Silence stretched. He could imagine her biting her lip with her upper teeth. He'd seen her do that so often in court, and it never failed to charm him.

"I am not sure what Fern wants. She wants justice for her sister. But whether that means she wants Joel to be innocent when she believes she saw him at her sister's murder scene, well, I don't want to speculate. I'm not sure she knows herself. I am afraid for them both." Her next words shocked him. "John, Joel believes Fern has a gun, and Fern hasn't denied it."

Bamber's stomach clenched. *A woman with a mission of vengeance. Would Fern Adams, a doctor sworn to heal, be willing to execute a man she believes is the cold-blooded killer of the sister she loved?*

****

Richard Phelan was already on the road, nearing the town where he'd been born and raised—if you could call his horrific childhood being raised. He allowed himself a little smile as he remembered the feel of his hands around his mother's neck, choking her life away, the expression in her eyes as she realized that she was about to die at the hands of the son she had used and allowed others to abuse, too.

Was she most upset about imminent death, or about the fact that she would never get a share of the incredible wealth that little lottery ticket had brought him? Richard grimaced. *He figured it was probably the latter; his money-grubbing parent had always dreamed of being rich and admired, sought after by a better quality of male than the ones who'd found their way to her door drawn by her reputation as a whore who'd do anything for money and gifts—even allow them access for playtime with her young son.*

Richard drew over to the side of the highway, threw open his car door, and leaned out to throw up on the gravel shoulder. Over and over his body was shaken with the violence that wrenched him. Finally, when he had recovered, he felt a steely new determination.

He was near Copper Junction, the town that had stood by while he was tortured and used. He was going to make the whole town pay—and especially that bitch of a nurse who'd aided that bastard doctor to get SueAnne Phelan to sell one of her twins and keep the other hostage as a money-making investment. He had to get to her before Joel and that interfering cow Fern got there, because the interfering nurse was sure to spill her guts about the things that had happened…

And then there's be one last loose end to tie up. Joel and Fern were going to go down in a blaze of glory. Then his brother would be moldering in a cold grave while he took off on a flight to a nice warm Caribbean Island where his winnings were stashed. He was going to lead a life that would heal his childhood…

Chapter Twenty-Two

The receptionist at the medical clinic had given them the address of retired nurse Hartnell who had worked for Dr. Stone at about the time the letters Joel had found were dated. They drove to the address, a sprawling bungalow in a quiet, working-class area of the town. There was a small front lawn, graced by a pear tree, leafless now as winter closed in, but decorated with several bird feeders that appeared to be very popular with the local redwings, chickadees, and grackles. A couple of fat robins took flight from the lawn as Joel and Fern walked up the paved path to the green front door.

"Mrs. Hartnell?"

The woman who answered their knock looked to be in her eighties, tall and big boned, her large frame stooped but still strong. The retired nurse cast a sour eye on Fern. "Who wants to know?"

"Mrs. Hartnell, we got your name and address from the receptionist at the medical clinic."

"That girl's a fool! She should know better than give out personal information to strangers. Now go away."

"Please, Mrs. Hartnell—if you could just spare us a moment of your time?" Fern tried again.

"No. I'm busy. I've got a soap opera to watch. And after that, another soap opera. No time for you." Her

Glenys O'Connell

voice dripped irony and made Fern think that perhaps this woman hated the idea of retirement, of not being busy.

She took out glasses from her sweater pocket and perched them on her broad nose. She looked more closely at Joel and then stepped back with a little gasp and began to push the door shut. "Go away, Ricky Phelan. I won't have the likes of you in my house!"

Fern's heart seemed to leap in her chest. Phelan was the name Glory had mentioned as being Joel's other persona. The bright day around her darkened, and she struggled not to give in to the shock and faint right away on this woman's doorstep. *Had she all the time being consorting with Joel's alter ego, the madman? This woman thought Joel was someone named Ricky Phelan. How could she tell which persona was in control?*

"I hate that we're intruding on you like this, Mrs. Hartnell, and I don't know who you think I am…this Phelan character? But you're probably the only person who can help me," Joel intervened quickly. "My mother died recently, and I discovered that she had a relative in Copper Junction, someone that Dr. Stone wrote to her about. A woman who was having a baby. This is thirty years ago, and perhaps you won't remember—"

"There's nothing wrong with my memory, young man. Nothing at all."

"Well, I wondered if maybe you could remember the names of some of Dr. Stone's patients…particularly someone called SueAnne? I don't have any other family, you see. I'd really like to see if this relative of my mom's is still around."

The old woman stared at him for a few moments,

chewing her lip as she considered his words. She'd lost her ruddy color, and Fern wondered giddily if this fainting thing was catching. But she wasn't prepared for the old woman's next words.

"You're not Richard Phelan, you say? Drop your pants, turn around, and let me see your butt, young man."

Joel spluttered, his face reddening with embarrassment. "I'm not exactly sure what—"

"Just do as I say. Let me see your butt. Otherwise, I'm on the phone to the police so fast it'd make your head spin. And don't think you can stop me. This little beauty here says not." Quick as a flash, the woman had reached into the corner by the door, and now Fern and Joel were staring into the cold eye of a gleaming shotgun.

"Dear God." Fern stepped back, heart beating frantically as she wondered just how good a shot the old woman was, and how fast she was on the trigger.

Faster than they could run, for sure.

"Dammit, Joel! Show the lady your butt and stop being such a shrinking violet." The words sounded strangled to her own ears, but they had a galvanizing effect on Joel. He finally managed to tear his gaze away from the deadly metal snout of the gun barrel and turn his back to them. Jeans snaps popped, zipper grated, and then the two women were gazing at Joel's interesting rear end.

"Well, smack me silly with a dead beaver's tail," Mrs. Hartnell finally managed. "Do you see that birthmark on his right butt cheek? The one shaped like a lopsided heart? Well, that there means that this young man is not Richard Phelan." The woman sighed and, to

Fern's relief, set the shotgun aside.

"You two young people had better come inside. Oh, don't forget to do up your skivvies, boy. Much as we might like the view here."

With a lewd wink at a still blushing Fern, she turned and led the way into her home.

So, a heart-shaped birthmark on his butt meant that Joel Alvarez was not Richard Phelan, the man Glory had been talking about.

Did it also mean he wasn't a murderer? Flimsy evidence, indeed.

Mrs. Hartnell's parlor, as she called it, was furnished with an overstuffed, comfortable settee and loveseat, and with an old, much used, recliner facing a large-screen television. A pile of magazines spilled out of the chair's pocket, and Joel glanced idly at the titles. The subjects ranged from nursing magazines to celebrity news to knitting and crochet. A woman of eclectic tastes, this Mrs. Hartnell.

And, it seemed, a connoisseur of men's rear ends and birth marks. His cheeks bloomed red as he remembered that humiliating moment on her doorstep when he'd given thanks for the luxuriant bushes that grew alongside the front steps and kindly hid his mooning from the rest of the neighborhood.

He glanced over at Fern, standing against a backdrop of violet-scattered wallpaper and crisp white lace curtains, and wondered if she'd read his mind because she grinned ear to ear when she caught his eye.

"You tell anyone about this, Fern Adams, and I'll—"

"What? You'll kill me?"

And the moment of relaxed humor between them

disappeared like good scotch at a doctors' convention.

Mrs. Hartnell bustled into the room, glancing curiously at the two young people who stood facing each other like armed combatants. She put down the tray she carried and began to pour tea into good China cups with saucers, and to offer around a plate of fresh baked muffins.

"Never had time for all this social nicety nice stuff, housework, decorating, and baking, not when I worked as a nurse. I've been retired twelve years now, and I've finally developed a few housekeeping and hospitality skills," she said, settling herself into the recliner. "When you two young folk quit staring at each other, maybe you'd sit down and get around to telling me what all this is about."

"Perhaps you'd answer a question for me first? Why did you want to see my butt?"

The woman's lips curled upwards in a mischievous smile. "Now, I may be old, but I'm not dead. Nothing like a firm young rear—"

"You know it was more than that." Joel wasn't smiling and he ignored Fern's snort of laughter.

The older woman added extra sugar to her tea and stirred thoughtfully, the spoon against the delicate China making a ringing sound in the suddenly quiet room.

"Let's say I want to hear your story first. Then, if it seems worthwhile, I'll tell you mine. You say you're looking for a relative or something to do with Dr. Stone?"

Joel hesitated. "As far as I can tell, it was SueAnne something. And my mom's last name was Alvarez, but that was her married name."

"Not much to go on, is it? Do you know how many patients Dr. Stone treated over fifty years in practice?" Mrs. Hartnell snorted.

"Mrs. Hartnell, it's possible the woman's name was Phelan," Fern put in, acting on a sudden hunch.

The woman's face paled. "Who are you really, and why are you looking for SueAnne Phelan? Tell me the truth, now."

Taken aback, Fern was lost for words. She saw Joel's questioning look and explained, "Glory Jordan, a lawyer, told me that a man called Chief had come into her office, claiming to be the father of Richard Phelan, who apparently is from Copper Junction and in some way we don't understand, may be related to Joel Alvarez here."

Joel just sat there, stunned. Shaking his head as if it would help clear his thoughts, he said, "Whoever this Richard Phelan is, he's not me. I've never set foot in Copper Junction before, and I've never heard of the Chief or of Richard or SueAnne Phelan. I got the name SueAnne from a letter my mother had kept. I don't know anything about…"

Mrs. Hartnell grasped the arms of her chair. Fern moved towards her; the woman's sudden paleness made her afraid she was going to have a heart attack. But then an odd look came over the nurse's face. Carefully she moved back into the seat, rocking herself backward and forward as she stared at a picture on the wall.

"That boy there is my son. Leon. He died in Vietnam. After he was gone, my husband never lifted his head. He died of broken heart less than five years afterwards. Oh, they called it cancer, but I knew it for what it was. His heart was broken because he lost his boy.

"You see, some parents love their children so much that when they lose them, they die a little themselves. Every day. Some parents care for their children, look after them, keep them safe. Because he couldn't keep our boy safe, my husband died himself.

"But life wasn't like that for little Richard Phelan. His mother was a flighty piece with lots of boyfriends, and she refused to let old Chief Joseph—or young Chief, then—even have the satisfaction of knowing if the boy was his or not. Though, she still took the money he gave her."

Fern had slipped back onto the settee beside Joel, but her tense body language said it all. She couldn't relax with him. Joel's hands curved into fists. *When he found out what was happening, what had turned his life—who had turned his life—into this living nightmare, there was going to be all hell to pay.*

Sarah Hartnell slumped back into her leather recliner, seeming smaller in stature as though she'd let out so much pain and anger that she'd shrunk. Joel started to speak, but Fern laid a hand on his arm to keep him still, her glance telling him that the nurse hadn't finished her story.

"Could you get me a glass of water?" the older woman said to Fern. "The glasses are in the cupboard above the sink."

When Fern had left the room, she returned her attention to Joel. "Why are you here? How did you know…Why did you come back?"

"I don't know what you mean. I've never been in Copper Junction before, and I've never heard of anybody called Richard Phelan until just now. I

273

honestly haven't a clue what's going on, but somehow it seems my entire life has been turned upside down. Everywhere I look, someone is accusing me of something awful that I didn't do, and I'm beginning to despair that I'll ever get to the bottom of it. You should know that I have been convicted of murder, the murder of a woman I met only once…"

Fern returned with the water. "Joel Alvarez has been convicted of murder, just so you know, but he's trying to convince everyone he didn't do it."

The nurse grimaced. "Well, honey, you must be pretty convinced of his innocence if you're traveling with him. And how come you're not in jail, young man? Do I need to be afraid?" Nurse Hartnell bit her lip. "So you're the one all the fuss has been about, that's supposed to have raped and murdered that young woman. I guess I can assume that you're not out and about on a good behavior pass?"

Joel tensed. Would this woman call the cops and hand him over? Had she already called them when in her kitchen under the pretense of being hospitable?

"I read about you. The woman you're with is the sister of the one you supposedly killed? What's she up to?"

"Gathering evidence to put him back in jail," Fern snapped.

"You see, Mrs. Hartnell, you may be the only person in the world who can help me prove my innocence. Except, that is, for the real murderer. And I need to get some evidence that exonerates me before the cops get here."

The older woman was quiet for a few moments. Then she turned to Fern. "Is he forcing you to be here?

Do you want to escape?"

Fern shook her head. "No, I'm sticking like glue with him until he either proves he's innocent or runs out of options."

"And if the latter happens?"

The look on Fern's face told the other woman everything she needed to know.

"So, Joel, what do you want from me? Why do you think I can help you?"

"Because you worked with Dr. Arthur Stone."

"Joel, or Richard, or whoever he is, was a hero firefighter in Toronto. He rescued a pregnant woman from a burning building, among other heroic acts. All his friends liked him; his coworkers respected him. He claims he had adopted parents who loved him..."

Nurse Hartnell sat up so suddenly drops of water spilled onto her crisp white blouse. "So, I am right. You have come back!"

"No, I told you—" Joel bit back his protest as the old woman held up her hand.

"I told you I knew who you are. I just wasn't sure *which* you are. But you don't look like the other one. I've often thought, over the years, that the eyes are the windows to the soul. When I look into your eyes, I see...I see something good. The last time I saw...the other, his eyes showed me...emptiness. Emptiness and hate."

The old woman fell silent again. After a few minutes, Fern stood. "I think we'd better go. We've upset you, Mrs. Hartnell, and I'm sorry for that."

"No, we're not leaving until—" Joel snapped.

Mrs. Hartnell nodded and gestured to Fern to sit. "It's time someone talked about what happened. I've held it in for a long time, but I never felt it was right. I warned Dr. Stone that no good would come of what he did. That Phelan woman, she was never fit to have a child. I actually thought it was a relief when Dr. Stone persuaded her to have an adoption. I vowed I wouldn't tell anyone. Dr. Stone, you understand, was a good man in many ways. He understood that sometimes children should go to parents who'll love them, but instead they are born to parents who aren't fit for the job."

Fern nodded in sudden understanding. "He arranged adoptions?"

Joel sat forward, his gut telling him that he was finally onto something that would explain the nightmare his life had become. "My mother had a letter from the doctor, saying that SueAnne was near to delivery, and he'd let her know when the baby was delivered."

"Yes, you see…your parents had agreed to pay Dr. Stone for his services, and SueAnne, who would get half the money, was agreeable to giving up the child for adoption. It never seemed wrong, although it was maybe against the law then. The rules were a bit muddy. When you saw the happiness it brought the adoptive people, and how it solved the problems of the reluctant mothers…

"But when she finally delivered, she gave birth to two little boys. Identical twins. Somehow Dr. Stone, who was getting on in years, had missed whatever telltale signs there might have been. We didn't have the luxuries of advanced testing and scanning that they did in the bigger centers, and SueAnne didn't have medical coverage."

Joel felt the blood drain from his face. This

explained so much. He was not one. He was part of another. He leaned back against the nubbly fabric of the settee, his face drained of color, and Fern shot him a worried glance.

"But what happened? Why weren't both babies adopted?" Joel asked in a voice so weak the two woman had to lean closer to hear him.

"Oh, that SueAnne, she saw a way to have her cake and eat it. She would only allow one child to go. She kept the other as a meal ticket. Both the Chief, who thought he was the father, and the social welfare department, paid her for the child's upkeep because she was a single, unemployed mother. Chief Joseph never knew about the other child.

"It was a living scandal in the town, how that boy was abused and neglected. And, and later…later there were rumors that various men paid her for…well, that the child was abused." Nurse Hartnell's ruddy cheeks had flushed crimson as she spoke.

Joel stood, hand over his mouth. "Can I use your washroom? I'm sorry…"

He rushed from the room as she aimed garbled directions to him.

When they were alone, Fern said bitterly, "So there are two boys, one of them brought up as a pampered only child, the other brought up to abuse, neglect— sexual abuse, perhaps. Do you think Richard Phelan could have grown to hate his brother?"

"My dear, Richard Phelan hated everyone. Himself, most of all. There's a rumor that he killed his mother when he left to go to Toronto. He won the lottery; they say the devil takes care of his own. And Copper Junction breathed a sigh of relief when he left.

We all hoped he'd never be back, and when I saw your young man at the door...well, you probably saw the expression on my face."

Your young man. Fern bit her lip. The niggling little thought she'd been suppressing since she'd first seen him finally emerged: in other circumstances, she was sure she'd have been happy to have Joel as her young man.

But after all she'd done, all she'd accused him of, after their past history, there was no way there would ever be a relationship between them. He would never be her young man.

And that thought left her feeling strangely desolate, as if she'd lost something very, very precious.

As they were leaving, nurse Hartnell put a hand on Joel's arm. "Take care of yourself, my dear. If you cross swords with Richard Phelan...well, he's dangerous, and he'll have no love for you."

Chapter Twenty-Three

Fern tossed and turned that night, sleep teasingly out of her reach as she tried to assimilate all that they'd learned that day. She and Joel had travelled back to the motel in deep silence, neither of them ready yet to discuss the implications of what the nurse had told them.

Yet the knowledge that what they'd learned could change everything hovered between them like a grey cloud that couldn't be denied. If Sarah Hartnell was to be believed, then Joel had a twin. An identical twin. They were hard to tell apart, she knew. When she was in school there'd been a pair of identical twins whose total likeness had allowed them to drive poor Mrs. Harrington, the teacher, out of her mind with their tricks.

Tears formed in Fern's eyes; tears she couldn't allow to fall. In her heart she searched the ramifications of what they'd learned.

The reality was that she may have given evidence that convicted an innocent man.

And worse than that, she had planned to deliver justice herself. A doctor. A woman committed to saving lives. And she may easily have robbed an innocent man of his life.

And how could she know? How could she possibly know the truth that Joel wasn't a murderer, especially when everything pointed towards him?

That ignorance was no excuse. *Could the man whose life she had ruined ever forgive her?*

Her heart ached with the desire to reach over, to touch him as he lay sleeping just a couple of feet away, to ask for forgiveness.

Then her mind threw up objections. There were other questions that needed answering before she stepped out of her safe zone. Was it even true that there was a twin, a living twin who was identical to Joel?

She remembered reading an article years before, about how identical twins were so close that, even when separated at birth, they recognized each other. Even felt the loss of the other one without being aware he or she truly existed. Fern had thought it really weird at the time, but now it threw up questions.

The obvious one being: what if Joel and his twin already knew of each other, were actually working together? A murderous, insane, tag team?

That would explain the attack on poor Lucy Lee Maxwell. If the other brother had done this, it gave a very real alibi to Joel… Just like when the twins back in her primary school had used their looks to tease their teacher. But these grown-up twins could be using their apparent identical looks to confuse law enforcement and witnesses while they went about committing terrible crimes? Both she and Glory had witnessed the fact that Joel was with them when Lucy Lee Maxwell was murdered. Or was he? How identical were the two brothers? With the doctor who delivered the babies dead, his records all destroyed, they only had the evidence of an elderly nurse that there even had been twins, one with a heart shaped birthmark on his ass.

Fern smiled at the memory of Joel's embarrassment. But how trustworthy was the woman's evidence, after all these years?

How could they prove who was a good guy and who an evil murderer?

Joel was shifting in the bed, the sheets pushed down around his waist. Looking over at him, Fern was ashamed to see that his wounds had not been attended to throughout their journey and were weeping through the fabric of his tee shirt.

Whatever she may think the man was guilty of, there was no excuse for her, as a doctor, to risk him developing septicemia or some other hard to treat, or even fatal, condition through her own negligence.

Swinging her legs out of the bed, she leaned over and gently shook his shoulder. Joel blinked, looking confused, and it took him several moments to realize where he was. When he saw the motel room, and Fern leaning over him, his face clouded. "I was dreaming," he muttered. "I was dreaming I was home in my own bed."

He didn't add that Fern had been part of that dream, and in that dream, she'd been looking at him in a far different way. A way that had made his heart speed up.

Then he awoke to reality. "What is it? Do we need to …"

"Your wounds need dressing. Hadn't you noticed it was leaking and sticking to your shirt?"

Joel looked down at himself. There was a widening circle of pinky clear fluid sticking his shirt to his flesh. Fern had left her bed and was returning with her small traveling medical case, which she opened and took out cleaning pads and bandages while Joel picked up the television remote and turned the set on to the national news. He winced and gasped a little as Fern gently pulled his shirt away from the reddened area, checking the surgical scar as well as the stab wound on his back. She clicked her tongue and reached for the cleaning pads.

"This is going to sting, but we have to clean it up. It's imperative that the area of the stitches be kept clean," she muttered.

"Oh, my lord!" Joel exclaimed, his face pale.

"Come on, it can't hurt that much," Fern muttered, pulling out another surgical wipe.

Joel grabbed her hand. "No, no, not the wounds! Look at the television, Fern! I'm on television but it can't be!"

Fern turned in time to see footage of Joel wearing a white coat and clutching a stethoscope, walking along what was obviously a hospital corridor.

"What the hell?"

"Look at the time stamp on the security camera footage, Fern. Look at the time stamp!" Joel winced as he tried to sit up on the bed.

Fern gasped, her face losing color. "That's yesterday's date. That's the Primrose Hill Hospital, I know it well."

"But what else do you see?"

Fern chewed on her bottom lip as the television footage moved on after the presenter described the "doctor" on the video as escaped prisoner Joel Alvarez, who had allegedly murdered a patient at the hospital while pretending to be an attending physician. She swallowed around the lump in her throat, and almost whispered: "That was yesterday. That's yesterday's date. And it can't have been you...you were here in Copper Junction."

Joel smiled. "Yes, I was here in Copper Junction, with you, not at a hospital masquerading as a doctor. And even if you try to deny it, at the time stamped on the film footage, I was with you and the nurse. She could testify for me that I was in her home at that time. I didn't murder a man in the hospital.

"And I didn't murder Lucy Lee Maxwell, because I was with you and Glory Jordan."

"But what about my sister? Who were you with then?" Fern snapped.

Joel's face clouded. "I was alone. I was walking around the lake, taking the scenic route, and wondering what it would be like to live in such a quiet, pleasant little town as Primrose Hill." He grimaced. "That little fantasy sure got shot to pieces. I wish to God I had never seen the place."

And he must wish he'd never met me, Fern thought, swallowing a sudden wave of sadness.

She helped Joel pull on a clean tee shirt and sweater and left him to finish getting dressed. "I just have to step outside, but don't go anywhere," she told him. She picked up her purse, checked her cell phone was inside and charged up, and stepped out of the room without another word.

Outside in the chill of a Northern winter, Fern shivered as she used her gloveless fingers to hit a number she knew by heart, So many questions, so few answers. Fern sighed. Then her eyes opened wide. The word DNA flashed in her mind like a beacon. Could DNA testing tell them apart? What about fingerprints?

Was there any way of knowing which was the Good Twin and which was the Evil Twin? Or were they both…?

A question she hoped the woman who answered the call, sounding groggy and obviously had just woken up from sleep.

"Morgan—I'm so sorry! Were you asleep?"

"Yes, Fern, I pulled an all-nighter last night and was catching up."

"Maybe I should call back later."

The other woman must have heard the disappointment in her voice because she immediately said, "What's wrong, hon? You sound, well, odd."

Fern was silent for as moment, shivering a little as she sought shelter from the biting wind in an alcove by the junk food dispensing machine. Then she swallowed and dove right in.

"Look, I can't talk very long. I am so sorry. I didn't realize what the time was. I can call back…"

"No, no. I know you wouldn't be calling at this hour unless it was important. Are you in trouble?"

"Everything's okay. Just…don't ask me any questions, okay?

She heard Morgan's sharp intake of breath. "All right, if you'll answer just one question first. You're not in any trouble, are you?"

Fern laughed—a sound that sounded false even to her own ears. If only Morgan knew the truth. Her fingers were slippery with a cold sweat as she held the cell phone to her ear. "Why do you ask?" She was sure Morgan must be able to hear the pounding of her heart, bad reception or no. She leaned back in the motel wall, her head against the cold cement block.

"Because that rather yummy detective—Bamber— was around looking for you, and he seemed a bit stressed. Or a lot stressed. Told me they'd tried to contact you at Glory Jordan's cottage, but you weren't there any longer."

Fern sat up suddenly, her stomach muscles clenching. "I called him to let him know I was taking time off. You know, with all this stuff about Joel Alvarez."

"Yeah, I can imagine you'd feel better out of the way until that creep's back behind bars."

"Morgan, we're friends, aren't we?"

"'Course we are, sweetie. What, do you want us to spit on our palms and vow friendship forever? Like we did as kids?" Laughter threaded through the other woman's voice.

"I need the answer to a question that's plaguing me, and I don't want you to tell anyone else that I asked, right? Or ask any questions. For the sake of our friendship."

"My, this is mysterious. Just what have you gotten involved with, Fern?"

"Can you do this for me, or not?"

Another deep sigh at the end of the line. "Okay, honey, but I want you to promise me you'll take care of yourself and tell me everything as soon as you can, okay?"

Fern had to stifle the little sob that threatened to spill out into the brightening dawn. "What I want to know, Morgan, is if someone had an identical twin, could they be differentiated by their DNA? Don't they have the same DNA?"

The silence at the other end was so thick you could

cut it with a knife. "Fern. I don't know where you're going with this. Have you heard from Alvarez? Is he trying to sell you the idea he had a twin? Because he's an only child, according to the records."

"No, really. This is for something else entirely. "

"Okay. I'm not sure I believe you, but you sound pretty desperate. Yes, identical twins do have identical DNA."

"It sounds like you have a 'but' in there." Fern swallowed hard.

"Yes, but there is more and more progress being made all the time. Probably if you go deep enough with the tests, there's a way of differentiating. It's just not a common test right now."

"But it is possible?"

"Some researchers are working on it, you know. Aller genomes and things like that. Apparently, it can be done, but it isn't often done. It's complicated."

"Nope, you lost me there, kiddo. I'm just a humble doctor. I leave that other stuff to the intellectuals like you."

Morgan laughed, and the strained link between them eased.

"Well, I'm off back to bed, then do a little walking in the woods tomorrow, then lunch out in the heated porch overlooking the lake." Guilt rose in Fern's chest about the convenient lie, but it was essential to keep up the pretense that she was relaxing at a lakeside cottage.

"Sounds like heaven. Take care of yourself. Don't run afoul of any stray hunters."

"I'll be careful, honest."

"And bring me back some maple syrup. It's a good area, up there. And Fern?"

"Yes?"

"If you are in trouble, you'll call for help, won't you?"

"You'll be first on my list."

Fern rang off and put the cell phone back in her pocket. There was one more call she had to make, but she had to think hard about it. Meanwhile, she needed to check on Joel.

****

The motel room, clean but worn, felt so empty after Fern had left. Her excuse about getting more junk food rang hollow, and he'd thought of going after her, but his mind felt empty after the initial excitement of Dr. Hartnell's revelations followed by the security footage on the TV news that showed someone who looked just like him, but wasn't him, couldn't be him. He had a brother? A twin?

His body was an empty chrysalis, dried in the sun, the life once there now flown away. At least, that's how he felt at that moment.

When Fern arrived back in the room clutching some snacks, she found Joel lying on the bed, pale and looking more defeated than she had seen him so far.

"Are you in pain? Have the stitches broken? You know you should be resting more."

He shook his head, and the lost, haunted look in his eyes almost broke through the icy barrier she'd tried to maintain between them. She sat down on the edge of the bed and took his hand, shocked at how cold his fingers felt in hers. "I'll get my medical bag. You might be running a fever." But as she began to stand, he held more tightly to her hand and pulled her back down.

His voice was low, almost defeated, as he began to

speak. "I always felt a bond between myself and Jim and Mattie Alvarez. They were my parents, Goddammit! The idea that they maybe weren't my parents is like a sledgehammer to the gut." Joel's hand moved to rest on his stomach, as if to protect himself from such a blow. "Now…now, I don't know who I am, who they were…and do I have a twin brother?

"And if I do have a twin brother, is he the same person who murdered your sister and then ran away? Is he, this Richard character, is he behind all the things that are happening? Everything I have been blamed for? Why would someone I have never met, my own flesh and blood, why would he hate me so much?" Joel's voice slid into a sound so like a sob that Fern's heart skipped a beat.

"I don't know what's happening, Joel," she began tentatively. "Everything has been turned on its head. I know you didn't kill Lucy Lee Maxwell. We were with you when that poor child was murdered, Glory and I."

"And I couldn't have killed the man who died in the hospital. I was on the road with you, and I doubt they'd consider you an accomplice. And yet they have footage of me, or a man they say is me, walking away down the corridors. If he is my brother, he must look a hell of a lot like me!"

Tears formed in Fern's eyes as she realized that the weight of evidence had shifted, and it now appeared that Joel might well be an innocent man. Her heart soared at the implications, and yet…and yet…

She got up quickly to go hide in the bathroom before she broke down. But Joel still held tightly to her hand, and she sat back down. Leaning over him, before she could even think of what she was doing, she

288

captured his mouth in a deep, hungry, desperate kiss.

Then she jumped up, pulled her hand from his, and rushed out of the room.

Tremors like earthquake shock ran through Joel's body, and he thought perhaps Fern was right and he must be running a fever. Because only with a high fever could he hallucinate such a kiss, or the surge of pleasure it brought. A fever that was heightened when Fern, her cheeks flushed, came tentatively back to him.

The relief he felt in knowing that he didn't have some sort of split personality, that he wasn't crazy, surged through him when he reached out to take Fern in his arms. How long had he wanted to hold her? And at the same time, he had battled with hating her for what she had done to him. But now…now all that mattered was the two of them together, the heat of their bodies burning through their clothes as their mouths met and melded and the world outside, the past, all had fallen away to be nothing more than this moment.

Wanting, needing, longing, suppressed rose in and joined the two of them like a fever as they pulled at clothes, desperate to feel heated skin and all the softness and hardness that heralded lovemaking.

As his hands found her breast, and Fern gasped with pleasure and slipped her hands underneath his T-shirt, she felt the dressings on his wounds and froze. "Oh, God, you have been through so much. You could have died in that jail, and it would have been all my fault."

Reluctantly Joel moved a little away, creating a slim space between them. "Whatever has happened, it's over now. I can't blame you for believing that I killed your sister, not when you saw someone just like me running away. In fact, I admire the tenacity that you followed up the desire to get justice for Rose, because you loved her.

"It's over now. We'll find my twin, or the police will, and then we will be free of all this. But just now, all I want in this world is to make love to you, to have this time together before everything hits the fan."

At his words, Fern melted back against his hard body, feeling herself becoming hot and boneless with a need so deep running through her that she thought she'd die if she didn't hold him, touch him, feel him plunge inside her.

Feeling him there was almost like a blessing, like forgiveness.

But would he forgive her for what she was about to do next?

****

Later, a much loving later, Fern stirred herself and moved reluctantly out of Joel's arms. She kissed him softly on the forehead, overwhelmed with a sudden flood of tenderness at the vulnerability of his sleeping form. But she had to act, and act now. She dressed and retrieved her purse with her cell phone from the dresser beside the television. She slipped on her coat and pushed her feet into her boots, but then she paused with her hand on the doorknob. Something was bothering her, making her question her decision of what she was about to do. If it all went wrong, if she was making a mistake, this could threaten to rip away the newfound happiness and budding trust between them.

She was convinced Joel had an identical twin brother. But there were still so many questions. What if it wasn't possible to prove Joel's innocence, after so much had been done to prove his guilt? Could DNA tests prove one twin had committed a crime and the other was innocent? They would need a sample of DNA from the other twin, and what if they never located this twin? What if Joel's brother disappeared and the only evidence that was left pointed straight at Joel?

She had listened to Joel talking about the future, about his release, about all the things he planned to do, and felt another whisper of sorrow.

He was innocent. Her testimony had framed an innocent man, and there was the awful fact that they might never be able to prove beyond a doubt that Joel's twin was the guilty one. *Would he ever be free to forgive her?* She sighed. There was no way she could ever be part of this glowing future that Joel outlined. She struggled to hold back tears as a dark sense of loss swamped her.

Earlier, as she finished changing his dressings, Joel had leaned over, placed his hand on her cheek, and kissed her with such tenderness that even the memory caused tears to rise in her eyes. God help her, his touch, the warmth of his hand on her face, was almost her undoing. She had wanted to press against him, melt into him, believe him.

They sat together quietly for a while, not caring that the coffee was terrible or that the world was still busy outside their cocoon.

Finally, Joel broke the quiet contemplation by asking about Lucy Lee Maxwell's murder and how it had been discovered.

Fern took a moment to marshal her thoughts. "It seems this young woman was studying for exams. She was at Queens University medical school, and she'd

291

chosen to spend some quiet time at the family cottage, right next door to where we stayed, while she worked. Her parents were due to join her the next day or two, but she was murdered, just like Rose, murdered overnight.

"A local police officer found her body. It seems Bamber had discovered that I was staying at a cottage and questioned Glory, who had admitted that I'd told her I wanted to be away for a while. He suspected that you might be holding me hostage and had sent an officer to check the cottage.

"When the officer couldn't get an answer from Glory's place, he saw a car was outside the cottage next door and went to see if the occupants had seen anyone. The Maxwells' door was open, and he peered inside and found that poor girl dead."

Joel was silent for a moment, looking as shocked as Fern felt. Then relief washed through him as he realized that he'd been with Glory and Fern the whole time. "I couldn't have gone next door. Even if I'd known there was a cottage there, I was hardly out of your sight for more than a few minutes.

"Don't you see. What happened to that poor young girl is appalling, but this is even more evidence of my innocence! I have a brother out there who's doing all these awful things. My God, why would someone I have never met hate me enough to kill two women and hang the crime on me?"

"Glory said the murder was exactly like Rose's. But our testimony might be considered to be tainted. Glory is your lawyer and I, well, I sheltered you after you escaped from the hospital. And there are copycat killings. The prosecution could argue that someone else could have killed Lucy Lee, copying the way you killed Rose. There were plenty of details in the news outlets from the trial.

"The only way we can prove your innocence is to find your brother and hope that our testimony, and that of Mrs. Hartnell, would carry enough weight. I don't know if there are tests to determine if there are differences in DNA between twins."

Fern went and put her arms around him. "Well, first I make a phone call. And then we go out and find out as much as we can about your brother. We're going to find him, prove your innocence, and punish my sister's killer."

Then Fern had gathered her purse and cell phone and slipped out of the motel room. She had an uneasy feeling that what she did next could make or break the fragile peace they'd found.

****

Oh, this has certainly been fun, but I'm starting to get a bit tired of the game.

The man who styled himself, in his own imagination, as The Puppet Master, was frankly getting a bit bored with being just a spectator as the characters he'd gathered seemed to be sleepwalking through the roles he'd given them

Of course, he'd not expected them to visit that old cow Sarah Hartnell's home. He'd deal with that bitch of a nurse later. Perhaps that Fern Adams was a better protagonist that he'd expected. Certainly, she was proving to be a much better challenge than her sister.

And that whimpering little girl with the lush body… Yes, he'd enjoyed little Lucy Lee Maxwell, would have considered taking her somewhere and keeping her for a while, but he had, so to speak, other fish to fry.

Chapter Twenty-Four

A uniformed officer poked his head around the door. "Sorry to interrupt, sir, but there's a call from that sergeant in Copper Junction. The officer says it's 'imperative'—his word, not mine—that he speak to you."

Bamber's pulse jumped. *Was this the information he needed to tie it all together, or was it another red herring that would muddy the waters more?*

He took the call back in his own office, swinging his chair around to look out on the increasingly wintry landscape. "Is that Detective Bamber? John Bamber?" A man's cigarette roughened voice inquired.

Bamber admitted that was who he was and waited for the voice at the other end of the line to identify itself.

"This is Cam Roberts, Sergeant Cam Roberts of the Copper Junction detachment. I have a potential situation here."

"What can I do for you, sergeant?" Bamber hoped his brisk tone of voice would make the man move on a bit, spit out what he wanted and get off the line.

"I think we can help each other, Detective. In reply to your info about a man wanted in your area, I sent material about a bad actor in my own area who had moved to Toronto, and the photo is identical to the photo of your guy, Alvarez? My guy has a record as long as your arm."

Bamber sat up straight, the feet of his desk chair hitting the floor with a clatter. "We still haven't located our suspect. I am not sure how he relates to your suspect, although the two men do look alike. You say you think he's somehow related to a suspect you have, or could they be the same man? We've been looking for him, though I'm not sure he'd be in any fit state to have got himself to your neck of the woods. He was seriously injured in a prison brawl before he escaped."

"Prison brawl, eh? Well, that sure sounds like the kind of thing my man would be involved in. Be right funny if I'd spent the last year looking for him, and you had him all tucked away in jail."

"Get to the point."

A short silence on the other end of the line spoke of the other man's disapproval. Then he spoke again. "Your Joel Alvarez is the split image of a man we've been looking for. This fella, he won the lottery, a big one, twenty million dollars, and took off for Toronto to collect his winnings. He never came back.

"A month later, his mother's body was found in her burned-out cabin. She lived in the backwoods off the beaten track, so to speak, in a spot not many people venture in the wintertime. No one's seen neither hide nor hair of her son since. We know he collected his lottery money but after that, he seems to have dropped from sight.

"Detective. We're looking to question him about his mother's murder. Her body was somewhat burned, and let's just say she'd gone to her Maker some time before she was discovered. Our sharp-eyed coroner up here noticed there were scratches on the woman's body we at first thought were due to animal activity." Bamber felt himself wince as horrible images flashed to mind.

"But it seems these were more like what you'd expect if her throat had been slashed with a blunt, saw-toothed knife. Hyoid bone broken, too, like she'd been strangled as well as having her throat cut. And it looks like the fire took place around about the time our man took off for the Big TO...

"Now, SueAnne—that's our murder victim—she and her son never did get along. He was a bad apple, but you know, they say they never fall far from the tree, and SueAnne would never have won Mom of the Year, if you get my drift."

Bamber's heartbeat sped up. Maybe this was their big break, after all.

"Our man, Alvarez, was convicted of the rape and murder of a local woman. He strangled her as he raped her, and then slashed her throat."

Cam Roberts let out a long sigh. "Was your victim by any chance a bit of a good time girl?"

"If you mean was she a prostitute, no. But if you mean did she hang out in bars and like to party, yes. Rose Adams was a wannabe performing artist. Sang for her supper in any bar that would have her."

Then the sergeant dropped a bombshell. "What you should know is I have information from a respected retired nurse that your Alvarez is here in Copper Junction. But that's not the end of it. It appears that this nurse assisted at the delivery of SueAnne Phelan's babies. I do mean babies, plural. Twin boys. Close to thirty years ago. According to nurse Hartnell, you couldn't tell them apart unless you knew where to look."

"So you think these may be two different men?"

"That's what the retired nurse claims."

"She's suggesting there are twins, identical twins. One is Phelan and one is Alvarez?"

Cam Roberts chuckled. "Well, I was so excited to see this picture, I forgot to mention that. According to nurse Hartnell, who I would trust, Phelan and Alvarez are twins who were separated at birth. Alvarez was adopted by a Toronto couple, and Phelan, well, Phelan was brought up by a woman who should never have had custody of a child. Let's just say, there was abuse."

Bamber finished their conversation, scribbled down a few notes, and thanked the other officer for the information. As he put down the telephone receiver, mulling over the information that had shed a whole new light on his case…and created even more confusion.

"Groves, get your woolies on. We're going to Copper Junction. Get a car and meet me outside. He almost smiled at the excitement that illuminated the young officer's face, but right now he was too tense to really enjoy it.

****

Richard Phelan's brain seemed to tingle with pleasure at the idea that this game was near its end. His brother and the woman who'd whored herself to him, both of them were going to pay dearly.

He'd deal with that bitch of a nurse who'd chosen to send his brother to a cushy life, and then handed Richard himself over to a monster.

And then there's be one last loose end to tie up. Joel and Fern were going to go down hard. Then his brother would be moldering in a cold grave while he

298

took off on a flight to the nice warm tropical island where his winnings were stashed. He was going to lead a life that would heal his childhood…

Chapter Twenty-Five

Bamber was just shrugging into his overcoat when the Geek, their forensics whiz kid, threw another spanner in their thinking. "Sometimes you just have to get back to basics. Technology is great, and the advances made in recent years have gone a long way to getting convictions where we couldn't before. But in Alvarez' case, he fell through the cracks."

"Just give me the potted version for now," Bamber snapped impatiently

"You see, identical twins have identical DNA. They're the only people in the world who do. Up until now, Álvarez might have been better off if he'd been caught up in this shitstorm before DNA became such a big deal. You see, while DNA can't easily determine the difference between identical twins, fingerprints can. If Alvarez had had to rely only on the fingerprints, there's nothing to put him at the scene.

"And now I've heard from my colleague at the uni, and it seems there is enough of a difference in the two DNA samples to add to the fingerprint evidence to be sure that Alvarez is not guilty of these crimes. The killer wasn't as clever as he thought."

"Amen to that, brother," Bamber muttered. "So, what can you tell us about the killer?"

"The fingerprints and the DNA seem to lead to a creepy kind of guy named Richard Phelan. Served a few months for rape and went on to be a person of interest in his mother's murder. And he's a lottery winner. The lucky bastard won something like $40 million on the Ontario Lottery. Who says goodness is rewarded?"

"But Phelan and Alvarez are one and the same person?" Lee looked as puzzled as Bamber felt.

The Geek smiled. "Oh, no. They are two different people. My friends, you're looking at the wrong branch of the identical twins."

Bamber's stomach clenched, remembering Glory Jordan's words. A woman with a mission of vengeance. Would Fern Adams, a doctor sworn to heal, be willing to execute a man she believes is a killer?

****

Joel was pacing, restless now. He'd awoken to find Fern gone, why, without leaving as much as a note to tell him where she was? A ripple of suspicion washed over him. Surely, after all that they'd said, all that they'd shared, just an hour or less ago, surely that wasn't a lie?

Then he remembered her touch, her whispered words, the pleasure they'd shared. The idea that he was in love with Fern Adams, despite all that had gone before, was both a shock and a comfort. But where was she? What was she doing?

His skin was crawling with anxiety, with the need to act. He knew the answer to everything lay somewhere in Copper Junction, but where to start? The nurse, Sarah Hartnell, had mentioned someone called Chief Joseph, who might be the father of SueAnne's twins.

It felt like a punch to his gut. This man might be

his father. His birth father. And there was only one way to find out. He couldn't go into the motel office and ask directions to the home of someone called Chief Joseph, not without setting alarm bells ringing, as he was sure to be recognized. But he could use the room telephone.

Where was Fern? What was taking her so long? She'd said she had another phone call to make. But that was before they'd made love. His spine prickled. *Had she gone to call the police? What would they do? Send a task force? Would he be gunned down as he stepped outside the room door?*

One thing was sure. He wasn't prepared to sit around here any longer. Weakness from his wounds had left him allowing Fern to run the show and, while he thought she now believed he wasn't guilty, it wouldn't stop her from bringing in the police, who may or may not believe all they'd discovered so far.

Apparently, this Chief Joseph was well known. The guy in the motel office had given Joel pretty good directions to the old man's house, without sounding the least bit suspicious. Joel's eyes lit on the set of car keys on the dresser, and again he wondered where Fern had gone. She couldn't have gone too far without the car.

His hand was on the doorknob when he heard his own name spoken, making him jerk his head toward the television news that showed footage of the front of a car detailing shop, with a man's photograph displayed in the corner of the screen. That man was himself—but it couldn't be. The other looked so like him, Joel was momentarily confused. The television presenter went on the say the photo was the man who was wanted for the murder of two women and a patient at the hospital in Primrose Hill. Police were adding the murder of a young woman at a Cloyne cottage to the list of issues that they suspected a man named as Phelan or Alverez was responsible for.

Nausea rose in his throat, and he just made it to the bathroom before throwing up the little food in his stomach, followed by painful dry heaving, until finally he rested his forehead on the cool porcelain of the toilet bowl. The rank smell of his own vomit brought another round of retching.

****

Fern had felt as though the walls of the small motel were closing in on her, and she was glad to get out into the fresh, cold air for a few minutes. She pulled in a deep breath, pausing to allow her heartbeat to settle down.

She had kissed Joel Alvarez. Made love with him, beautiful, tender love. Joel Alvarez was an innocent man.

The words ran around in an endless loop in her head. One moment, she believed them. The next, she didn't. Yet the evidence was solid. Not even a man with a split personality could be in two places at once. Certainly not three different places. But what about the DNA evidence? The evidence from the staff at the Wild Turkey pub? The only answer could be that Joel was the Good Twin, as she'd started to differentiate them in her mind.

She found an alcove near the vending machines that was more protected from the bitter winter wind that was sweeping across the car park and pulled out her cell phone. Her fingers shook as she hit the number that Detective John Bamber had said would connect her directly with his own phone.

As it rang, she almost panicked and cut the connection, but then she heard the reassuring voice of the detective.

"Detective Bamber? It's Fern Adams. Dr. Adams."

His angry reaction was palpable across the ether. "Dr. Adams—exactly where are you and what the hell do you think you're doing?" The edge of irritation in his voice almost made her cut the connection.

"I don't have much time. Joel Alvarez is here with me and he's innocent, detective." She hurried on with the speech she'd written in her head when she'd decided to make this call. "You need to speak to a woman named Sarah Hartnell, a retired nurse who can tell you that she helped deliver twin boys. Joel was adopted, the other stayed with an abusive mother. His name is Richard Phelan."

"Dr. Adams, we know about the existence of Phelan…and an hour ago I was given evidence that Alvarez and this other are identical twins. We can identify them by DNA using a new process. Where is Alvarez now?"

"We're booked into a motel, the Copper Break, as you come into Copper Junction…"

"We're almost there. Should be with you in twenty minutes. Keep Alvarez with you and don't tell him we're coming. He's not out of the woods yet. A police officer from Copper Junction by the name of Cam Roberts may meet you at the hotel. And Fern? Watch your back."

The detective clicked off and Fern stood for a moment listening to the dead air. *So the police knew that Joel was probably an innocent man! They knew about the twin and had DNA evidence that should prove conclusively that Joel was innocent.*

She felt weak with relief, despite the warning voice that reminded her of Bamber's words: *Alvarez isn't out of the woods yet.* Ignoring Bamber's order, she fully intended to tell Joel about this call.

Sighing, she turned on the path to return to their motel room when she walked right into a solid male chest. Joel must have been worried and come to find her. But looking up, the face of the man looking down on her with a strange smile on his narrow lips, was Joel, and wasn't Joel.

With a jolt of surprise that he had crept so close, crowding her, she looked into the face of the man standing before her and she knew this was Richard, the Bad Twin.

But her stomach roiled at the incredible likeness between the two. Only the cruelty in the smile and the deadness in the dark eyes alerted her. How long had he been there? How much of her call had he heard?

"Well, well, I wondered when we'd finally meet up."

Fern shuddered involuntarily, poised to scream and run, but she reacted too late.

****

Richard Phelan had driven slowly along the main stretch of highway on the outskirts of Copper Junction, carefully scanning the cars parked at the two down-at-heel motels. He gave a whoop of victory when he spotted Fern Adams' vehicle in front of one of the rooms in the least scruffy of the two motels. Even better, he could see the woman herself, sheltering against the wind as she spoke into her cell phone. "Got you! Now to have some fun, dear brother!"

He congratulated himself on having the foresight to take down her vehicle registration on one of the clandestine visits he had made to the Adams' family farmhouse. He felt a stirring in his loins as he remembered peeking in one of the windows of the old farmhouse and seeing Fern dressed only in a skimpy lace camisole as she sat with a glass of wine and a book she was studying so intently that she never noticed the man at her window.

Richard smiled, an ugly humorless expression as he considered that he might have the opportunity to play with Fern and to act out an X-rated fantasy on that lush body. Maybe he would force his damned brother to watch.

Wouldn't that just be a sublime Karma? Oh, my, my. What a delicious little thing she was! It's like being at a smorgasbord. Do I take the hated brother first, or his pretty lady?

Of course, it would be nice to have them both together, and that had been his plan. But they were separate now and that made it more complicated. He didn't need the silly bitch to start screaming and have Joel, unfettered, leaping to her defense.

Decisions. Decisions.

Chapter Twenty-Six

"I'd like to get to Copper Junction in one piece, not in an ambulance! Slow down, Lee!" Bamber admonished his partner as they drove towards the small northern town where so much of the information about this case was leading them. They'd arranged to meet with Sergeant Cam Roberts at the police station there and had apprised the Copper Junction officer of the latest information about Alvarez' whereabouts.

"I thought we were in that life and death rush? Who knows what Alvarez and his psycho brother might be doing up there in the sticks," Lee replied, not taking his foot off the gas pedal.

"We are in a rush, but I prefer life to death and the way you're driving in this weather is downright dangerous. We're in an unmarked car and I'm surprised we haven't been stopped by some alert uniform in a cruiser," Bamber snapped back.

The early December weather was quickly degenerating into the depths of Canadian winter. Out of a clear gray sky, snow had started to fall in fluffy white flakes, falling slowly at first but they gathered momentum as they built up a slippery layer on the highway. Pretty soon the road surface would have morphed into a treacherous mass of ice and snow that wouldn't be comfortably passable until the plows and sanders had been by. Already they'd passed a small car that had skidded onto the central reservation and now rested there, looking pathetic as snow built up on it. A CAA tow truck had pulled off the road to rescue the little car and its occupant, who was standing alongside the vehicle, blowing on his hands and looking thoroughly pissed off.

"Ah, winter in Ontario," Bamber said, noting as they passed that a police cruiser had also stopped to see if the driver needed help. "We don't want to join that guy on the side of the road," he told Lee.

His companion just grinned and said, "Not a chance in the world of that happening in an unmarked like this. Have you seen the snow tires on this baby?"

Bamber sighed and made a mental note never to let his partner drive again. Then he turned his mind to the problems they might face once they arrived in Copper Junction. He was mightily curious as to Sergeant Roberts' remarks about how the nurse—what was her name? He checked his notebook and saw the name Hartnell—as to how nurse Hartnell could tell the identical twins apart and was sure that Alvarez was not his evil twin. Dr. Adams had given just a brief indication that the nurse had some definite evidence but hadn't explained further.

By now they were pulling into the outskirts of the town and passing a couple of motels. "That must be the one that Adams and Alvarez were holed up in," Bamber said, "But I think we need to coordinate with the local police first, get a proper idea of what's what."

Lee looked crestfallen at not stopping immediately at the hotel to roust out Alvarez, imagining himself kicking in the motel door, gun in both hands, just like on the American television police shows. He cast a quick, guilty glance over at Bamber, knowing what his superior officer would have to say about such a fantasy. Then he sighed and carried on at a much slower pace, following the GPS to the local police station.

****

Fern had put up a hell of a struggle as Richard grabbed her. He'd brought his car up close to where she stood after he had seen her, so engrossed in her cell phone conversation that she hadn't even noticed him until it was too late. Her struggling made him both horny and angry, her nails raking his face had pushed him over the top into fury, and he hit her hard enough to daze her while he pushed her into the back of the vehicle. He drove around to the rear of the motel, parking near the garbage cans, and quickly silenced any protests Fern might make with a strip of duct tape over her mouth, then tied her wrists together. She was still dazed from the blow, and a sense of power roared through him at her helpless state.

But he would have to wait to enjoy the delights ahead. He had bigger plans for Dr. Fern Adams and his pampered twin. *Oh, yes, he had plans, all right.*

****

"I wondered how long it would be before you found your way to my door. Come inside."

Joel tentatively crossed the threshold of the small log cabin at the old man's invitation. Looking about him, he was impressed with the sense of peace and quiet that pervaded the home. He took in the packed bookshelves, the old-fashioned record player, and stack of records in tattered sleeves. An old mongrel dog raised his head to look at the visitor, sighed, decided there was no danger here, and then resumed sleeping peacefully in front of the glowing wood stove.

The place seemed to suit and reflect the old man who stood back to let him enter his home. Chief Joseph was tall and straight-backed, his gray hair in a traditional plait, his hands gnarled with arthritis and hard work, but his expression still serene and confident. In other circumstances the atmosphere would be soothing, a time to sit and talk and relax. But right now, Joel was so tightly wound with worry about Fern that he could not sit still, pacing the small area of the great room until the old man rounded on him and demanded he sit down and make sense with his anxious scattered words.

As Joel moved into the room, he was surprised to see that Nurse Hartnell was seated there on an old rocking chair covered with a vintage quilt. She smiled, but her expression changed as she looked to the Chief who stood behind Joel.

"Joseph, no!"

"Don't turn around, son. I've heard of all you've done. You are a damaged soul, but I can't have a son of mine going about doing what you've been doing, boy. It's not right. It's on my conscience. Perhaps I should have done more for you. Maybe I'm as responsible as you are for what you done. But it ends here, now. I'll kill you myself."

Nurse Hartnell rose and rushed to stand between Joel and the Chief, pushing the barrel of his rifle up into the air away from Joel. "He's the other twin, Joseph, the boy who's already been punished for the behavior of your other son."

"I don't understand. I only have one son."

"Joel, come and sit alongside me on the couch.

Joseph, please sit down in your recliner, and I'll explain to you."

Joel swallowed around his growing anxiety over Fern's whereabouts as he allowed the older woman to take his arm to settle him beside her on the comfortable-looking couch. Indecision crossed the old man's face, but moments later he moved to his battered old recliner and sat stiffly. Tension tightened Joel's chest as he noticed the old man had not put the gun down.

"I hope you can explain this, Sarah." The Chief said, never taking his sharp eyes from Joel.

Nurse Hartnell drew in a long breath and then released it. "We've been friends—sometimes more than just friends—for a long time, Joseph. You know you can trust me, yes?"

The old man nodded, still watching the younger man, and his strong fingers clutched the hunting rifle. Somewhere in the rear of the room a grandfather clock began to chime the hour. Joel pushed down the increasing urgent need to question the couple about Fern's possible whereabouts as nurse Hartnell began to speak.

"You knew SueAnne was pregnant, and you believed that you were the father?"

The Chief nodded, and Joel noted the tear on the man's rugged cheek was swiftly wiped away.

"I was there when she gave birth. Joseph, there were two baby boys. I swear this to you because I helped deliver them. Dr. Stone didn't know there were twins and had already made arrangements for one baby to be adopted by a couple from Toronto. I didn't think it was legal, but we'd talked about it and decided it was in the child's best interests to allow SueAnne her wish not to be burdened with a child.

"Money exchanged hands. I don't know how much. After the first baby was delivered, cleaned, and wrapped up, and we were ready to…well, SueAnne's contractions started up again, and she delivered another baby boy. I know now they were identical twins."

The old man looked at the nurse with injured eyes. "As you say, we've been friends a long time. How come as a friend you never told me this?"

The nurse's cheeks colored. "I know I should have…I am so sorry. I was so torn between doing the right thing for you, for SueAnne, for the babies, and then Dr. Stone swore me to secrecy. Dr. Stone was afraid of legal action, I think, and I was glad that the child wasn't going to be brought up by SueAnne. But then the second baby came, and SueAnne decided she wanted to keep him.

"I told myself being a mother could be the making of her. Having a child to love and raise could stop her wayward ways and give her a sense of responsibility. I was just trying to reassure myself, and I couldn't have been more wrong."

Chief Joseph was silent for several minutes, digesting the news. Then he asked, "If they are identical twins, how could we know which twin is sitting right there in my home?"

Joel blushed, and nurse Hartnell laughed.

"I don't think we need to show…" Joel said, pleading in his voice. Dropping his pants again for an audience wasn't an idea he relished, even to prove he was the good twin.

"Just trust me on this. Joel is Richard Phelan's

twin, and he is your son."

Chief Joseph studied the young man sitting opposite him, and Joel had the uncomfortable feeling that the man was able to see through to his soul. Finally, Joseph nodded as though satisfied. "So, why do you come to me at this late date?"

Now he was there, Joel didn't know how to start. So many questions tumbled in his mind. He took a deep breath and began, "First of all, you must know that I knew nothing of your existence until recently. I thought I was the only child of two very good parents in Toronto. When they both died, I…I was feeling lonely. I had no other family." He explained about finding a letter addressed to his mother that seemed to suggest friends or family in Copper Junction. "I had some time off coming from my job with the fire department, so I…well, to cut a long story short, I received an anonymous letter saying I should go to Copper Junction. I set out for here, had a car breakdown in Primrose Hill, met a lovely woman—a doctor." He glanced briefly at nurse Hartnell, who smiled encouragingly. "I thought I was falling in love.

"Then all hell broke loose. A woman was murdered, the sister of the doctor I was dating while waiting for my car to be fixed. Then out of the blue, I was arrested. Seems the woman I thought I was in love with had accused me of being the man running away, covered in blood, from her sister's apartment.

"Then a barista in the local pub said I'd been sitting with the murdered woman, drinking and laughing all afternoon…and DNA evidence said I was the killer. I don't know how it came to this, but before I could take a breath, I was sentenced to twenty-five years in prison as a murderer."

He told his story as succinctly as he could, but his voice faltered as he spoke about being attacked in prison and then being helped to escape from the hospital. Joel wondered how to explain meeting with Fern and challenging her to help him prove his innocence or let her sister's murderer go free. He rushed through the story, explaining how he had no idea he had a brother until this day.

"He seems to blame me for every bad thing that ever happened in his life, and he has sworn revenge in the very worst way."

Joel glanced for what seemed like the fiftieth time at the clock on the wall. He rubbed his eyes, anxiety about Fern growing by the minute. He visibly startled when his cell phone rang just as he was about to explain that he feared she had been taken by his twin.

"It's Fern," he told them as he saw the name on the cell phone, relief evidenced in his voice. "I've been so worried about you. Where are you?"

He reared back and paled at the sound of male laughter that came through the cell. Not Fern, after all—

"I'm so glad you're worried about me, brother, but I'm fine. Better than fine, actually. Having a lot of fun with your girlfriend. Pretty little thing, isn't she?"

"I swear to God, whoever you are, if you hurt Fern—" But his threat was cut off by laughter and then the caller was gone.

Joel leapt to his feet. "I've got to find Fern. God knows what that animal might do to her." His stomach clenched at memories of the photographs shown in court of Rose Adams' dead, mutilated body. Vomit rose in his throat, and he rushed to the door and outside to throw up.

He came returned, pale and exhausted. "I'm sorry. I just couldn't…"

"My son, you needn't worry about that."

"Joel, you need to rest. You're still weak from the attack in prison, and I think you should let me look at your wounds before you go anywhere."

Joel shrugged off the concern from them both. "I'll see to that later, when I know Fern is safe." He paced anxiously across the room. "But where can she be? Where would he have taken her?"

There was silence in the cabin for a few minutes. Nurse Hartnell bit her lip and seemed to be fighting back tears, but Chief Joseph's face reflected anger and determination. He stood and went to pick up his hunting rifle again. "I know where he'll be," was all he said as he strode to the door.

"This is my fight, too!" Joel leapt up and went toward the older man. "Where would Richard have gone? Where would he have taken Fern? You know, don't you?"

Chief Joseph swung around and looked Joel in the eye. "Yes, I know. He'll have gone where all of us need to go when we're in trouble. He's gone home."

"But the cabin burned to the ground!" Nurse Hartnell exclaimed.

"It did, but there's an old log barn. That's where he'll be. He slept there quite a few times when he couldn't handle being around his mother anymore."

****

Joel paced the length of Chief Joseph's living room, eager for action, itching to rush out and find his

315

brother and Fern but finally he agreed with the old man and nurse Hartnell that they needed a plan. His first thought had been to start searching the town for any sign of his brother and the woman he loved, but he'd soon been persuaded that would be a waste of time because the Chief was right.

In times of trouble, we all want to go home.

And home for Richard Phelan was a falling-down old log barn alongside the burned-out log building where his mother had died. Or been murdered by the son she chose to keep.

His mother. Their mother. The woman Richard had hated so much that he'd finally murdered her in a fit of rage when she'd tried to get a share of his Lotto winnings, according to the two older people who filled him in on some of his twin's past. An appalling past that had spawned an evil personality.

His gut told him the old man was right and that Richard had probably gone to ground on his home territory. "I just wish to God, Fern is safe, but there's no telling what that madman might do," he worried.

"He won't hurt her, not yet." The Chief sounded so sure of himself that Joel wheeled around, demanding, "How can you be so confident? Do you know what he has already done to two women?"

The Chief quietly walked towards the door, hoisting his hunting rifle over one shoulder. "He's succeeded in what he wanted. He's wrecked your good name, your hero status. He's had you imprisoned for murder, and he's set the authorities on you further with the second death. And a third death. Now he wants to really hurt you, to rob you of all you have that he can never have. And he'll keep your woman alive so that you can witness what he does to her before he kills her. He intends to destroy you…May the lord forgive me for saying that about my own son."

Chapter Twenty-Seven

"Let me go, you bastard!" Fern struggled against the hard hands that held her as Richard mercilessly ripped the duct tape away from her mouth and she tasted her own blood.

He mercilessly tore the duct tape from her wrists, the pain causing momentary flashes of purple before her eyes. Richard's smile grew wider.

Desperately, she reached into the pocket of her sweater, seeking the snub-nosed gun she'd been carrying around with her. But her fingers came up empty, and when she raised her eyes, it was to see her captor holding the gun up and grinning savagely.

She took comfort from knowing that she'd never loaded a single bullet into the weapon. Indeed, she'd been ashamed that she'd even bought it.

Now, with the man who held her prisoner standing before her, his expression of cruel enjoyment, she saw that he was nothing like Joel. The two men were like night and day, or evil and good.

Whatever might happen, she vowed she wouldn't give him the satisfaction of making it easy, or of showing her fear. She looked down at the ground, her expression that of a lamb to the slaughter. Waiting.

And when Richard moved closer towards her, as she'd known he would, she braced herself then launched her body towards him, beating at him with her fists, tearing at his face with her nails.

She got a moment's satisfaction from the bloody marks she'd left on his skin, but the blows she landed on his back and head seemed to make no impression on him, other than to widen his malicious grin. Seemingly without effort, he dragged her into the tumbling-down log structure and pushed her into a broken stall onto a sleeping bag over a pile of ancient straw.

Fern threw herself clumsily to her feet, struggling for balance as the world spun around her. She launched herself in a clumsy run, heart pounding madly, but he caught her easily, pulling her against him and forcing a savage kiss on her bruised lips. She bit him, and he slapped her so hard the world turned momentarily black.

"That's right, sweet thing, fight me! I'll teach you a lesson you'll never forget."

"You bastard!" she screamed, and he hit her several vicious blows that knocked her to the floor. Again, Fern tasted blood on her lips. *Was it his or hers?* She spat to clear her mouth.

"Yes, I'm a bastard, and so is that wimpy twin of mine, the one you've been mooning over all this time. The one who killed your sister!"

Fern was taken aback for just a moment that this man could suggest he was innocent, and Joel was the murderer.

She shook her head, trying to clear her thoughts.

****

Joel and Chief Joseph agreed that nurse Hartnell would stay behind. She was to go to the police station and sound the alarm about Dr. Fern Adams' kidnapping and their belief she'd been taken against her will by

Richard Phelan to his old homestead. She was also to tell them that Joel and Chief Joseph were going to the homestead, but to leave out the fact the two men were armed.

Just as she was explaining everything to Sergeant Roberts, the detectives from Primrose Hill arrived in a screech of tires. Bamber rushed into the station, and Sergeant Roberts introduced the elderly nurse to them and insisted that Bamber and Lee listen to her story before they set off on what had now become a manhunt. The situation added danger of the life of an innocent hostage hanging on the actions of the police. Bamber worried that the two men, Chief Joseph and Joel Alvarez would act precipitously, and the whole situation would become even more of a nightmare and lives would be lost.

When she came to the part that Richard and Joel were identical twins, Bamber held up his hand to silence her. "We know about that, ma'am, but what we don't know is which twin is which—and which carried out the murders. Or if they were working together."

The nurse issued a few words her friends and former colleagues would have been shocked to hear coming from her mouth. "I can tell you those two boys are only identical in looks. But there's one way to tell them apart, and that's without their pants." She frowned at Lee, who'd sniggered. "But their characters are like night and day. Richard's soul is so black, he'd never bat an eyelid to kill a police officer, Joel, his father, or the woman he's kidnapped. So I suggest, gentlemen, that you get your rear ends out to that old barn and pray you're not too late."

Bamber looked at the station sergeant, his raised

eyebrows silently asking the question, *Can this woman be trusted?*

Roberts, who was busy giving orders to his own troops, nodded. "I've known nurse Hartnell for years. I think she maybe the midwife who brought me into the world...I certainly have known her all my life, and I trust not just her truth, but her judgement."

Bamber and Lee exchanged glances, but Bamber indicated he would accept the judgement of the seasoned cop who certainly seemed to know his town and its people.

Often, in the public eye, law enforcement seems to move like molasses in the winter, making careful plans. But when the police do move, they move with speed. Marked and unmarked cars went hurtling through the town and onto the unmarked gravel road that led through heavily wooded land toward the old burned-out log cabin, going full circle to the place where this tragedy had begun, nearly thirty years ago.

****

Joel and Chief Joseph were about thirty minutes ahead of law enforcement, driving without lights up the meandering driveway where trees dressed with frost glittered in the moonlight and pressed against the road. Ahead were the charred and blackened ruins of Richard Phelan's old home; the log cabin where he had allegedly murdered his mother and burned the building to the ground; the home where, according to Joseph and nurse Hartnell, Richard had experienced a childhood so nightmarish, it had warped him for life.

What would it have been like to be a child in a place like this? Joel wondered. The quiet rural setting could have been heaven on earth where a child could run free and play, but not apparently for his twin brother at the hands of a selfish, drug and alcohol addicted mother. An unsought pang of guilt at his own easy, well-loved upbringing temporarily swamped Joel. Then he straightened his shoulders. If his brother hurt the woman Joel loved, any sympathy would evaporate, and all bets were off

He swallowed the threat of nausea as he thought of the woman he loved in the hands of a man incapable of love, capable only, it seemed, of extreme cruelty. He stopped the car some distance from the overgrown clearing where he could just pick out the ruined skeleton of the old log and frame home. Opposite, half hidden in darkness, was an old log barn with a faint light glowing between the unmortised logs. Joel's heart beat loudly as he thought of Fern in that building—her at Richard Phelan's mercy, or perhaps already dead at the hands of his brother.

Pushing away that thought, he commented to Chief Joseph…his father! "What a weary, depressing place this is." He took in the tall pines and cedars towering over the lane. Nature was slowly taking over the road and clearing.

Silence hung heavy, broken only by the shushing whisper of the tall pines.

"It wasn't always like this," Joseph replied. "In fact, this was once a pretty, well-kept property."

"That must have been some time ago, judging by how it looks now."

"It doesn't take Mother Earth long to start reclaiming her own."

"So, how do we do this? I think we've probably lost the element of surprise. It's so quiet here that

Richard, assuming he is here, must have heard our vehicle." Joel swallowed back the fear that they'd made the wrong decision, that perhaps Richard had taken Fern to some other location where God knows what atrocities could occur.

"He is here." Chief Joseph spoke with authority. "And we need a plan, because I'm sure he has your woman with him and will try to use her to hurt you."

Fear ran again on icy feet down Joel's spine. He shivered and pushed it back, knowing he'd never forgive himself if Fern was hurt because he hesitated to help her.

As they sat, Chief Joseph pointed out the slight flickers of light that could be seen through the gaps in the logs at the far end of the barn. "He's here. My other son, he's here." Chief Joseph unbuckled his seatbelt and reached for his rifle. "I am going in there alone. This is my battle. He's my son and I am responsible for his…his…" the old man couldn't bring himself to end the sentence. Instead, he unlocked the door of the passenger side and made to move out of the car.

"No." Joel stopped him with one word and a hand on his arm. "If we go in now, we go in together. We both have a lot to lose."

"I think I can talk to Richard…talk some sense to him. Perhaps get him to come with me and we'll find help for him," his voice tailed off. Reality told him there was probably no help for Richard, that the dye was already cast by the boy's actions.

"Maybe we should wait for the police. I'm sure that Nurse Hartnell will have told them what's going down here." Even as he said the words, Joel knew that there wasn't the time to waste, not if he was to get Fern safely out of Richard's clutches.

After a few minutes' discussion, they decided Richard would probably be well aware that both Joel and Joseph were searching for him, and that the old man had probably guessed they were on their way to the old homestead.

"We're going in there together," Joel said firmly, grasping an elderly hunting rifle Chief Joseph had supplied. Even now, he wasn't sure he could use it against another human being.

Just as they stood at the rickety barn door, two police vehicles came hurtling up the driveway, stopping some distance behind Chief Joseph's old pickup truck.

****

Inside the barn, Fern gasped with shock at Richard's assertion that Joel had killed her sister.

"I don't believe you! You killed Rose, just as you killed poor little Lucy Lee Maxwell!"

"You're wrong, there. The blame rests on my whore of a mother, the father who refused to recognize me, and my holier than thou pampered twin. In fact, the entire population of this fucked up town who abandoned me and turned the other way when her boyfriends did horrible things to me as a helpless child. Those who pretended I wasn't covered in bruises and marks from the beatings—the people who didn't lift a finger to help me—they're the ones who are responsible for the things I did, for the murders, and for my whole damned, screwed up life."

"No. That's just a copout. No one forced you to do these evil things." Fern flinched as Richard's grip on her arm tightened painfully, but she refused to let him see her fear. "You chose to do what you did. No one forced you to be an evil monster. You decided that for yourself. Oh!" She gasped as Richard grabbed her by the hair and dragged her toward him. He pressed his body against hers, and she had to fight to keep from throwing up as he roughly explored her breasts. Only the cruel grin on his face gave her the strength not to give in to the fear that threatened to drag screams from her. "Do you think your pretty boyfriend will want you after I'm finished with you?' Richard grabbed Fern's breast with a rough hand and pressed a bruising kiss against her mouth.

"Stop it! Let go of me! Don't you think you've hurt enough people already?"

"No. No one gave a damn about me. Why should I care about them? I did what I wanted, took what I wanted. No one gave me anything, not even a meal or a kind word. And now I'll make sure my brother, who wants you, never gets you. My father, who's so well respected in the town, did nothing to help me except look lovesick whenever my mother showed up looking for money from him."

"You're right. I should have done something."

Richard whirled around at the quiet voice.

Chief Joseph stood just inside the barn, a hunting rifle in his hand and tears in his eyes.

Richard pulled Fern closer to himself, her body pressed against his as he used her as a human shield. He grinned bitterly when he saw Joseph and Joel standing shoulder to shoulder, his brother's face pale with pain from his wounds, but determined. With his tongue clamped between his teeth, Richard made a show of rubbing his hands over Fern's breasts and sliding his fingers between her legs. His smile showed how he enjoyed the rage and fear on Joel's face as he roughly fondled the woman his brother loved.

"Well, well, isn't this just the prettiest little family gathering a person could want?" Richard's eyes glittered cold in the moonlight filtering in through a trapdoor in the barn roof.

Fern's heart gave a little leap as she saw the man she loved. Standing proudly alongside Joel was an old man wearing gray braids. Even from that distance she saw there was a resemblance between Richard, Joel, and this man. And despite how much the two brothers were alike, it was the cruelty shining in Richard's eyes that had made her see the difference between the two brothers. Back at the motel, she'd recognized who was behind her there but too late…

"Let her go, Richard. She hasn't done anything to you. This is just between you and me, and it's me you want to hurt." Despite his fear for Fern, Joel's voice was strong and calm. That seemed to irritate Richard even more.

"And how could I hurt you even more than letting you take responsibility for the death of this woman?" Richard snapped back.

Joel's heart hammered in his chest. His brother was truly evil or truly insane—more than Joel could ever have imagined.

Chief Joseph walked farther into the barn, his back straight as he held the gaze of his son.

"So why didn't you do something?" Richard addressed him. "When I was a little kid, I used to pray. I prayed to a God who'd cast me aside as well, because no one came to help me."

Tears glittered in the old man's eyes. "I could tell

you that I didn't know how bad things were for you. I could tell you that I didn't know how bad SueAnne was behaving. About all the boyfriends, the drinking, the drugs…and it would be true on some level. But on another level, I knew, and because I loved her, I fooled myself to thinking things couldn't be that bad."

"But if you really thought you were my father, you could have helped, done something—anything…" Richard's words ended in a sound like a child's sob.

"SueAnne and her parents wouldn't let me anywhere near you. An Indian wasn't good enough for her, but she wound up partying with any guy who came along. I know that. I tried to get her to stop drinking and whoring, asked her to marry me over and over. She laughed in my face. In her mind she thought the world of soap operas really existed. That rich, glittering life was what she wanted for herself. She was an intelligent woman who believed in fairy tales.

"I'd been in love with SueAnne since we were children, and that never changed, no matter what she did. And I would have loved you, too, whether you were mine or not. I told her I'd take good care of her and you, that I'd marry her or just be there for her—whatever she wanted. She told me to go to hell. Her father was a harsh, unyielding man, and he wouldn't give his only daughter to an indigenous man. Just about every other man in town was, though, provided he could flash a fat wallet. I knew this, and yet I still did nothing. I share the blame for everything done to you and what you have done."

Richard's eyes fell to the rifle held so competently in the Chief's hands. "So, are you going to shoot me down like a savage dog? Is that your solution?"

Chief Joseph was silent. Hanging his head, he murmured, "I thought I could do that. I thought for you that would be the best answer. But it was really just a selfish thought, that if I killed you, I'd finally have taken some responsibility. Seeing you standing there, the image of your brother and yet so different...I can see who you might have been if I'd had some courage and followed my conscience. It was the talk of the town. Everyone speculated about what was going on here. No one did anything. But the truth is, you grew up into a monster. The monster we made you into."

Joel came forward, trying not to look at Fern's fear-filled face. If he focused on how scared she was and the rapidly swelling bruises on her pale cheeks, he was afraid he'd lose all sense of caution and leap at Richard, prepared to tear him apart.

But a move like that could result in Fern's being badly hurt or killed. He knew he was still physically weak, and his brother was ruthless and cold-hearted and would laugh at his attempts to rescue her. So instead, he stopped a few yards away from where Richard stood, Fern held tightly against his body, and he asked, "Why do you hate me so much? We've never met. I've never done anything to you! Lord knows, I didn't even know you existed until yesterday."

Richard's eyes blazed, and for a moment Joel thought he'd made the worst mistake as his brother's arm squeezed more tightly around Fern. "Never done anything to me? You really think that?" Richard slammed his fist against one of the barn supports and stopped to look at the blood that oozed from his knuckles. "You were the favored child. You got the cushy life. And what did I get? I got abuse, starvation, beatings."

"Richard, I am so sorry for that. But I didn't know. I was just a kid myself, like you. I didn't choose to be adopted."

"It doesn't matter whether you knew or not. It's time for you to pay for your good life!" In a swift movement, Richard pulled a deadly sharp knife out of his jacket pocket, holding it against Fern's throat. Joel's vision seemed to telescope until he could see nothing but the face of the woman he loved, and that of the monster who held a shining blade against her soft pale throat.

"Don't, please don't! Tell me what I can do to make amends. Tell me what you need."

"I want you to hurt, to hurt forever and ever. And this is a good start, isn't it, *brother*?" Richard pressed the knife slightly, and a tiny trickle of blood appeared on the alabaster of Fern's throat. She went even paler as she felt the warm moisture on her skin.

Joel thought his heart would fly out of his chest, it pounded so hard.

Then everyone in the barn went on alert as armed police and emergency medics rushed into the dimly lit building, climbing swiftly over debris. Detective Bamber and several armed officers led them into the barn, coming to a shocked full stop at the tableau before them.

Joel saw the weapons bristling in the hands of the officers and thought his life was over. He muttered a prayer that they would realize that the man they wanted, the murderer, was the one holding a knife against Fern Adams' throat. But would they know what moves to make? Would they be able to prevent that knife going deeper, cutting off Fern's life as Richard extracted the ultimate revenge?

After all, his brother had nothing to lose.

Then the knife in Richard's hand flashed, blood spirted, and all hell let loose. For a mind-reeling moment, Joel thought Fern's throat was cut, that the rich red blood was hers. Then he realized that in one fluid movement, Richard had thrust Fern to one side and stabbed himself in the chest, hitting an artery and releasing a torrent of his own blood across his shirt. The spray stained nearby straw and wooden poles of the barn's structure.

Without thinking clearly, Joel rushed to enfold Fern in his arms. He was almost lightheaded with relief to see that she was safe. The keening sound of grief filled the barn and he turned so see Chief Joseph cradling his dying son. Joel turned and fell to his knees alongside Joseph, his arm still around Fern. The old man was holding his son tenderly, his lips moving in silent prayer as Richard's lifeblood ebbed. Seeing Joel beside him, Richard managed to rally a little, grinning at his twin. "I wish we could have been brothers," he murmured. "You didn't win in the end." Then he coughed up a huge gout of blood and was gone.

Fern slipped her hand in Joel's, and he held her tightly in his arms.

"Why? Why did he kill himself?" Joel murmured, shock still muddling his thoughts.

"Because he had nowhere to go. Because he wanted to be in control of how this ended."

Joel looked up at Detective John Bamber and saw the regret and pity in the other man's face. "It's over, now, Joel. You can go home."

The barn reverberated to the sounds of police and forensics and other specialists working around them, but Chief Joseph stood in an island of silence. Joel and Fern stood with the old man, and when he spoke, his words were filled with pain for the loss of one son and love for finding another.

"I had two sons. One walks in the light, the other walked in the dark. Now it is up to me to bring him into the light so that the Great Spirit and the ancestors can know him and heal him. I will hold a traditional burial ceremony for my boy Richard. I want his spirit to know the love he never had when he walked this earth as a boy and as a man. We will mourn him as we would mourn a child who has gone missing and lost, and we will hold him to the light so that he may find his way home.

"I hope that you will come to that ceremony and show your brother your forgiveness, to increase the love and light that surrounds his spirit."

Joel nodded, and Fern reached out to hold the hands of both men.

"It's over," she whispered the words like a prayer.

Chapter Twenty-Eight

The old farmhouse was filled with light and laughter as friends gathered with Fern for a celebration of Rose's life and to welcome in a New Year. She paused for a moment to look over the crowd, seeing so many people who'd been kind to her and supported her through the awful events of the year. The rooms sparkled with lights and Christmas decorations, and a warmth more than she could ever remember being there, even when her parents were alive.

There were only two people missing—her sister, Rose and Joel Alvarez, the man she had been through so much with. Yes, when she listened to the talk, the laughter, the impromptu music, Fern was sure she could feel her beautiful sister's lighthearted presence. How Rose had loved parties! *Perhaps her spirit had come to spend time with the people she cared so much about and to enjoy one last fling.*

Fern's eyes filled with tears as she thought about all the might-have-beens.

They'd talked about her sister and shared memories and stories. There'd been laughter and some tears. Now everyone was settled to enjoy bringing in a new start to life, to the opportunities traditionally attributed to a brand new year.

"Why so sad, my friend?" Dr. Morgan James handed Fern a glass of wine and touched her own glass to it in a gentle toast. "To you, to Rose, and to Joel Alvarez, wherever he is."

Fern sipped the wine. "Rose would have loved this," she said, smiling against the tears that threatened. "There weren't many parties as we were growing up. Nothing like this one, for sure."

"Well, there you go, my dear. Here's to a new beginning."

"I'll drink to that," said Mrs. Kanjorski, the elderly neighbor who'd sat through Joel's trial every day with Fern.

"Me, too," agreed Angie Rainier, from the garden center where Rose used to work when she wasn't off singing and dancing at various concerts and on cruise ships.

The toast soon spread around the room, with everyone raising their glasses to toast Rose, Fern, each other, the New Year, and new beginnings.

Just then headlights brushed against the frosted windows, highlighting the glittering snowflakes dancing outside.

Heart beating fast, Fern ran to the hallway, grabbed a jacket, and flew outside into Joel Alvarez' waiting arms. He tilted her chin up so that he could look into her beautiful eyes, his own expression full of love, and opened his jacket to enfold her in his warmth.

"Sorry I'm so late. The roads were bad. But I see the party's still in progress," he murmured.

"I think it's just getting underway," Fern replied. "And you're here now. That's what matters."

Joel's arms tightened around her. "Yes, the papers are all signed, everything is settled. I'm a free man, and I'm here now. If you'll have me, I'm never going away again."

She raised her face for his kiss as people chattered excitedly and began to stream out of the house into the crisp air. They surrounded the couple as the church bells rang out their ancient song across the small town and welcomed in a new year full of love, laughter, and promise.

A word about the author...

Glenys O'Connell writes romantic suspense and comedy. Her interest in criminal psychology began when covering the crime beat as a journalist for a large daily newspaper. She holds a degree in psychology and is qualified as a counselor. As well as romance, she also writes non-fiction on mental health issues, children's books, and is an award-winning playwright. She has lived and worked in the UK and in Ireland, and is now settled in rural Ontario, Canada, with her husband and two spoiled cats.

You can read more about her at her blog, https://romancecanbemurder.blogspot.com/ or on Facebook at www.facebook.com/glenys.oconnell.

Thank you for purchasing
this publication of The Wild Rose Press, Inc.

For questions or more information
contact us at
info@thewildrosepress.com.

The Wild Rose Press, Inc.
www.thewildrosepress.com